Praise For Robert J. Conley and
FUGITIVE'S TRAIL

"In Kid Parmlee [Robert Conley] has created a second-hand Billy the Kid who will charm your damned ears off and send you down a trail of fun, frivolity, and adventure. Go buy it right now, read it and enjoy it."

—Max Evans, author of *The Rounders,*
The Hi-Lo Country, and *Bluefeather Fellini*

"[Conley is] versatile: poetry, humor, historical Western, mystery, even horror. Now, Kid Parmlee. Neither a traditional general Western character, nor a super hero of anti-hero caricature, he is simply Kid Parmlee, a human being. In his pathetic way, Kid Parmlee is not a very good person, but also only as bad as survival requires. Simply clever, good and bad, sad and funny, failure and success . . . 'The Kid' holds up a mirror to the human condition."

—Don Coldsmith, author of
the Spanish Bit Series and *Bearer of the Pipe*

"Kid Parmlee ain't much shucks with the King's English, but he's loud and clear when he talks with his six-shooter."

—Elmer Kelton

"Conley's newest Western . . . [has] wit and a plot that bounces from one trouble-brewing scene to the next. Simple yet charming prose." —*Publishers Weekly*

**St. Martin's Paperbacks titles
by Robert J. Conley**

Fugitive's Trail

A Cold Hard Trail

A
COLD HARD
TRAIL

Robert J. Conley

St. Martin's Paperbacks

This is a work of fiction. All of the characters, organizations, and events portrayed in this novel are either products of the author's imagination or are used fictitiously.

A COLD HARD TRAIL

Copyright © 2001 by Robert J. Conley.

All rights reserved.

For information address St. Martin's Press, 175 Fifth Avenue, New York, NY 10010.

ISBN: 978-1-250-09199-4

Our books may be purchased in bulk for promotional, educational, or business use. Please contact your local bookseller or the Macmillan Corporate and Premium Sales Department at 1-800-221-7945, ext. 5442, or by e-mail at MacmillanSpecialMarkets@macmillan.com.

Printed in the United States of America

St. Martin's Paperbacks edition / April 2001

St. Martin's Paperbacks are published by St. Martin's Press, 175 Fifth Avenue, New York, NY 10010.

10 9 8 7 6 5 4 3 2

Chapter 1

If you ever heared a me atall what you mighta heared is that I run off from my home in Texas when I was just only fourteen year old 'cause a the fact that I had done kilt me a man. The man what I had kilt was named ole Joe Pigg, and I kilt ole Pigg 'cause a the pure and simple fact a the matter that the son of a bitch had shot my poor ole dog Farty. I kilt him with a ax handle, and then my ole paw give me ten bucks and a swayback horse and tole me to get the hell outa Texas.

Well, that was all a few year ago, and in the course a me traveling all through them years, well, I learnt me a thing or two. First off, I learnt me how to be a good cowhand, but only I never could seem to keep hold of a job. Seems like ever time I was to get me a good job, along come a Pigg what had it in for me 'cause a what I had did to ole Joe. So I had to kill another Pigg. Oh, yeah. The other thing what I learnt was how to handle a six-gun pretty damn good, and I really had to learn that, 'cause I ain't got much size on me.

Then somewhere along the way come another family, this one called the Hookses. I kilt me one a them, and it was all for a good enough reason, I guess, but then the rest of them Hookses never seemed to agree with me on that matter, so they got after me too, and for a while there it seemed to me that the whole damn world was populated with nothing but Piggses and Hookses. Seemed like ever'where I went up popped another one a them bastards. Anyhow, come a time when I final figgered I had done got rid of all of them, so I could kinda relax just a little bit.

Another thing you mighta heared if you heared about me atall is that I partnered up with an ole boy what called hisself Zeb Pike but only I come to find out that the real Zeb Pike was long dead and gone and my Zeb Pike just only used that name 'cause he liked it, I guess. Anyhow, he was my pardner, and his main and only real ambition in life was to sniff out a big bonanza a gold, and I learnt something about gold sniffing from him too.

And then of all folks to pop back up into my life was my own ole paw what I had never thought really give a shit about me till he give me that ten dollars and that old swayback and told me to get outa Texas for my life. But he come around after folks had done got to calling me a regular Billy the Kid, what I kinda resented till ole Paw seemed to be so proud a my new reputation. I damn near even carved notches on my gun butts, but a wiser head come along and stopped me from doing that. Hell, I even cut out keeping a count a the folks I kilt. I guess I figgered out that killing folks ain't nothing to be too proud of.

But anyhow, circumstances had worked around me in such a way that I was riding along with ole Zeb and my ole paw, what I really wished had never come back into my young life. You see, I never had no real love for Paw, 'cause he had never really showed it that he had none for me. Not till he seed it that I was coming to be knowed as a real bad gunslinger, and a course, Maw never had seemed to keer too much about me neither.

The last thing I remember about Maw she had slapped me real hard across the face.

Well, I was all outa jobs, and I didn't really have nothing special to do with my young life, so when ole Zeb said he wanted to go sniffing again, I said that I didn't mind too much. We rid up into the hills and commenced to panning a little just for what old Zeb called pocket money, and we was piling up some too, but it come to be too much work for Paw. We was setting at our little camp late of a evening, sipping some coffee around our campfire when Paw commenced to bellyaching.

"Why the hell don't we get down outa these damn mountains?" he said.

"We're a-making money, Paw," I said.

"There's heap better ways a doing that," he said. "Hell, I ain't seed a woman or a bottle a whiskey in so long that I wonder would I know what to do with either one if I was to see it again."

"You don't need to go seeing no women," I said. "Not unless you go on back home to Maw where you had oughta be anyhow. I ain't never yet figgered out what you're a-doing away out here in Colorady when Maw's home all by her lonesome."

"Well, now that ain't none a your damn business, Melvin," Paw said.

That set me off like nothing else could. I had told him before that if he ever was to call me that name again, which really by the way is my name what they had give me when I was borned, that I would kill him dead. Well, I never kilt him dead. He was my paw, but whenever he said that after I had told him what I told him, I just kinda went crazy like, and I whipped out my Colt six-shooter, and I shot the lobe right offa his left ear. I was some mad, I can tell you. Melvin ain't no right name for a gunfighter or for a cowhand neither. 'Course, I weren't really being neither one a them just then. I were out a-hunting gold. Still it pissed me off considerable.

Now, before you go to thinking that I'm bragging about that there shot, I should oughta tell you that ole Paw had real big ears with long hangy down earlobes, and so it weren't no real special shot after all, and I did scratch his neck just a wee bit too. But anyhow, whenever I done that I kinda felt bad about it, 'cause he was my paw.

Well, Paw went to screaming and hollering, and he clapped a hand up to the side a his head. He come up on his feet a-dancing around and a-howling, but all that done was it made him sling all that blood around him 'stead a just letting it run down his neck and all. I put my gun away. Ole Zeb, he just set there a-waiting to see what was a going to happen next, I guess. Final, ole Paw got tired out a-dancing around the way he was doing, and he come back to where he had been setting before, and he set down again. He brung his hand down from the side a his head and held it in front a his face and looked at it all bloody with his eyes real big like something weird in the night. Then he looked over at me.

"Boy," he said, "you like to a kilt me. Your own paw."

"I shoulda," I said. "I done told you that I would if you was to ever call me that name again. Didn't I? You recollect that time? I told you."

"Well, yeah, but I—"

"I woulda, too, if you wasn't my paw. And something else. I never like to a kilt you, 'cause if I'd a meant to kill you, you'd be dead right now. I shot a man's ear off once before, and I done that a purpose. I done exact what I meant to do with that there bullet. Your damn earlobe was too long anyhow."

Well, ole Zeb, he couldn't hold off no longer on that one. He bursted out a-laughing and went to rolling on the ground. I could see that made Paw some angry, but he was a-holding back, 'cause he knowed what I thunk about ole Zeb, and he weren't about to do nothing to piss me off again, knowing that he still had one good hangy down earlobe for me to shoot at. It's a good thing too. Facing a man and being right-handed, it's a mite tougher to pick off a right lobe than it is to nip the left one.

Pretty soon ole Zeb quit laughing and set back up and went to wiping the tears out a his eyes. Paw was setting still with a heavy pout on his face, and I was feeling bad on account a what I had did. I figgered I had best say something.

"It'll scab over here in a minute or two," I said, "and it won't hurt too much neither. A earlobe ain't much of a loss."

Ole Zeb musta decided just then that he'd oughta help out in calming the whole situation down some. He stood up and walked over to his pack and shoved a arm way down in it. He kinda scrambled around in there for a while. Then he come out with a whiskey bottle. It was nearly full too.

"I been hiding this here back for emergencies," he said. "I reckon this might be one."

"By damn," Paw said. "I ain't never felt more emergent. Let me have a swig a that."

Ole Zeb walked on over and handed Paw the bottle, and ole Paw, he tuck him a real long swig. I thought that brown liquid would never stop glug-glugging, but he did final bring it down and hold it back out toward ole Zeb. Ole Zeb tuck the bottle, and Paw let out a loud sigh like as if he hadn't never felt such relief in his whole long and worthless life. Zeb tuck him a drink and handed the bottle over to me. I didn't really want none, but I didn't want to say so, so I tuck me a little drink and passed the bottle back to Paw.

"You might be right, Parmlee," Zeb said.

Paw had to lower the bottle to answer.

"What?" he said. "Right about what?"

"About getting back to town," Zeb said. "I reckon we been out here in the wilds about long enough. A little touch a civilization might do us all some good. We got us a little pocket money in them sacks a dust. We can take us a break from all this work. Get us a bath. Run some whores. Get drunk. Stock up on supplies. Then we can come back out here on the trail. I'm getting a mite bored with this gethering up a pocket money anyhow. I'm kinda itching to get outfitted for a serious search for the mother lode."

Before we all final settled down for the night, that last bottle was empty, and it was ole Paw what drunk the most of it. Hell, he was so drunkened up that he damn near forgot all about his left earlobe. I don't think he really went to sleep neither. I think what he for real done was he just passed on out. Me and ole Zeb crawled on into our bedrolls. We was quiet for just a little while, and then I said, "Zeb?"

"What is it, Kid?" he said.

"Do you think you'll ever find that mother lode? For real?"

The next morning, we packed up and headed on down. We had our three saddle horses and Zeb's Bernice Burro. We had us a long enough ride just getting our ass on down outa them mountains, and come noontime, our bellies was all a-growling, and so we had to stop and fix ourselfs something to eat, but we was mostly outa them kinda supplies, so what we et was just only beans. That's all. I was wishing that we had the makings for biscuits, 'cause ole Zeb, he could really whomp up some good ones whenever he had all the stuff what he needed for it. But anyhow, he didn't have, so we et them beans, cleaned up and moved on.

I had let ole Zeb take the lead with Bernice Burro right behind him, and then Paw was next, and I was a-taking up the rear. We was on a kinda narrow trail coming down outa the foothills, so we had to ride along like that, and then ole Paw, he commenced to farting on account a them beans, I guess. I cussed him something awful, and I begun to think that I was real glad I had shot his earlobe off, and I was thinking about shooting off the other'n. Riding behind him like I was, I coulda hit it easy enough, but then the bullet mighta gone on up ahead and nicked ole Zeb, and I didn't want that, so I just cussed ole Paw was all, but whenever we got offa that narrow trail, I made him move on back to the rearmost position. I weren't about to ride along behind him no more.

We was final down on the flat, and it was some easier to have a conversation thataway, so I hauled on up beside ole Zeb.

"Zeb," I said, "where you reckon we're a-headed?"

"Well," he said, "Fosterville's about the closest town to us. If we're in a hurry to get drunk, we might oughta head for Fosterville. That is, unless there's some other town you'd ruther to get drunk in. We don't have to go to Fosterville."

"Fosterville's just fine," I said. I never bothered asking ole Paw. I didn't figger it was none a his business which town we went to, and if he had some different idea, why, he could just go on and head for wherever he was a mind to. I didn't really want him hanging around me no how. But he never said nothing, riding back there behind us where he was. Instead he just only cut another fart. I was sure glad that I weren't riding back behind him no more.

I got to recollecting about Fosterville, which was where ole Jim Chastain was the sheriff. I hadn't liked ole Chastain worth a shit whenever I first met up with him, but I figgered that was 'cause I didn't have much use for lawmen in the first place. In my wild-ass adventures I had managed to get myself hooked up with two of them in spite a my feelings, and I had wound up liking them both. Ole Chastain was one a them two. The other'n was a Texas Ranger who had gone on back to Texas.

But I got to thinking that it'd be good to see ole Chastain again. Hell, I knowed he'd have a drink or two with us. He might even get drunk with us. He was that kinda good ole boy even if he was a lawman. Yeah, I was getting anxious to see the old bastard again. Paw blowed another fart just then.

"Damn," I said, "I sure hope you get all farted out before we ride into Fosterville. It'd be damned embarrassing to be with you in town and you letting all them farts one after the other like that."

"It's them goddamned beans we et," Paw said. "It ain't my fault."

"My beans don't make you fart," Zeb said.

"It's just only you a-doing it," I said.

"Well," Paw said, "it's them damned beans."

"You drink too much whiskey at night," Zeb said, "it'll make you fart the next day."

"Beans," said Paw.

We had to camp on the trail that night, and we didn't have no more whiskey, so Paw, he was real grumbly. We final got him to shut up and go on to bed, and I guess he went on to sleep. We didn't have nothing but beans to eat neither, so we all kinda decided that we'd just wait till morning. We wasn't too far away from Fosterville by then, so we knowed we could get us a good breakfast by mid-morning. We decided to tough it out. I figgered that ole Zeb was right about the whiskey on account a ole Paw was the only guilty one amongst us, but still I didn't want to take no chances on getting myself humiliated in town by my own paw's gaseous condition.

We had it figgered about right. We rid into Fosterville just about ten o'clock in the morning, and we didn't waste no time neither. We hauled our ass up right in front a the first eating place we come to, and we hitched the horses and ole Bernice, and we went right on inside and ordered up three big breakfasts a steak and eggs and taters and biscuits and gravy and lots a coffee, and we set there and et for a while. I can tell you, it sure tasted good. I stuffed my skinny ole belly till I thunk that I had might near bursted it.

After we had did that, we figgered that the next thing we had oughta do, seeing that we had done tuck keer a our own needs, was to go on and take keer a the critters. We paid for our eats and went outside where we unhitched them four and headed on down to the stable with them. We set them up real good, and then we went looking for a place to cash in our gold dust, which thing we done right quick. I knowed that my lazy-ass ole paw didn't deserve nearly the same share what me and ole Zeb tuck, but Zeb, he divided it all up in three even parts anyhow and give Paw his share. Then we all three of us stepped out onto the sidewalk with plenty a money in our pockets.

"Well, what now?" I asked.

"Whiskey," Paw said.

We walked down to the nearest saloon and went inside and bellied up to the bar and ordered us each a glass a whiskey. I knowed ole Paw would drink three or four glasses and then pass on out, and ole Zeb could suck on the stuff all day long. Me, I never had got to where I could handle too much a the stuff. A couple a drinks, and I wouldn't be worth nothing for a while. I figgered I'd just sip on my one for as long as I could. After all, it weren't even noon yet.

Ole Paw, he downed his first one real quick like, and he went to hollering for the bartender to bring him another. There weren't too much business in the saloon that early in the day, so Paw got service right quick, but when the man went to pour, Paw stopped him. He pulled some cash outa his pocket and slapped it on the bar.

"Just leave us the bottle," he said.

He picked up his glass and the bottle and headed over for a table.

"Let's set," he said.

Me and Zeb follered him on over to the table, pulled us out some chairs and plopped our ass down. Paw poured his glass full, but me and Zeb was still working on our first ones. I got to thinking about how the last time we was in Fosterville, we had kilt ourselfs some Hookses. Well, it weren't really the last time. We'd had us a big fight in town, and one a them Hookses had got away. Then me and ole Zeb had went to climb his mountain. You know, Pike's Peak. And that last Hook had follered us up there and got hisself kilt, so we had come back to Fosterville to let ole Chastain know about that. We had left to go on up into the mountains right after that.

Anyhow, I was thinking about all that and being glad that it was over with and me having nothing to do but only to figger out how to get ole Paw to turn his bony ole ass back toward Texas and Maw and then to go back on the gold trail with old Zeb and see if we couldn't find that there mother lode he was always a-talking about. That's what I was a-thinking, and just then ole Red come a-walking in the place.

Now if you heared about me before then likely you heared about ole Red. Ole Red was a whore, and that's the truth, but even so, she was the bestest gal I ever had. I don't know how come I hadn't been thinking about her riding back into Fosterville like that, but I never. But when I seed her, I was sure glad of it. I guess she was glad to see me too, 'cause she let out a yelp and throwed her arms out wide and come a-running.

I stood up to meet her, and when she run into me, she like to of knocked me over backwards, but I managed to keep on my feet. Well, she hugged me real hard and kissed me till I was plumb embarrassed, and then she went to doing the same thing to ole Zeb. She never hugged and kissed on my paw though. Whenever she final cut it all out and looked at Paw, I said, "Red, you know my ole paw?"

She said howdy to him and set down with us, and I signaled the bartender to fetch us over another glass. I poured her a drink.

"Where have you been?" she said.

"Aw, we just went up into the mountains," I said. "Ole Zeb, here, he smelled us out some gold, so we come back down. That's all."

I was glad I never had to tell her about no killings nor nothing like that. My life had plumb settled down, and I was satisfied with that. I didn't want to be no gunfighter, and I didn't want no one calling me no "regular Billy the Kid" no more. If I was to do anything besides just only hunt for the mother lode with ole Zeb,

I reckoned it would be to find me another cowboying job somewheres. I hope you believe that.

Anyhow, I was just setting there a-sipping at my whiskey and being real glad to be seeing ole Red again, and even thinking about how soon maybe I might be able to get her into a bed with me somewheres whenever I noticed that her eyes opened kinda wide and she was a-staring at something back behind my back. I looked back over my shoulder, and damned if it weren't ole Jim Chastain, and I'd a been real glad to see him again too, but for one thing. Ole Jim, he had a real sternlike look on his craggy ole face, and he was a-holding a short shotgun what was pointed right at us.

Chapter 2

Well, I can tell you what, by God, I was never so surprised in my whole damn short life. Here I figgered ole Jim Chastain was a friend and all that, and I was kinda looking forward to seeing him again and maybe even getting drunk with him, and here he was with his badge just a-shining and that shotgun pointed right in our damn middle.

"Jim?" I said.

"Don't move a muscle, Kid," he said. "I know how good you are, so if I see your eyebrow twitch, I'll cut loose."

"Get him, boy," ole Paw said. "You can do it."

"Aw, shut up, Paw," I said. "Even if I was to get him, that's a scattergun he's got there. He'd blast us all four a-setting here. I ain't moving, Jim, but just what the hell is this all about?"

"You'll find out soon enough," he said. "Red, you better get up and get outa the way, but stay over there where I can see you."

Ole Red got up and moved over to the bar, and she looked plumb astonished, I can tell you. Me and Paw and ole Zeb just set there, skeered even to take a drink.

"Kid," Jim said, "stand up with your hands held high."

I done what he said.

"Now, real slow, reach down and unbuckle that belt and let your rig drop to the floor. Be careful now."

I done that too, and it sure was a empty feeling hearing the sound of my Colt rig hit the floor thataway. Then ole Chastain made Paw do the same thing and then ole Zeb. I was trying to figger out what the hell he was up to. Far as I knowed, even though I had kilt me all a them men, I wasn't wanted for nothing. Fact a the matter is, all a the men what I had kilt was wanted men it turned out, and I had even been a depitty a ole Chastain's for a short time there, and so we was killing the same men so to speak for a while. With all our guns on the floor, ole Jim had the barkeep come out and gether them up and take them behind the bar.

"I'll pick them up later," he said. "All right, you three, head for the jail. You know the way."

Well, I led the way, but I was damn sure embarrassed walking through the streets a Fosterville with my hands up in the air like that and no gun strapped on me. I felt nekkid and foolish, and I could tell that my face was a-blushing red. I really hated that, and I told myself that I'd figger a way to get my ass outa this mess, and then I'd just kill ole Chastain for humiliating me like that. It seemed like a reasonable way to deal with the situation. All the way over to the jailhouse, I was sure for certain that ever'one on the street was a-looking at me.

Once we made it over there, ole Chastain made us go into a cell and back up to the far wall, and then he come over to the cell, still holding that damn scattergun on us, and he slammed that door and locked it. I felt just sick. I had been chased all over the damn country and shot at, but I hadn't never been locked in no jail cell like a sorry-ass criminal before.

"Now maybe you'll tell us what the hell this is all about," I said.

Jim walked over to the gun cabinet on his wall and put up the shotgun, and I was glad it weren't pointed in my general direction no more. He walked around behind his big desk and set down in his chair. Then he rared back and propped his big feet on the desk and crossed his arms over his chest.

"You boys know anything about the stage being robbed up north of here about a week ago?" he asked.

"Hell, no," I said. "We only just come down outa the mountains. We ain't heared nothing. That's a hell of a thing to ask old friends anyhow."

"The driver was killed," Jim said. "Gold shipment was taken. Stagecoach turned over trying to get away from the robbers. Couple of passengers got banged up a little."

"Well, so what?" I said. "I mean, I'm sorry for them and all that, but what's it got to do with us?"

"Anyone see you three over the last month or so?"

"No," I said. "It was just only the three of us up in the mountains. We was panning for gold."

"Got some too," said Zeb. "You can check. We cashed it in right here in town."

"Gold dust?" said Jim.

"That's right," said Zeb. "Several bags full. I got a nose for it."

"It was bags of gold dust that was taken from that stagecoach," said Jim.

"Well, damn it all, Jim," I said, "you didn't even know we had no gold dust till ole Zeb here just told you. How come you to go and throw down on us like you done?"

Jim raised his feet up off the desktop and dropped them down onto the floor. Then he leaned forward and pulled open a desk drawer. He hauled a piece a paper outa that drawer and looked at it a minute without saying nothing. Then he started in to read.

"Three white men, one young, skinny, scrawny one, one older, also skinny and needing a shave, the third one short, stubby, and old with gray whiskers. That's the description we got on the three men that held up the stagecoach," he said. He tossed the paper down. "Sound like anyone you know?"

Well, I reckoned that I was kinda skinny and scrawny, and ole Paw did for a fact need a shave, and Zeb, well, he was stubby and bewhiskered, sure enough.

"I guess there could be a whole bunch a young skinny fellers out there," I said. "And could be there's a few of them running around with a couple a old codgers."

"What do you mean, a couple a old codgers?" Paw said. "I ain't a old codger like him."

"Don't you go calling me no codger," Zeb said.

Just then the front door a the office come open and Red come a-flying in. She whirled right over to ole Chastain's desk, stopped right quick and stood there a-glaring at him with her hands on her hips.

"Jim Chastain," she said, "what do you mean by putting these friends of ours into a jail cell? You ought to be ashamed of yourself. They just got into town, and you come a-sneaking—"

"Hold on, Red," Jim said. He picked up that damned paper again and handed it to her. "Read this before you go flying off the handle. I'm just doing my job is all."

Red tuck the paper outa Jim's hand and read it. She looked over at us for a bit and then she read it again. She put down the paper and come right over to the cell. I was standing right up front a-hanging onto a couple a bars. She come right up to me so that our two noses like to a touched through the bars.

"Kid," she said, "did you pull that job?"

"No," I said. "I never. We never."

"Don't lie to me, Kid," she said, and I swear, the way she was a-looking at me, if I'd a wanted to I couldn't'ta.

"Red," I said, "I ain't lying. Me and Zeb and Paw has been alone in the mountains ever since we last seen you till just now. We didn't rob no stagecoach. I swear it to you, Red."

She stared right into my eyes for what seemed like five minutes, but I bet you it weren't, and then she whirled around and flounced back over to ole Jim's desk.

"They didn't do it, Jim," she said. "You got the wrong men."

"All I can go on is what they sent me on it, Red," he said. "I got to hold them here till one of the witnesses can get down here and take a look at them. If they're the wrong men, the witness will tell us, and I'll let them go."

Well, Red fussed some more with him, but she never got nowhere, and final she left, a-stomping all the way out. Jim, he settled back down behind his desk. Ole Zeb come a-sidling up beside me.

"Who's the witnesses?" he said.

"Who's the witnesses?" I asked out loud.

"Shotgun guard," Jim said, "and two passengers."

"Them same passengers what got all jostled around when that there stage turned over?" Zeb whispered.

"The same passengers what got all jostled around when the stage turned over?" I asked out loud.

"I reckon," Chastain said.

"Hell," said Zeb, "they'll identify any skinny kid with two older fellers. They was likely seeing double anyhow."

I opened my mouth to repeat what Zeb had said, but then I changed my mind. I never said nothing out loud.

Instead, I turned around the other way and walked back toward the back wall a couple a steps. I was thinking about what ole Zeb had just said.

"You know, Zeb," I said, "likely you're right about that. I reckon it wouldn't be the first time a innocent man got hisself hung to death."

"Three innocent men, you mean," Paw said.

I didn't believe my ole paw had been innocent since the day he was borned, but I didn't bother saying so. I did know he was innocent a that damn stagecoach robbery though. He had been in the mountains with me and ole Zeb. There just weren't no way he coulda slipped off to rob no stage without us a-knowing about it, and even if he coulda, why, what was the chances a his finding another ole codger like Zeb and another skinny kid like me? It just didn't make no sense atall. No sir. I knowed that we was all three of us innocent a the charges.

"Well," said Zeb, "what're we going to do?"

"You shoulda tuck him back there in the saloon," Paw said.

"Shut up about that," I said. "I told you how come I never done nothing back there, and I was right. Why, even if I'd a shot him, his finger coulda twitched and he'd a blowed all of us straight to hell. Red too."

"You watch how you're talking to your old man," Paw said. "You ain't wearing your fancy gun in here, and I might just take it into my head to whip your skinny ass once more before they hang us."

"You do it, old man," I said. "You do it, and then you wait and see if they hang us up or if we get out, and if we get out, I'll get my gun back, and if you whipped my ass, I'll kill you dead. I don't give a damn if you are my old man. You never acted like it but just only one time in my whole life nohow."

Zeb stepped in between me and Paw.

"You reckon we might could get outa here?" he said.

"There'll be a way," I said.

I went over and laid my ass down on a cot what was against the wall, and I folded my hands behind my head and crossed my feet one over the other and commenced to thinking. I thunk about what ole Zeb had said that them folks might just up and say that we was the ones even if we really wasn't, and if they was to say that, why, we'd get ourselfs hung up no matter if we was innocent or not. We'd be just as dead and wouldn't nobody give a damn neither. Well, maybe ole Red would, at least for a little while, and then I wondered if Maw would give a shit that Paw never come home again. He was gone a awful lot as it was.

"Paw," I said, "if I can figger a way to get us outa here, will you go on back home to Maw?"

"Well, sure I will," he said. "Don't I always?"

"I mean right away whenever I get us outa here," I said.

"Well, now, I don't like making no promises like that," he said. "Who knows? Something might come up and cause me to break my word if I was to give it like that."

"Well, think about it thisaway," I said. "If I was to come up with a way a getting us outa here, I mean, breaking us outa here, you know, then the law'd be after us 'cause they think we done that robbing and they'd be after us too 'cause we broke outa jail. Right?"

"Right," said Paw.

"The safest place for you to be would be back home in Texas and not up here with all the laws looking for you."

"Yeah," he said. "You're right about that."

I figgered I had him then.

"Well?" I said.

"You get us outa here," he said, "and I'll run back home to your maw faster'n you can say shit."

"All right," I said. I smiled and laid back again the way I was. 'Bout then ole Chastain got up. I heared him shove his chair back, and I raised my head up a bit so I could take me a look at him.

"I'll bring you boys back some lunch," he said. He was a-heading for the door.

"Don't bring no beans," Zeb yelled.

I heared the door shut, and I went back to my thinking. Now I had done tuck keer a one problem. I had figgered out how to make Paw go on back home. I felt real good about that. All I had left to do was just only figger out how to get us outa the damn jail. If I was to be able to get my hands on a six-gun, I knowed for damn sure that I could get us outa there, but I couldn't figger how I was going to do that. I had heared about folks digging their way outa jail, and I didn't know no one more experter than ole Zeb when it come to digging.

"Zeb," I said.

"Yeah?"

"Can we dig our way outa here?"

Zeb looked around at the floor and the walls, a-studying for a spell. Then he said, "Hell, no."

"Ain't no way?" I said.

"No way."

I laid back again and thunk harder. Seemed like to me I had heared about someone somewheres in a jail what had gouged the bars outa the winders and pulled them loose, just one or two of them, enough so he could squeeze hisself through and get out.

"Can we pry them winder bars loose?" I asked.

Zeb went over to the winder and tuck hold a two a the bars and tried to give them a shake but they never budged nor wiggled nor nothing. He kinda scratched around at the bottom a the bar for a minute.

"Keep a-thinking," he said.

"No good?" I said.

"No good."

Well, I couldn't hardly think a nothing else 'cept only that ole Chastain was a-fixing to bring us something to eat. I set up and studied on the cell door and the front wall a bars there. There weren't no way he could give us no food without he was to open the damn cell door first. I was thinking that maybe we could jump him when he done that.

"Listen," I said.

Paw and Zeb both come up close to me.

"You come up with something?" Paw asked.

"I got it," I said. "Listen keerful. Ole Chastain, he said he was a-bringing us some food, didn't he?"

"Sure he did," Paw said. "It's crawling on 'bout noontime. He has to feed us. It's the law."

"What's he going to bring that food on?"

"Well, I reckon he'll be a-bringing it in on a tray," said Paw. "What else? And what has that got to do with getting our ass outa here?"

"He'll have to open that there door to get a tray in here to us," I said, and then Paw's eyes opened up some, and so did ole Zeb's.

"Oh," said Paw.

"Whenever he opens that door," I said, "we'll jump him. All three of us. And we'll get his guns, if he's got them on, and we'll get outa here and lock him up, and then we'll go get our horses and guns and get the hell outa town."

"That's good," Paw said.

"It oughta work," said Zeb.

"The important thing is," I said, "to not go looking

suspicious whenever he comes back in here. Don't be looking sneaky like. Just stay casual, like you ain't thinking a nothing in perticular 'cept maybe what's to eat. You got that?"

"Yeah," said Paw.

"I got it," Zeb said.

I heared footsteps then, and I said, "Here he comes. Watch out."

I laid back down, and Paw, he went over to the winder and kinda stared out, and ole Zeb went and set on the other cot across the cell from me. He commenced to humming some old song. Chastain walked on in all right, and he was a-carrying a tray with a rag throwed over the top of all the food to keep all the flies off, I guess. He walked over to his desk and put the tray down. Then he got the keys, and then the son of a bitch went to the gun cabinet and got the damned shotgun. He pointed that damned thing right at us.

"Get over against the back wall," he said. "All of you."

Well, we done that.

"Face the wall," he said.

We done that too, and I could hear him unlocking the door. Then I heared him a-taking some steps, and I figgered he was fetching the tray, but I also figgered he was still a-holding that scattergun in one hand. I never moved a muscle. I heared it when he put the tray down on the floor, and then I heared when he shut and locked the door again.

"Have at it, boys," he said.

Paw looked me right in the face.

"Real bright idea you had there, son," he said.

Well, the best thing about it was that there weren't no beans on the tray. We all of us went and et like we was at some fancy eating place and not in no jail, and the food was pretty good. Then we drunk some coffee. It was on the tray too, but only it was just one cup for each of us, and I wanted some more. We finished up ever'thing what was on that tray, and then I went and laid back down and Zeb did too.

"I ain't got no place to lay down," Paw said.

Chastain got up and got his gun and keys again. He come back over to the cell and unlocked the door.

"Come on," he said.

Paw stuck a bony finger on his chest.

"Me?" he said.

"You," said Chastain. Paw walked out and Chastain shut the door again and locked it. He went on over to the next cell and opened it up. "Go on," he said, and Paw went in there. Chastain shut the door and locked it.

"How come you to do that?" Paw asked him.

"There's just two beds in a cell," Jim said. "Now you got two. Take your pick."

Well, we lounged around the rest a that day, and Paw done some grumbling, but final the sun went down and it come dark outside. I heared a horse whinny out loud like something was really a-bothering it, and then it made some more noise and final went stamping away. Chastain got up and hurried to the front door, jerking it open and running on outside to see what was the matter. Then I heared a voice from outside the cell winder.

"Kid," it said. "Kid."

I looked around me, but I didn't see no one, and so I set up. The voice come again.

"Kid, hurry up," it said. "We ain't got all day."

I looked around me kinda stupid like, and then ole Zeb, he said, "Go over to the winder, you dummy."

I got on up and stared over at that winder, and I wondered who the hell could it be a-calling to me like that and what for, and then that voice come at me again.

"Kid, are you there?"

It was a female voice, for sure, and it just had to be good ole Red. It couldn't a been no one else. I come real excited then. I don't know what I thunk a female gal would be able to do for me and Zeb and Paw, but somehow in that moment a my desperation, I didn't think of ole Red as just only a female gal. In my wishfulness she come into my head like a true angel a mercy, and I knowed that she was going to be the saving of us.

Chapter 3

I hurried right on over to that there winder, and I stuck my face in it smashed against them bars, and sure enough, there she was. It was ole Red, all right, and she was a-holding my own Colt six-shooter up towards me a-pointing the barrel right at my nose.

"Red," I said, "point that thing some other way."

"Oh," she said, and she turned it off to the right somewhat.

"What're you doing with that anyhow?" I said.

"I fetched it over here to you," she said.

"Well, how in the—"

"Never mind all that," she said. "We ain't got time. All I done was slap that horse on the butt real hard a couple of times. Jim'll figure that out pretty soon and be back in here. Here. Take this thing."

I reached out the bars and tuck hold a my Colt and drawed it inside with me. Paw and Zeb, both their eyes got real big.

"I got the rest of it too," Red said. "It's with your horses out back. Don't worry. No one saw me."

"But Red," I said, "how did you—"

But I shut up then on account a she had done hurried on off, and so I was just a-talking out the winder to myself. Good ole Red. She never let me down yet. Here

I was trying to figger out how to get us outa jail, and damned if she didn't bring me my own six-gun. I just didn't hardly know what to think about that.

"You better hide that damn thing," Paw said. He was talking at me through the bars from the next-door cell.

"Yeah," I said. I turned back away from the winder then. Chastain hadn't come back in, so I just kinda laid back down on the cot the same way I had been before, but I tucked that Colt in under the piller that my head was a-resting on. "I told y'all I'd figger a way to get us outa here," I said. Then Chastain come back in. I just laid there.

"Well?" Paw said.

"This here might not be the best time," I said. "Hell, it's broad daylight out there."

Ole Zeb squatted down beside me and kinda whispered into the side a my head.

"Yeah," he said. "It's broad daylight, and someone's liable to go walking along behind the jailhouse and see our horses out there. Then when's it gonna be the right time? Huh?"

I set up then. He was right. And Red had said she had put the rest of the stuff with the horses, and I couldn't figger what she meant by that 'cept maybe Paw's gun and Zeb's, so Zeb was right. I had to do something right by God then before someone was to come along and find our critters and guns a-waiting for us out back. Ole Chastain was a busy at some kinda paperwork at his desk, so I slipped that Colt out from under the piller and stood up with it behind my back. Then I sidled over to the bars.

"Hey, Jim," I said.

"What?" he said, without even looking up.

"Jim," I said, "come on over here a minute, will you?"

He looked up then, and he said, "What is it? I can hear you."

"I just want to talk to you," I said. "I been trying to figger out how come that there description a them robbers was to go out sounding so much like me and Paw and Zeb when we never had nothing to do with it."

"We'll get those witnesses out here and clear the whole thing up," Chastain said.

"Men has been hung dead by mistake," I told him. "I've heared about it. More than once. What if there's another scrawny kid out there, something like me, you know, and a couple a old farts with him, and they done it, and them witnesses sees us, but they never really got no good look at them other three, and so they says, yeah, that's them, but only we ain't. Not really. What about that? Come on over here, Jim."

"Kid," he said. "I'm busy, and I don't want to get into that kind of discussion with you anyhow."

Well, I give up trying to get him over to the cell. He just weren't going to go for it, so I just went on ahead and pulled that Colt out from behind me and thumbed back the hammer, and ole Jim, he heared that sound all right. He looked up then, and he seed that he was looking right into the barrel a my shooter.

"Stand up slow, Jim," I said, and he did. Real slow.

"Kid," he said, "you don't want to do that."

"I don't want to set in your jail and wait to see if you wind up hanging my ass up in the wind," I said. "Walk on over here, but pick up them keys on your way."

Well, he done what I told him to do, and I had ole Zeb to get his gun and the keys.

"Open the door, Zeb," I said. Ole Zeb, he reached on out through the bars and twisted his hand around so he could put the key in the hole and turn it, and he did get the door opened. Then he hurried on out and went over to unlock the cell ole Paw was in. Paw was really faunching too. I was still holding my shooter aimed at ole Chastain, and I went out last.

"Now you can get on in there," I said, "and see how you like it."

"Kid—" he said, but I cut him short.

"Whenever I wanted to talk," I said, "you wasn't interested, so now I ain't interested. Just get your ole ass in there."

Ole Jim got in the cell, and Zeb shut the door and locked it.

"Now you can start taking off your clothes," I said.

"What?"

"You heared me," I said. "Strip yourself nekkid."

"What do you want to do that to me for?" he said.

"At first I wanted to kill you for the way you embarrassed me out there on the street while ago, marching me around in front a ever'one with both my hands stuck way up in the air and all that," I said, "but I reckon embarrassing you back is just about as good. Maybe even better. Now do it."

He crossed his arms over his chest and put a real stubborn look on his face.

"I ain't going to do it," he said.

Ole Zeb walked over to the gun cabinet and picked up that greener that Chastain had pointed at us back in the saloon. He cocked both hammers and aimed it at the cell that Chastain was in.

"You ain't, huh?" he said.

Ole Jim, he turned white as processed cotton. "Hey, old man," he said, "if you just touch that trigger, you'll splatter me all over this cell."

"Then you best do what the kid says," said Zeb.

Ole Jim likely never stripped so fast in his life, not even for a whore, and each time he pulled off a piece a clothes, I made him hand them through the bars to me, and then I made ole Paw gether them up to bring along with us. Final I told Zeb to bring along the scattergun and the keys to the cell.

"Kid," said Jim, "if you take the keys, how'll I get out of here?"

I looked back at him, and he sure did look silly standing there nekkid in the cell, all long and gangly and bony and hairy, but I never laughed out loud. Instead I just give a shrug, like as if to say, I sure as hell don't know. Then I looked back around at my two partners in evil doings.

"Zeb," I said, "take a peek out that back door and tell me what you see."

Ole Zeb peeked, and then he said, "I see our critters out there all right."

"Any folks?" I asked.

"Nary a soul," he said.

"Then let's get outa here," I said. The three of us went out the back door and clumb up on our horses, and ole Red, she had even brung along ole Bernice Burro, so Zeb tuck hold a her line to bring her along with us. We rid slow and easy till we got plumb out to the edge a town, and then I figgered that someone might spot us riding on out, so I kicked my ole horse in the sides and give a yell. Paw and Zeb done the same, and we went tearing on the hell outa that place.

We never said nothing, not a word, till we got us a couple miles outa town and final slowed our critters down so as not to run them to death, and then we just kinda moved along slow like for a spell without saying nothing still. Of a sudden ole Zeb, he bursted out laughing. Whenever he final stopped long enough to draw in a breath, I asked him what was so damned funny.

"Ole Chastain nekkid in his jail," Zeb said.

Well, then me and Paw commenced to laughing, too, at the thought of it and the remembrance a how ole Jim looked back there whenever we left him, and then I told Paw, whenever we got done laughing like that, to drop ole Jim's boots. He done that, and we rid on a ways, and I had him to drop Jim's shirt, and on like that till the poor bastard's clothes was strung out for several miles along the road. The last thing we had was the keys to the jail cell, and I tuck them and throwed them as far offa the road as I could. I figgered no one would ever find them again.

"Reckon how long it's going to take for ole Chastain to get outa that there cell a his?" Zeb said.

We all commenced in to laughing again.

"Well," I said final, "the first thing is he'll have to yell his head off to get someone's attention."

"Then whoever it is hears him will go into the jailhouse," Zeb said, "and see him in there locked in his own cell nekkid as a mole."

We laughed some more at that thought.

"Then he'll have to have them to go find him some clothes," Paw said.

We laughed some more.

"And once he gets some new clothes to cover up his nekkidness," said Zeb, "then they'll figger out that he ain't got no cell keys, and they'll have to hunt up someone to cut through them bars or something."

"He'll be all day a-getting his ass outa there," I said.

We went and laughed even more, and my belly and sides and jaws was all a-hurting, but we final got stopped laughing like that and we rid along quiet like for a bit there, and then ole Paw spoke up and he was real serious.

"He'll kill you for that if he ever gets the chance," he said.

"What?" I said.

"Chastain," said Paw. "He ever gets the chance, he'll kill you."

I didn't say nothing, but I done some deep thinking on that, and I figgered that ole Paw was right for sure. Why, ole Jim had tuck my shooter away from me and made me walk down the street with my hands stuck up in the air, and I had told myself that I would kill him for humiliating me in front a folks thataway. Now, I reckon I weren't humiliated none compared to what ole Jim was going to be whenever he was discovered nekkid in jail like that. No, sir. That was a mean thing I done, and I final realized the full and complete meanness of it just then.

"I reckon he can try if he's a mind to," I said.

None of us said nothing more for a spell till ole Paw said, "Where we headed anyhow?"

"You're headed for Texas," I said.

"I ain't so sure about that," said Paw. "I hate to go home to your maw without my pockets full a cash. You know I always bring her cash money and groceries whenever I go home after a trip."

Well, I didn't know no such thing. I did recollect that sometimes after he'd been gone off for a long spell, he'd maybe bring home some groceries all right, but I don't recall him ever giving Maw no cash money. More likely he'd done drank it all up before he come home. Anyhow, I never said nothing about that. Instead, I dug into my pocket and pulled out what I had in there. I hadn't had no time to spend hardly any of it, so I still had all that money I got for my share a the gold dust we had cashed in. 'Course, I knowed that Paw had his too, and he had got the same amount as what I had got. I kept me a little a that cash and handed most of it to Paw.

"I know you've already got more than that in your

own pocket," I said. "With this here you oughta have plenty. Now, you promised me, you old son of a bitch. You said you'd go home to Maw if I was to figger us a way outa that jail."

"You never figgered a way out," Paw said. "It was that redheaded gal what brung you your six-gun. She figgered it out for you."

"The law's going to be after your ass here in Colorady," I said. "You'll be safe at home in Texas."

"Well," he said, "there's some truth in that."

"Well, head for Texas then," I said.

"I ain't made up my mind yet," he said. "The law's going to go after you worse than me, and I ain't heared you talking about getting outa the state. Maybe I'll just string along with you."

I slowed my ole horse and kinda faded back on the trail till I was back behind ole Paw, and then I pulled my Colt and cocked it. Paw heared it all right.

"You made me a promise," I said, "and if you don't keep it, I'm fixing to shoot off your other earlobe right now."

"Well, boys," Paw said, "it's been fun, but I got me a woman a-waiting at home. I'll be seeing you around."

Then he kicked his horse in the sides and let out a yell and tuck off so damn fast I couldn't hardly believe it. I eased the hammer down on my Colt and put her away.

"You reckon he'll really go home?" Zeb said.

"I ain't going to foller him to make sure," I said. "At least he'll be gone from us."

"He was right about one thing," Zeb said.

"What was that?"

"Me and you'd be better off outa the state too. They're going to be a-hunting us. 'Special ole Chastain after what we done to him. We ain't going to be safe no place in Colorady. Maybe up in the mountains. Maybe they can't find us up there, but even if we was to go back up there, we'd have to come back down again sometime. What if we was to head north, say up into Wyoming, and then we could go on up in the mountains up there? Maybe Californy. I can sniff out that gold any-wheres. What do you say?"

"I don't know, Zeb. I ain't too anxious to leave the state."

"Kid, they're on our trail. You know that. And when-ever they catch up with us, Chastain or whoever, they're going to commence shooting without asking no ques-tions. They'll shoot to kill, on account a they know how good you are with a gun. They won't be wanting to take no chances."

I just kept riding along. I didn't say nothing.

"You hear what I said?"

"I heared you, Zeb. You go on. Go to Wyoming or Californy and hunt that mother lode. I got me other things to hunt."

"What? What you got to hunt? What's so important you'd take a chance on getting yourself kilt over it? Tell me that. What is it?"

"I'm going to hunt me up three men," I said. "A scrawny, skinny kid and two old men."

"Are you crazy?" Zeb said.

"Well, I reckon that there question ain't yet been an-swered," I said. "I might be, but I just know only one thing."

"What? What's that?"

"I don't like being on no one's wanted list, Zeb. I ain't no way comfy with that fugitive stuff. I been there before, and I don't like it, I tell you. I mean to get busy and find them three outlaw bastards what really done that stagecoach robbing and killing and bring their ass in and prove to ole Chastain and ever'one else that it weren't us what done it. I mean to clear off our good names."

"How the hell you going to go about the doing a that?" Zeb said. "Where you going to start? Where you going to look? We don't even know who they are. Who you looking for? Hell, we don't know whichaway they tuck out after they went and done their evil and nefarious deed."

"What's that mean?" I said.

"Never mind," he said. "Hell, they could a gone anywheres. Canada or Mexico. Chicago maybe. They got enough cash outa the deal, they mighta even got on a boat and headed to China."

"They wouldn't a gone to China," I said, "lessen they could talk Chinaman. I don't mean to cuss and discuss it no more. Like I said, you go on wherever it is you want to go. My mind is made up all the way total. I'm going to find them three no good son of a bitches and bring them in or kill them dead. I mean to do it."

Chapter 4

Well, ole Zeb, he got me a good one, he did. I thunk that I'd had him, but he turned it right around on me.

"All right," he said. "All right. You win. I'll string along with you. Hell, you knowed I would, didn't you? Don't I always? Don't I do whatever it is you say most ever' time? All right. We'll hunt them killers and stagecoach robbers. We'll hunt their ass down. Where we going to start?"

Well, I couldn't rightly answer him that. I didn't have no idea where the bastards would likely be at. The robbing and killing had tuck place north of us, but that didn't near mean that they was still up there. Like ole Zeb said, they coulda headed for China for all we knowed.

"Well, shit, Zeb," I said, "let's us just ride up into the mountains for a spell and think on it a while."

"Now that there's a good idea," he said. "Let's do her."

A course, it was Zeb's idea in the first place. I knowed it, and he knowed it, but he never rubbed it in. He just acted as how it was my own latest idea, and I never said nothing about it not being that neither.

"There's a place just up ahead where we can turn up towards the high country," he said.

We rid on for a space, and then there it was. The place what Zeb had said would be there. I knowed it would be, 'cause Zeb, he knowed them mountains. I reckon ole Zeb knowed them mountains better than any living critter, 'cept maybe mountain goats and mountain lions and such. Anyhow, he turned his horse up that trail, leading Bernice Burro, and I turned my own ole horse and follered them. We rid on for a considerable distance without talking no more, but once whenever the trail leveled out just a little, I turned to look back. I hadn't never got used to them high spots like that. I was still fascinated by being able to look out for miles and miles, and I just wanted to take me a look, was all, but I got more than what I was bargaining for, I can tell you that.

"Zeb," I said.

Ole Zeb stopped his horse, and Bernice walked right into its ass end. Then she stopped too. Zeb turned around in his saddle and looked back at me.

"What is it?" he asked me.

"Look there down below," I said.

"By damn," he said, "that there sure has the look of a posse about it."

"It does, don't it?" I said. "You reckon they'll see where we turned off and foller us up here?"

Zeb clumb down outa his saddle and walked back to where I was at, and he looked off over the edge a the drop off there.

"What do we do," he said, "if it is for real a posse, and if they does come up the trail after us? Will you shoot a couple of them to make the rest turn around and go back? What'll you do, Kid?"

"I can't shoot no lawmen, Zeb," I said. "Hell, I want to prove we ain't guilty a that other business. If I was to kill me a lawman or two, I'd be guilty a that for sure.

Then the other thing wouldn't matter none no more, would it?"

"I reckon you're right about that," he said, "but if they've got us all slated to hang anyhow, what's the difference?"

"The difference is that I aim to prove we're innocent," I said. "If I can do that without shooting me no lawmen, we'll be all right."

"I don't know if ole Jim Chastain will feel thataway about it," Zeb said.

"How come?" I said.

" 'Cause we're damn sure guilty a breaking outa his jail and locking him in it and leaving him nekkid in there, ain't we?"

"Yeah," I said. "I reckon we are at that, but that ain't no hanging offense. Least, I don't think it is."

"Hey," he said, "looky there. They're a-coming up this way for sure."

He run over to one side a the trail and put his back against a rock and commenced to shoving at it by propping his feet against another rock. It come loose a little.

"What're you doing?" I said.

"You said you can't shoot them. They can't blame you for a little rock slide, can they?"

"I don't want to kill no one, Zeb," I said.

"It'll just block the trail, is all," he said. "Come on. Give me a hand."

Well, I didn't know what else to do, so I swung down offa ole horse and moved over to that there rock beside ole Zeb. With both our backs at it, it come loose all right, and it commenced to tumbling and rolling down the trail, a-bouncing offa one side and then t'other, and along the way, it picked up and kicked loose some other rocks, and pretty soon, by God, we had us a regular rock slide running down the trail.

That trail was winding and narrow, and before the rock slide reached all the way down to the posse, it stopped all right, and it just kinda jammed up the trail there above one a the sharpest turns.

"It stopped, Zeb," I said.

"That's all right," he said. "It done just what you wanted it to do. It stopped them dead, and ain't no one hurt. They can't get over it, though, or around it. They'll just have to turn around and go back where they come from. That's all."

"Zeb," I said, "you got them spyglasses on you?"

"I'll fetch them," he said, and he walked back to his horse and reached into the saddlebag. I follered him and tuck them from him, and then I looked through them down the trail, and by God, I seen ole Chastain hisself. He was dismounted and standing in the trail a-looking at them rocks what blocked his way, and he tuck the hat off his head and throwed it down real hard. I could tell that he was plenty pissed off.

"It's ole Jim all right," I said, and I handed them glasses back to Zeb.

"Has he got his clothes on?" Zeb said. I never answered him, 'cause I seed that he was putting them glasses up to his own eyes and so he'd see for hisself. "Yeah," he said. "He found hisself some britches all right."

Ole Zeb, he laughed some at that, and he walked back to his horse and put the glasses back in the saddlebag. Then he clumb on up in the saddle. Well, I done the same thing, and then Zeb started in to riding, and I commenced to foller. We come at last to a kinda plateau where ever'thing leveled off for a while, and we turned north and rid thataway. Neither one of us said nothing, but I was glad that Zeb had turned us north, on account a that was the direction a that stagecoach robbery, and

I kinda wanted to hunt around some in that direction, even though I wasn't sure atall that them three criminal bastards would still be hanging around loose anywheres up thataway.

Anyhow, we rid most a that day away till the sun was getting real low in the western sky, which that didn't take too long 'cause a them mountains, you know. The sky was getting gray, and it didn't look to me as if we'd have much daylight left to us, and then ole Zeb, he spoke up.

"We'd oughter stop along here," he said, "and make us a camp for the night. Riding along here after dark, a feller just might fall right offa the edge."

I'd heared Zeb talk thataway before.

"Would he fall all the way to China," I said, "and never be found?"

"If he was to be found," Zeb said, "it'd be by a Chinaman."

Well, we stopped, and we pitched our camp all right, and we even built ourselfs a little fire on account a the night air was fixing to chill up some that high up in the mountains, but we didn't have us no vittals to cook, so we just set around hungry and kinda grumpy on account a that. By and by, we crawled underneath our blankets and went to sleep.

We both of us woke up kinda early the next morning, and I believe we'd a fought each other over a damned ole chicken egg. Anyhow, we broke camp and was saddling up our horses, when we heared the loudest bang I had ever heared. It sounded to me kinda like thunder but only not quite, and besides that there weren't no storm clouds in the sky and no lightning a-flashing. I like to a jumped right outa my britches, and our three critters jumped and stamped around, a-neighing and braying out their own concerns.

"What the hell was that?" I said.

"Someone's blasting up ahead," Zeb said. "They're either onto a hell of a big strike, or they're too damn lazy to dig. Let's mount up and go find out."

Well, I weren't so sure, but I mounted up to foller him, 'cause what the hell else could I do but 'cept to just trust him up in them mountains the way we was.

"Zeb," I hollered out, "what if we was to ride on up there where they're a-blasting, and just get our ass blasted right offa this mountain and on down into China?"

"Not a chance," he said. "I can tell where they're a-blasting at."

Well, I was still nervous, but I did believe him what he said. He was a old hand at them mountains, and he knowed ever'thing there was to know about gold, whether it was panning or digging or blasting. At least, he said he did, and I believed him—mostly. But I was nervous. Then there come another blast, and it was ferocious. Ole horse, she jumped sideways and like to of skittered right offa the edge, but I fit her back over onto the trail. It tuck all I had in me though.

"Damn it, ole horse," I said. "You want to wake up being meat for some Chinee dog?"

Zeb, he just rid on like there wasn't nothing the matter, so I kept follering. We went on like that for another while, maybe it was a hour, maybe more, and then Zeb just stopped. Bernice run into his horse's ass, and then she stopped. I stopped too.

"What is it, Zeb?" I asked him.

"Well, I be damned," he said.

"What?" I said. "What is it?"

"Come on up here, Kid," he said.

The trail was a little more accomodating just there, so I moved over and rid past Bernice so I could come up alongside ole Zeb, and then I seed what it was that had stopped him like that. He was a-staring straight ahead with big wide-open eyes at a whole damn little town just up ahead of us.

"Damn thing weren't here when I was here last," he said. "Someone musta run onto something. Just look at that, Kid. They's mining shacks and sluices and ever'thing. There looks to be several houses too, like as if some families is in on this together."

He reached back to pull the glasses outa his bag again, and he tuck hisself a long look, and while he was a-looking, he was a-talking.

"Yeah," he said. "Sure enough. I see womenfolk. I see some kids too. It's a sure enough town all right. A gold-mining town. I be goddamned all the way straight down to blackest hell. It's a gold-mining town in the mountains."

"Well, what'll we do, Zeb?" I said.

He set still for another minute or so just a-staring through them glasses, and then he brung them down and turned a bit and stuck them back in the bag.

"Let's ride on down there and meet them," he said. "Likely they got some food, and I'm hungry as a hibernating bear."

Well, we done like he said. We rid on for a while, but then whenever we come close enough for the folks in the mining town to see that someone was a-coming, I seed three men run for rifles, and I could see that they all cranked shells into the chambers too.

"Zeb," I said, "you see that?"

"Don't pay it no nevermind," he said. "That's the way a feller gets when he's got gold. They're just being keerful. We'll ride on in easy like. They won't do us no harm. Just stay calm, Kid. Leave me do the talking."

"I ain't going to argue on that one with you," I said,

and I slowed ole horse down so that pretty soon I was
back riding behind Bernice Burro again. We rid on into
that town single file, and when we come in close, ole
Zeb stopped. He kinda held his hands up to show them
that he wasn't planning on no hostilities.

"Howdy, folks," he said. "I'm ole Zeb Pike. That
there skinny kid back there is my pardner, Kid Parmlee.
We're just a-traveling this here mountain trail, and we're
mighty hungry. Thought we'd try your hospitality."

It stayed quiet, and I couldn't handle not knowing
what was going on up there, so I raised my own hands
up some and rid on around. Them three with the rifles
was a-standing and staring real hard at ole Zeb, and
when they seed me a-coming around, they give me
pretty hard and cold looks too.

"Your pard looks like a gunfighter," one a the three
said.

"Ah, he's just a kid," Zeb said. "That's how come me
to call him that. Kid."

"Whenever I had me a job," I said, "I was a cowhand.
Then I done me a little placer mining with ole Zeb here.
He taught me."

"You're not a gunfighter?" the man said.

"No, sir," I said. "I've learnt to use my six-shooter
for when I have to use it in defense a my own life and
limb or my pardner Zeb, but I wouldn't call myself no
gunfighter."

"You ain't working for Morgan?" the man said.

I give Zeb a look, and he give me one.

"Morgan?" he said. "I don't know no Morgan. You
know a Morgan, Kid?"

"No, I don't," I said. "Me and ole Zeb, we ain't working for no one. We ain't got jobs right now."

Them three men looked at each other, then one of
them lowered his rifle, and so did the other two.

"Climb on down, men," the one said, "and welcome. We're sorry for the rude greeting, but we can't be too careful these days. My name's Willie Weaver."

Weaver stuck out his hand, and ole Zeb shuck it. Then Weaver turned to me, and I shuck his hand.

"These men are Charlie Raspberry and Larry Tucker," Weaver said. "You're welcome to come in and rest a spell and have something to eat."

"Thanks," Zeb said, and me and him shuck with Raspberry and Tucker.

"Follow me," Weaver said.

He led us over to a white canvas tent with a chimbley poking out its top, and we went in. It was a big tent, and it was pitched up on top of a wood frame. There was long tables and benches in it along with a cookstove, and we could smell the beans and stuff a-cooking before we even went inside. Weaver made a motion toward a table and bench.

"Sit down," he said. Then he turned toward a woman who was standing nearby. "Myrtle," he said, "we have guests, and they're hungry."

"Well, we can sure take care of that," Myrtle said, and she went to busying herself over some pots and pans. Weaver, he poured out two cups a coffee and brung them over to us. Then he went back and poured another'n and come and set down with us.

"Thank you, sir," I said.

"Just call me Willie," he said.

"Willie," Zeb said, "who's this Morgan you was asking about?"

"If you keep on riding that trail you were on," Weaver said, "you'll find him. He's just over on the other side of the next rise, and he's set up a gold camp there, but he wants ours. He's been trying to run us off of this mountain. Well, first off, he tried to buy us out. When we told him we weren't interested, he started threatening, then worse. He's got some thugs working for him. Ever' now and then, some of them slip over this way and do what they can to sabotage our equipment, harass us, to scare us off or slow us down. Anything they think of to try to get us to change our minds."

"You musta come across a good vein here to put up with that kinda nastiness," Zeb said. "And to be a-blasting like you was."

"That was Morgan blasting," Weaver said. "We don't blast. And you're right. We have a good thing here. I don't know if it'll make us all rich or not. We have twelve families here. It ought to make us all a decent living though. Maybe give us each a good enough stake so we can go down off this mountain eventually and open us each up a business of some kind. That's all we want."

"But Morgan wants it all," I said.

"Yes, he does," Weaver said.

"It's a damn shame there's got to be folks like that in this here world," I said.

"I don't know if there's got to be," Weaver said, "but we sure do have them."

Just then that Myrtle brung us over plates, and Weaver sure enough told the truth whenever he said that she'd fix us up real good. We had us some mountain goat meat cooked ever' bit as good as ole Zeb ever cooked it, and some beans, and some fresh bread, and some taters, and it was all good, good as ever I had, and skinny as I am, I et two plates full, and then I drunk me a few more cups a coffee. All the time we kept a-visiting with ole Weaver and hearing tales a the hard times him and his folks had been putting up with in them mountains all on account a that Morgan feller.

"Willie," I said, "is there any way for us to ride around that Morgan when we leave outa here? I don't really cotton to meeting up with him."

"I suppose it's possible," Weaver said, "but it would be a rough ride. The trail goes right through his camp. You could go back the way you came in, or try to ride up higher without the benefit of a trail. That would be a rough go."

I thought about falling all the way down to China, and I said, "I don't want to try to ride around up here without no real trail to ride on."

But I looked at ole Zeb just then, and I seed that he was a-giving me a look too, and I figgered that we both of us was recollecting just exact how we had done ruint the trail back t'other way. 'Course, we neither one of us never said nothing about that to ole Willie. We kept that little secret to just me and Zeb. But that was ole Weaver's only way out too, 'cept unless to just go straight through ole Morgan's camp, which a course he wouldn't want to try, and so he might not appreciate us blocking him in the way we had did. The other thing, a course, was that we wasn't wanting to tell no strangers, even if they had fed us real good, that we was on the fugitive trail.

It takes too much explaining and excuse-making to tell folks what don't already know you pretty good that the law is a-wanting you but it ain't your fault. The more you talks, the more guiltier you sound, 'cause a real guilty feller will be a-doing the same thing. He'll be proclaiming that it was all a mistake, and that he's as innocent as a newborn nekkid babe, and he got mistook on account a this and that. He'll go on and on thataway with a real pitiful look on his face. So if a feller really and truly is innocent a whatever awful thing he's been accused of, why, what is there to tell him from that other feller, the guilty one? They both acts just the same damn way. So there just ain't no sense in even talking about it.

Chapter 5

Well, ole Weaver and them put us up for the night, and then they went and fed us a good big breakfast and lots a coffee, and we thanked them kindly and packed up and hit the trail. We headed north, figgering it couldn't hurt nothing to just ride on through that there Morgan's camp and go on our own way. We seed the camp whenever we topped the next rise, just like ole Weaver told us we would, and then ole Zeb, he stopped to study it a while before we rid on down into it.

"It ain't much of a gold camp," he said. "I can see where they been blasting that mountain back there behind them though. Looks like to me like they ain't doing no good. That's how come them to want Weaver and them's place. Well, let's ride on through. Ain't nothing else for it."

So we headed on, but when we got down into Morgan's camp, the same thing happened to us what had happened back at Weaver's. We was met by men with guns. These wasn't holding rifles though. They was four of them, and they was just standing across the trail right smack in our way with their arms crossed over their chests and six-guns slung low on their thighs. They was gunmen all right. One thing I learnt in my last few years a life, I learnt to spot a gunhand. We stopped.

"Some problem?" Zeb said.

"You just come riding out of that gold camp over the hill," one of the gunnies said.

"It's right on the trail," Zeb said. "No way around it. Same as yours. We're just headed north, is all. Can we pass through?"

I was thinking that I might could get all three of them before they was to get me or Zeb, and I might coulda done it too, but it woulda been a real fool move to try it, 'cause you just never know. One a them might actual a been better'n me, or one a them coulda been just luckier that perticular morning. It don't hardly pay to buck them kinda odds lessen you absolute have to. I set quiet.

"I don't know," the man said. "I think maybe Mr. Morgan might like to have a word with you before you move on."

"That'd be right neighborly," Zeb said. "We'd be tickled to stop for a visit."

Morgan had a big tent kinda like the one Weaver had tuck us into, and that's where this feller led us, but only whenever we went inside, ole Morgan's tent was more like a saloon than a eating place. That one gunslinger pointed us to a table not far from the bar where there was a feller in a black suit and a string tie a-setting and playing with a deck a cards all by hisself. When we come over there, he looked up.

"What is it, Shark?" he said.

"Couple a strangers wanting to ride through," Shark said. "They come out of Weaver's town. I thought you might want to see them before they move on."

Morgan, he looked at Zeb and then he looked at me. He put down his cards.

"Gentlemen," he said, "my name is Randall Morgan."

"I'm Zeb Pike," Zeb said, "and this here is my pardner, Kid Parmlee. We're just passing through, is all."

"Sit down," Morgan said. "Can I buy you a drink?"

"This time a day, Mr. Morgan," I said, "I'd rather have coffee, if you don't mind."

"What about you, Mr. Pike?" Morgan said.

"I reckon I could stand a snort a brown whiskey," said Zeb.

Morgan waved a arm and had our drinks on the table in front of us right quick. He was a slick one—I could tell that, and I could tell just as well that I didn't like his ass worth a damn. I picked up the coffee though, and had myself a sip.

"So you just came from Weaver's town?" Morgan said.

"That's right," said Zeb.

"Came from where?" said Morgan.

"Well, we come up on the mountain south a Foster-ville," Zeb said, and I could tell he was picking his words real keerful like. "Got up to the trail and headed north. I been up here before, couple a years ago maybe, and weren't no one along here then. Your place and Weaver's is all new to me."

"What's your business?" Morgan said.

"We thought to do a little placer mining," said Zeb, "when we find the right spot. Be farther north. Not any place around here."

"That's good," said Morgan. "All the places around here are taken."

"Looks thataway," said Zeb.

"You sure you were just passing through Weaver's place?" said Morgan.

"Why, sure," said Zeb. "That's what I said. What else would we be doing over there?"

"Maybe you work for Weaver," said Morgan. "You look like a prospector all right, but your young pard, there, has the look of a gunfighter to me. Weaver might think he has need to hire him a gunfighter."

"I ain't no gunfighter," I said, "and even if I was, I don't work for Weaver nor no one else. Right now, I ain't even got me a job."

"You looking for one?" Morgan said. "I might be able to use you."

"We ain't looking," Zeb said.

"I didn't ask you, old-timer," said Morgan.

"I ain't looking," I said.

Zeb tossed down his drink and stood up. I had only just had me a sip or two a coffee on account it was hot, but whenever Zeb stood up, well, I did too.

"I think we'll be on our way, Mr. Morgan," Zeb said. "Any reason we can't be on our way?"

"Why, no," Morgan said. "It's a free country. Why would I try to hold you up? Next time you're along this way, stop in for another visit."

Zeb turned and headed out the door, and I follered him. Outside, we mounted right up, and we made our way back over to the trail and turned north on it. I seed tough-looking faces eyeballing us as we rid along. Then we come close to the far edge a the camp, and I seed some men come up from behind some crates and stuff with guns in their hands, rifles and revolvers.

"Look out, Zeb," I said, and I turned ole horse and headed back. Zeb turned quick too and come along right behind me. We rid hard through that camp till we come back to where Shark and them others had stopped us on the way in. They was back there at their posts again, and they stood across the trail just like before. We hauled up.

"What is this?" Zeb said. "Morgan said we could go on our way."

"This ain't your way," Shark said. "This is the way you come from."

"Some men over at the other end a the camp pulled guns on us," I said. "It didn't seem too safe of a way to go."

"Maybe you better just stay a while," Shark said.

"Maybe we don't like it here," I said.

All four a them bastards went for the guns, but I seed that ole Shark, he was the fastest. I whipped out my Colt and sent a bullet into his right hand what tuck off his thumb. The barrel a his shooter hadn't yet cleared the holster. Then I pointed quick at the next one. His hand was just on the butt a his gun. He stopped still, and so did the others. I moved my gun barrel from pointing at one to the other and they all kept still. Shark was a-groaning and a-cussing.

"Drop them gun belts," I said, and they done what I said. "Ride on through, Zeb," I said, and he did. I waited till he was well along, and then I rid on past them bastards too. I caught up with ole Zeb, and I said, "Hit it," and we continued our journey at a fast pace. Them three what still had thumbs musta all picked up their shooters, 'cause just about then the bullets commenced to popping behind us. I knowed they was wasted shots though. We had done rid outa six-gun range.

We kept on a-riding hard for a while, and then we slowed her down again. I looked behind us, and I didn't see no pursuit, so we rode on easy all the way back into Weaver's town. When we come into the town, I didn't see no sign a Weaver just then, but I seed Raspberry a-walking toward us.

"Back so soon?" he said.

"It looks thataway, don't it?" I said. "Weaver around?"

"I think he went over to the tent to get him some coffee," Raspberry said.

"Mind if we head on over thataway?" I asked him.

"No," he said. "Come on. I'll go over there with you."

Ole Raspberry walked on toward the tent, and me and Zeb, we rid along real slow behind him. Pretty soon we tied up our critters there by the front door a the tent, and then the three of us went on in. Ole Weaver was there all right. We went and set down there at the table across from him.

"Well," he said, "I can't say I'm too surprised. Morgan and his bunch give you some trouble?"

"Damned if the bastards didn't try to kill us," Zeb said.

"First thing," I said, "whenever we rid in there, just on our way through, you know, why, three gunslingers stopped us and made us go meet Morgan, and then he commenced to quizzing us all up, and then he said we could go on our way, but when we got over to the far side a his camp, why, some gunmen popped up, so we turned around and headed back thisaway. Then them same ones what had stopped us a-going in blocked our way again. But that time, I went and shot one of them, and we come hightailing it back over here."

I had to take me a breath after all that talking, and just about then ole Myrtle, she come on over and asked us if we wanted some coffee. We all said that we sure did, and she went to fetch it.

"What'd they quiz y'all up about?" Raspberry asked.

"Mostly about you," Zeb said. "I mean about your camp here. They seemed to think that we might be a-working for you or something. Accused the Kid here a being a professional gunfighter."

"We told them we was just a-passing through," I said.

"So what will you do now?" Weaver asked.

"I guess we ain't rightly had no time to think on that," I said.

"We was headed north," Zeb said, "but I reckon we ain't now."

"You could go back south for a ways," Raspberry said, "and then take the trail down the mountain. That's the way we have to go in and out. Matter of fact, we have a load of supplies coming in that way right now."

"It's a little late," Weaver said. "I'm starting to worry a bit about it."

Me and Zeb give each other looks on that, on account a if their supplies was a-coming up the same trail what we come up, well, we sure knowed how come they was delayed, and it was 'cause we had pushed all them rocks in on the trail and closed it up. We didn't neither one of us say nothing about that though.

"Say, Willie," said Raspberry, "what say you and me mount up and ride back that way to see if they're coming up all right?"

"I was kind of thinking that myself," Weaver said. "We got plenty of daylight left today. Let's just go on and do it."

"All right," Raspberry said. Then he looked at me and ole Zeb. "You want to ride along with us? It'd get you on your way."

Now that kinda put us in a spot, 'cause we didn't really have no notion a going back the way we come. There was that posse outa Fosterville with ole Jim Chastain a-heading it and mad as anyone could be at me on account a me leaving him nekkid in jail like I done, and there sure weren't no reason for us to go on back down there and head south. But we had to say something, and since I couldn't think a nothing to say, ole Zeb, he spoke up.

"We'll ride along with you," he said. I agreed by nodding my head. Weaver and Raspberry went on out ahead of us to get their horses ready, and since mine and

Zeb's was done saddled and ever'thing, we just set there a-finishing our coffee.

"Zeb," I said, "how come are we a-going along with them? For one thing, we know that there trail is blocked."

"We can help them get it cleared," he said. "It's the right thing to do."

"And then once we clear it off again," I said, "then what? We don't want to ride south, and we sure don't want to go back through Fosterville."

"Let's just go along," Zeb said, "and play it by ear. We'll help these ole boys get their supplies on through, and then we'll just see what we can see. Maybe we'll have to ride south. Or maybe we can take a wide swing east and ride around Fosterville heading north."

"Well, yeah," I said. "I s'pose we could do that. We'd get us on up north eventual if we was to do it thataway."

Well, we slurped our coffee on down, said thankees to Myrtle, and went on outside. Ole Weaver was already a-headed back our way with a saddled horse, and in another minute, here come Raspberry. We all mounted up and headed outa the camp going back south on the mountain trail. Ole Zeb opined that we'd oughta hit that camping spot what we had used on our way up before full dark, and we could camp there. If we was to do that, then we'd oughta get back to the trail down the mountain kindly early the next day, maybe mid-morning or so. Weaver and Raspberry agreed with him on that. We hadn't rid along very far outa Weaver's camp whenever the Morgan bunch commenced their blasting again, and we had to fight our skitterish horses and ole Bernice to keep them from sidling offa the edge and maybe taking us with them. Anyhow, we done okay, and we made it on to the camp site about when ole Zeb had figgered we would, and then we unpacked and settled in for the night.

Next morning, we had us some breakfast and coffee—Weaver and Raspberry had brung along supplies—and then we got us a pretty early start. We was far enough away from the blasting by that time that we didn't have no more problems. I asked Weaver if they'd ever had trouble with Morgan south a their gold camp, and he said they never. Ole Morgan, he just pestered them from over at his camp what was north a theirs. I reckoned that I had ought to keep myself alert just the same. You never know who or what might could pop up out on the trail like that.

When we come to the turn going down the mountain, ole Weaver, he hauled a watch outa his pocket, and it was just ten o'clock. Zeb had hit it right on the head. He sure was a humdinger when it come to knowing just about ever'thing they was to know in them mountains and a course, ever'thing about gold too. We had to slow down and take her real easy going down, on account a the trail got steep here and there, and it woulda been easy to slip just a little and then wind up sliding down the mountain for a while, and that with a horse a-sliding on top of you. Anyhow, we rid a ways like that, and then Weaver, who was riding out front, seed the rocks in the way, and he called a halt. I stretched my neck on out, and I could see down the trail on the other side a that long rock pile me and ole Zeb had made was a couple a men and four packmules. The men was busy a-moving rocks.

"Is that there your supplies?" I said.

"That's them," Weaver said.

"Well," Zeb said, "I reckon we best get busy on this end and see how fast we can meet up with them."

All four of us dismounted, and we commenced to

tossing rocks and rolling boulders and such, a-trying to clear out that there trail, and I can tell you, I ain't never in my life worked so hard as I worked that day. It was cool on that mountain trail, but it weren't no time, and I was sweating like hell. I called back to mind ole Chastain and that posse, and how come me and Zeb done what we done, but moving them goddamned rocks that day, I got to thinking that if I was to have a choice in the matter, I'd ruther be fighting the damn posse than moving the damn rocks.

When Zeb had come up with that idea, and I had gone along with it, it never come into my mind that I would be headed back the same way and so be clearing off the damn trail. If that thought had come to me, I'd a not did it. I can tell you that. Ever' now and then, whenever I got me a chance to catch his eye, I give ole Zeb a real mean look to let him know what I was a-thinking, but if the truth a the matter was to be told, I figger he was probably having basic the same kinda thoughts as what I was having.

We worked the rest a that day away, and they still couldn't bring them mules through, so we all just had to lay our ass down along that steep trail and sleep the best way we could manage, and it was sure a long night being uncomfortable the way we was. I was glad when daylight come, but whenever I went to stand up, I couldn't hardly manage it I was so sore on account a all the hard work the day before and then sleeping the way I done. I groaned somewhat, but no one else seemed to have no complaints, so I didn't say nothing too much. I didn't want to turn out to be the only sissy in the bunch, and whenever the others went back to work, why, I did too.

Well, final at last we got the damn trail cleared off, and the two men and the four mules come on through.

Weaver interduced me and Zeb to them other two, and they said something about us going on our way, but we said that we figgered we didn't want to make the ride on down just then, and that if they didn't mind another night a our company, why, we'd just head back up to the campsite with them and wait till morning to make our way on down offa the mountain.

That there likely didn't make no sense, 'cause it was just as far one way as tother, but no one said nothing to argue with us, so all of us headed back on up. We didn't talk much for the rest a the trip till we got to the campsite and unpacked and made us our sleeping spots and cooked us our food and coffee. Whenever we had done et and was all just a-setting around the fire like that and thinking about calling it a day, why, that's when the conversation got going. For a while, all we talked about was the rock slide and what a pain in the ass it had been to get the trail cleared off and all, and ever'one a-wondering how it had got started in the first place. Me and Zeb give each other looks whenever that subject come up.

Then Weaver asked them two what was bringing the mules back if they'd had any trouble along the way, and they said that they had got ever'thing what they had went after all right and hadn't had no problems.

"We witnessed a bank robbery though," said one of them what was named Binger.

"In Fosterville?" Raspberry asked, and his eyes was wide.

The other'n, called Bobby Crash, nodded his head. "In broad daylight," he said. "It was three men. They killed a man in the street for no reason."

"The sheriff there," Binger said, "come running out

of his office just as the three bank robbers was riding
out of town, and he was sure a-cussing."

"Yeah," Crash said. "I guess he knew the outlaws too.
I heard him say, 'That damn Kid Parmlee,' and then he
called for a posse to ride after them."

Chapter 6

Well, me and ole Zeb looked right into each other's saucer eyes at that, and Weaver and Raspberry give us quick and puzzled looks too. I was trying to figger out if I was a-going to have to draw out my shooter to get us away from them four men, but Weaver was a-thinking all right. He turned back towards ole Crash and ole Binger.

"When did this robbery take place?" he asked them.

"It was day before yesterday," Binger said. " 'Long about, I'd say, eleven in the morning."

"Kid," said Weaver, "you were up here with us. What's going on?"

"Well," I said, "I reckon since you know as much as you do, I might just as well go on ahead and tell you the whole story. A while back my ole paw was a-riding with me and Zeb, and we rid into Fosterville after we had been in the mountains for a spell, and ole Chastain, the sheriff, he throwed down on us without no warning. Said we had robbed a stagecoach somewheres up north and kilt a man. We never."

"He had a description," Zeb said. "Two old guys and a skinny kid."

"Sounds like these bank robbers," Binger said.

"Anyhow," I told them, "whenever we rid into your

camp, we was running from ole Chastain and his posse. See, we broke outa his jail."

"But now you can prove that you're innocent," Weaver said. "If the three that robbed the Fosterville bank are the same three who robbed the stagecoach, we know you were up here during the bank robbery."

"Only thing is," I said, "if we was to ride down into Fosterville, even if you was to go along with us, ole Chastain, he mightn't wait to hear what you got to say. If he was to see me and ole Zeb here, he just might start in to shooting first and asking questions later."

"What kind of lawman is he anyway?" Weaver asked.

"One what the Kid here left locked up in his own jail cell stark staring nekkid," Zeb said. "That's what kind."

"You done that?" Raspberry said.

I just kinda shrugged. "It slowed him down some coming after us," I said.

Raspberry shuck his head real slow. "I can't blame the man if he did shoot first," he said. "That's an awful thing to do to a man."

Well, shit, I knowed that, and I already felt just a little bit guilty about it, but on the other hand, I kinda figured that ole Chastain sorta deserved it on account a he throwed down on us with that shotgun without even bothering to ask us to tell our side a the story, and then he embarrasssed us by walking us right down the street in broad-ass daylight with our hands a-sticking up in the air, and him s'posed to be a friend a ours. Why, we had fit Piggses and Hookses together.

"I guess it was kinda low-down," I said.

"Let me think a minute," Weaver said.

"What?" I said.

"Just a minute," he said.

I pulled the makings outa my pocket and rolled myself a smoke. Then I leaned over close to the campfire to get a light, and I like to of burnt the end a my nose, but I didn't let on none. I set back to puff on my cigareet and wait to hear what ole Weaver was a-thinking on.

"You two have a problem," he final said. "We have a problem. Maybe we can help each other out."

I come up real suspicious like all of a sudden, and I raised a eyebrow up on one side a my head, and I said, "What are you a-thinking, Willie?"

"You can't really go back down this southern trail, can you?" he said. "Not without taking a chance on facing that Fosterville posse."

"Well," I said, "it'd be kinda chancey all right."

"You can't go north on the mountain road. You already tried that and had a run-in with Morgan and his men."

"That's the truth," said Zeb.

"You're wanted for murder. Both of you."

"What're you getting at?" I said. I was starting to get aggravated at ole Willie about then.

"Just this," he said. "Suppose you two stay up here with us for a while. Suppose you help us keep Morgan and his gang at a distance. Then, once we have what we want out of our claim up here, we all go down and go into Fosterville, and we clear your name with the authorities. Why, by that time, they might even have caught up with the real robbers, and you'll find that you've already been cleared."

"Of the robberies and killings maybe," Zeb said, "but not of the jailbreaking and sheriff-exposing what we done."

"That's a whole lot better than a hanging offense," Weaver said. "Well, what do you say?"

I had to admit that his idea was considerable more worthwhile than anything what I had in my own head just then. I didn't answer him right off though. I give the matter some thought. I figgered that it wouldn't hardly be safe for me and ole Zeb to try to go after them outlaws just then on account a ole Chastain was likely right on their trail, and if we was to ride in on the deal, he might spot us before spotting them, and that could cause a major disaster for me and Zeb. And the other thing I figgered was that maybe ole Weaver was right. Maybe if we was to hide out in the mountains for a spell, and them outlaws was to keep on a-pulling holdups, why, maybe ole Jim Chastain or some other lawman would just catch up to them. Then they'd find out who they really was, and then it'd be might near safe for us to go back amongst them.

"We'll give her a try," I said.

Well, the next day we rid on back into Weaver's gold camp, and the first thing I done was to beg myself a bath on account a I was filthy dirty from all that rock moving and sweating and sleeping on the ground, and so Willie and ole Myrtle, they come up with a tent for me and Zeb to live in. It was a fair size, not one a them little bitty ones, and they got me a tub a hot water in there, so I soaked my ass real good and scrubbed up with soap too. I felt better after that, but my muscles and bones was still sore from the whole entire ordeal. Anyhow, it was still daylight when I come outa the tent dressed in clean clothes and my Colt strapped on. I walked over to the big tent for some grub and coffee.

It was the end a the work day by then, and so most ever'one in the whole camp was in there, and Willie Weaver made a big announcement and interduced me and ole Zeb to the whole crowd. He told them that our job was to keep the Morgan gang offa their backs while they done their work. All of a sudden, I felt like a for-real hired gunslinger, and that was something that I had been denying I was all along. I wasn't sure how I felt about that. I said so to ole Zeb.

"Well, Kid," he said, "look at it thisaway. S'pose now that this here gold camp was a regular town. It's kinda like one, ain't it? Got women and kids and all."

"Yeah," I said. "I reckon it is kinda like a town."

"Well, look at it thataway," he said. "It's a town, and over that next rise north a here, there's a element a troublemakers—outlaws, you might say."

"Okay," I said.

"Now what would a town do about a situation like that?"

"I reckon they'd hire them a lawman," I said.

"Well?" he said.

I tuck his point all right, but then I couldn't figger out what was worse, being a hired gunslinger or being a lawman. I just went on over to our tent a-fixing to go to bed but only I never made it. I heared someone a-hollering like hell.

"Stop him. Stop, thief."

I run back outside real fast and looked around for what it was that was wrong, and I seed a figger a-running like the dickens towards the north side a the camp. Someone come up aside a me and pointed right smack at that running figger.

"Stop him," he said.

I didn't ask no questions 'cause there didn't seem to be no time for it. I just whipped out my Colt and fired a shot right in front a the feller what was a-running. He stopped all right. He looked around. There was a saddled horse at one a the shacks not far from where he was at, and he turned and run and jumped on its back and headed south.

"Stop him," this feller said to me. But I didn't know

what the man had did, and so I hated to just shoot him dead like that.

"What the hell did he do?" I said.

"He's got our claim papers," the man said.

'Bout then, ole Weaver had come a-running up on account a he'd heared the commotion.

"You say he got our papers?" Weaver said.

"I saw him come out of the shack over there," the man said. "I yelled, and he ran. I went into the shack and saw that our papers're missing. He's got to be one of Morgan's men."

"What can he do with your papers?" I asked.

"The only thing he could do," said Weaver, "is take them down to Fosterville, forge some signatures and re-file."

"Get me a horse," I said. "I'll stop the son of a bitch."

In another minute I was riding after the bastard, but I wasn't riding too hard and fast 'cause the sun was done down and it was dark. That mountain road was dangerous even in daylight, so it sure weren't no place to get in a hurry on after dark. But I knowed I had to stay after him. See, he mighta been damn fool enough to ride down that there trail at night. He mighta been desperate enough, 'cause what he had meant to do was to steal them papers and sneak back over to his own camp in the dark, but he had been saw, and he had been forced to run the other direction. I figgered that meant he would ride all night, unless, a course, he was to fall off the edge and land way down in China. Well, that meant I would ride all night too, but only it wouldn't be no fast riding, I can tell you that.

That there turned out to be the longest and most scariest ride I had ever tuck in my whole entire lifetime. That ole horse they had give me slipped and skittered a time or two, and I had me some awful visions a falling through the black night for hours and hours before I come back to earth and got all smashed up into little bitty pieces. Once I even got off and walked up front, a-pulling that horse along by his reins.

I was sure relieved when we come to the turnoff what run on down the mountain. It was still dark as hell, and it would still be easy as pie to take a tumble, but on that going-down trail, a feller would tend to slide a while ruther than just get pitched right through midair. All the time I was trying to look through the dark and listen real hard, too, in case I was to come up on the bastard I was follering. I never seed nor heared nothing. I knowed I was on his trail though, 'cause that was the way he had run outa the gold camp, and there weren't no other place for him to be but 'cept on that trail. He was out there in front a me all right.

Way before daylight hit, I was hungry and tired and sleepy, but I just kept on a-going 'cause there wasn't nothing else for it. By the time the ole sun managed to creep out and peek over the edge a the eastern horizon and give a little light to the sky, I was almost to the end a the trail and down offa the mountain. I could see on down there too, and I didn't see no sign a the paper thief. I sudden come a little nervous thinking about ole Chastain and his posses too. I rid on down and out onto the flat road. There was mountains to my left and flat prairie off to my right. I sure felt like as if I was in a real touchy position there.

The road I was a-riding on tuck a curve a-follering the line a the foothills just up ahead a me, and in a few miles after that, it would run right on into Fosterville. I figgered that I had to catch up with the bastard and stop him well before we come to that point. When I rid around that curve, I seed him. I had been pretty close behind him all right. He musta been at least as skeered

a that high mountain road as what I was. I kicked that
ole horse in the sides to move up on the crook a little
faster.

I covered about half the distance between me and him
before he heared me a-coming, and then he tuck a look
back over his shoulder. He kicked his horse, ruther, the
one he had stoled, and I hurried on after him.

"Hold up there," I yelled out, but he didn't pay me
no mind. I pulled out my Colt and fired a shot up over
his head a-purpose. I didn't want to shoot him in the
back, but I wanted to make him stop if I could. He
heared the shot, and he looked back, but he kept on a-
keeping on. Then he went around another curve, and I
lost sight of him for a minute. Whenever I rounded that
curve, I seed the horse he had stoled kinda ambling
around confused like. There wasn't no rider on his back.
I hauled back on the reins a my borried horse real quick
like, and it's a good thing I did too, 'cause a shot come
at me from somewheres just then. I yelped like a coyote
at night, tuck me a headlong dive outa the saddle towards my left, and when I hit the ground, I rolled on
over towards the rocks at the base a them foothills.
When I come up behind a big ole boulder, I had my Colt
in my hand.

The reason I had yelped the way I done was on account a I didn't have no idea where the bastard was
hiding at, and I figgered that if I yelped and left the
saddle that he might just get convinced that he had shot
me. Then if I was to stay still long enough, he just might
come outa hiding to hunt for me or for my corpus,
whichever it turned out to be. 'Course, I didn't intend to
be no corpus when he come around. I stayed low, and I
waited.

It sure enough seemed like a hell of a long wait as
hungry and tired and sleepy and cold as I had got making

that all-night ride down that mountain. Once or twice I damn near fell for my own trap what was to come outa hiding and go look for the feller, but I never. I reminded myself that in a situation like what we two was in, the one what lost his patience first was the one most likely to end up dead. I stayed hunkered down behind that rock.

Both horses was milling around out there in the open. They even kinda come together. They knowed each other, both of them being from Weaver's camp like they was, and I figgered that they tuck some comfort in that fact after what they both just been through. I also knowed that two saddled horses without no riders out like that a loose would sure as hell stir up some interest if anyone was to come riding along, and I was thinking that if anyone done that, I sure did hope that it wouldn't be no Jim Chastain posse.

Then of a sudden I had to piss so bad it was a-hurting me to hold it back, and pretty soon, why, it weren't no matter a hurting no more. It become a matter a not being able to hold it back no longer. I was fixing to piss my pants if I didn't make a proper decision right then. I thought about getting myself kilt, and I thought about showing up wherever I would show up with pissy pants, and I stood up and hauled it out and let go. Oh, but that was a whale of a physical relief, I can tell you, but at the same time it was real nervous making.

I was standing behind that rock I had been hid behind, and I was pissing all over it on account a the fact that I sure didn't want to turn my back in case that bastard should come a-looking for me the way I intended for him to do in the first place. But the problem was that it just wouldn't quit. I musta been plumb full a piss, as skinny as I was. It just kept a-coming. I was using my left hand to aim my stream and still holding my Colt in my right hand, and if that feller had come a-walking up, well, he woulda been able to see me from about my belly up standing behind that rock. And that's just what happened.

He come a-walking out in full view, and he was moving slow and looking around, hoping to find me a corpus, but then he seed me, and I was a-standing on my own two feet, not dead atall. He was a-holding his six-gun in his hand. I seed him just a instant before he seed me, and I hollered right out at him, a-hoping that he wouldn't be able to tell what it was I was a-doing.

"Just throw that shooter down," I said, "and I won't kill you."

Well, he never, the dumb son of a bitch. Instead he raised it up and swung it around and snapped off a shot what skidded on that boulder I was a-pissing on, but I raised my Colt up and blasted his ass. My shot tuck him right in the chest. He kinda jerked and staggered, and then he went limp all over and crumpled up there on the ground. I watched him real keerful, and he never moved after that. I final finished up my business and put ever'thing away. Then I walked out around that little wet boulder and headed for my latest victim. I thought about ole Paw. He woulda wanted to keep count, but I had give that up.

I moved out slow on account a I was pretty sure that he was dead, but you just never know. Sometimes a shot man will hang on long enough to surprise you and shoot you before he goes on to croak, so I watched him real close. I walked on up to where I could reach out with the toe a my boot and kick his shooter away. Then I holstered my own and rolled him over on his back. He was dead all right.

I squatted down and rummaged through his pockets, and sure enough, there was them papers what they had said he had stoled. I tucked them into my own pocket, and then I tuck hold a him and dragged him over behind the boulder what I had wetted down and left him there. Then I went and rounded up the two horses. I started to head back for the up the mountain trail, but something held me back. I wasn't quite ready to go back up there and hide out. I had a urge to do something different, and I didn't have no Zeb nor no one else with me to fuss about it and talk me out of it.

I mounted up the same horse what I had been riding, and I led the other'n along behind me. I headed them north, but only I didn't stay on the road. In just a little while, I turned kinda northeast like as if I meant to swing wide around Fosterville. I rid on like that for a spell till I could see the damn town up ahead. There wasn't no one riding outa town and coming in my direction, so I got to feeling a little more puffed up and confident in my plan, what really, a course, hadn't been give too much thought. Well, off over yonder to the east there was a grove a trees. It looked to be nice and quiet and cool and dark. I figgered it'd hide me out all right, and I headed over there with my two horses.

I rid my ass on over into them trees and got down outa the saddle. I tied them two horses where they could get to some good grass, and then I set down on the ground and stared over at Fosterville. I dreamed about ole Red and all a her many female charms, and I sure did want to get my ass tangled on up in them. I meant to wait out the whole entire day till dark set in, and then I was a-going on into town.

I can tell you, it aggravated me something fierce to think on how them three outlaws had just damn near ruint my young life, not to mention a couple a older ones as well, and then on top a that, how ole Chastain, what I had called my friend and had gone a-looking for a-purpose to have a drink or two with, had turned on me so easy like, a-believing that me and Zeb and Paw coulda been them cold-blooded bastards. That just really chapped me for good and all.

Chapter 7

Well, I musta set there a hour or so when I seed what looked for all hell like a posse a-riding outa town headed south, and I couldn't be real actual sure for certain, but it looked powerful like ole Chastain a-riding out front. The only thing what I could figger was that he had done looked ever'where he could think of a-going north, so he was fixing to search the other direction some. I was hoping that he wouldn't take that trail up the mountain again and this time find it open and clear and go on up there and come onto ole Weaver's camp the way me and ole Zeb had did, but only if Chastain done it he'd find ole Zeb up there a-hiding out without me.

Then it come to me that with ole Chastain outa town, why, I'd likely be pretty fair safe in there. I made up my mind right quick to just go on in, and that's what I done. I was a-wanting to see ole Red, you know, and I kinda wanted some whiskey too, but the main thing just right at that very minute was that I was ferocious hungry. I mounted up on my borried horse and tuck the reins a the other one and rid on into Fosterville, but I rid in on the backside a the main street. I went on down the way like that till I come up on the backside a the stable, and I tuck the horses in there to get them feed and all. Then

I walked down the way to a eating place what I knowed, and I had myself a big meal. I felt some better then.

Being well fed like that and knowing that ole Chastain and his posse was outa town musta made me feel just plumb cocky too, 'cause whenever I got up to leave that place, I just walked out the front door right onto the main street and stood there a minute a-looking the place over like as if I was fixing to buy the whole town or something. Then I seed ole Red. She just come outa a shop across the street and down a ways, and she walked along at a pretty fair clip for a few strides before she happened to glance over my way and see me a-standing there. Well, she hustled her pretty ass on over to me.

"Kid," she said, "you damn fool, what are you doing in town?"

"Well, the sheriff and the posse is gone outa town, ain't they?" I said.

"Yes, but—Oh, come on." She grabbed aholt a my arm and looked up and down the street. Then she pulled me along with her across the street and in between two buildings there. When we come out on the backside, she turned us to the right, and we walked on down to where a stairway was on the back wall a one a the buildings there. I reckanized it, and I knowed that it would take us right on up the room what she stayed in. We went up and then down a hallway and on into her room. She shut the door and locked it.

"Jim is really mad at you," she said. "I think he'd shoot you on sight if he had the chance. Why, half the town went into his office just to get a look at him in the jail cell like he was. And he was cussing and shouting out orders and blushing all over his whole body."

"It didn't hurt him none, did it?" I said. "He oughta learn to take it a little better'n that."

"Where's your paw and ole Zeb?" she asked me.

"I sent Paw back home to Texas," I said. "Ole Zeb, he's safe holed up with some folks we run into."

"Where at?" she said.

"If I don't tell you," I said, "then can't nobody make you tell them. I had some business I had to take keer of that brung me close into town, and being so close, I figgered I'd just come in and drop in on you. I was going to wait till dark, but then I seed the posse ride out and figgered this would be as good a time as any."

"You crazy fool."

"Listen," I said, "I got me and Paw and Zeb all cleared a them stage robbing and killing charges. The folks we're a-staying with can prove that we been with them for a few days now, and we just heared that them three what folks think is us done robbed the bank right here in Fosterville."

"That's right," said Red. "They did, and Jim is sure that it was you."

"Well, I can prove that it weren't," I said. "We was with them other folks away from here. Only thing is, them folks got a problem theirselfs, and they can't hardly afford to leave home and come down here till we get it solved for them. I'm kinda hoping that ole Jim catches up with the real crooks even before that, so he'll know the real truth about it on his own."

"Oh, Kid," she said, "you sure got yourself into a big mess this time."

"I never got me into it," I said. "It was them three crooks, whoever they are, and ole Chastain for believing that they was us."

She throwed her arms around me just then and smacked her lips right up against mine and give me a long and sloppy kiss. It surprised me real good, but it was just what I was a-wanting. Then, whenever she final broke loose, she tuck aholt a me and led me on over to the bed, and we commenced to pulling clothes offa each other till we was both stark staring nekkid, and then I started in to laughing. Red give me a hard look for that.

"What's so funny?" she said.

"I was just thinking," I said, "that if ole Jim was to come in here and see me like this here, he'd most likely march me right down the middle a the street without letting me get back into my clothes."

She laughed too then.

"He'd prob'ly handcuff you to a hitching rail out front and leave you nekkid there for a while," she said. "Likely at least a day or two."

We both of us laughed, and then we wound up rolling around on the bed in each other's arms, and then of a sudden, we wasn't laughing no more. We become down-right serious over each other's nekkidness, and we sure had us a time for a while. I don't know how long we kept it up, but when we was all did, we just laid there side by side in that sweaty bed a-panting like two dogs.

"You want a drink, Kid?" she said.

"Well," I said, "I don't reckon one would hurt me none."

She got up to go pour us a couple a drinks, and while she was a-doing that, I set up on the edge a the bed, reached into my shirt pocket and pulled out the makings. I rolled me a cigareet and lit it, and she brung the drinks over. I give her a drag offa my smoke, and I tuck me a sip a the drink she had brung. Then we heared the sound of a bunch a horses, and she went over to the winder and tuck a peek out.

"Jim and the posse," she said. "They're back."

"They got any prisoners?" I asked, right hopeful that they had come onto them real crooks.

"No," she said.

I tuck another sip a my drink and then another drag on my cigareet.

"Now that they're back in town," she said, "you better stay right here till after dark. I don't want any of them to see you. Especially Jim."

"Well," I said, "if I got to lay low, I can't think of a better place to do it in."

We finished up our drinks and my smoke, and then we went to playing around a little more, and we done that sorta thing for most all the rest a that afternoon. When it come on toward evening, ole Red, she got dressed and went out, and in just a little while, she come back with a whole mess a food, and we et ourselfs full and had another drink. Then she suggested to me that late night weren't the safest time for me to go sneaking outa town. Early morning before daylight was the best, she said. Ever'one what had stayed up late would be sleeping real sound. Well, I never argued with her over that, and I made up my mind then that I'd just stay right there with her till the wee hours a the morning. Then I would go on and slip outa town and head back for ole Weaver's gold camp.

I had done found out all the news and it weren't good. Ole Jim still thunk he was after us, and he hadn't even come near to catching the real outlaws, so we had to keep hiding out till Weaver and them was ready to come down and clear us. The good news a course was that I had stopped ole Morgan's man from getting into Fosterville with them papers. I figgered that on account a them papers, Weaver and the others was likely worrying about me and what had happened, and I bet that ole Zeb was some concerned too, but I figgered it wouldn't hurt them none too much to wait just a few more hours to get the word.

And ole Red, she had saw Chastain whenever she had

gone out after our dinner, and she had talked to him
some. She told me that he was still for damn sure and
certain that it was me and Paw and Zeb what was doing
all that wickedness around the countryside, and that
nothing she had said had went even a inch towards convincing him that he might be mistook in his feelings.

Anyhow, I had me a whole lot more fun that night,
and just before time for the sun to come a-creeping
around, I dressed and slipped out the back way and went
on down to the stable and got my two borried horses.
By the time I had rid back to where I had shot that
Morgan man, the sun had just peeked up the tiniest
bit. I stopped and loaded the stiff onto the extry horse.
It weren't too bad on account a the nights and even
the days a little bit was starting in to be kinda cool. I
made it back up that mountain without no trouble, and
I woulda stopped for the night along the way, but only
I didn't have no food packed in, so I just kept on a-
going. It was into the night whenever I made it back to
Weaver's gold camp.

They was two guards there, and they stopped me, but
whenever I told them who I was, they let me ride on in.
I found the dead man's horse what he hadn't been able
to get to whenever I tuck my first shot at him, and I
switched him from the horse he had stoled to the one
what was his own or else Morgan's, and then I sent that
there Morgan horse on the way back to ole Morgan's
camp. Someone woke up Weaver to let him know I was
back, and he dragged me into their food tent and heated
up some coffee and dug out some cold meat and biscuits,
and I et them, and they was all right. I was that hungry.

I give Weaver back the papers that owlhoot had tuck,
and he was sure glad to get them back into his own
hands, I can tell you. Before I was able to give it all up
and go on to sleep, it seemed like as if most near the

whole entire camp, including ole Zeb, had woke up and come to see me and to find out what had happened.

I lied to them all just a little bit whenever I told them that I had saw the posse what was a-looking for me and Paw and Zeb, and I had gone into hiding till the coast was clear again. It was about half a lie, I guess. Anyhow, they all tuck that as good enough reason that I had been gone for so long. Final they was all satisfied, and they let me go on and get some sleep. I sure as hell needed it too.

I was up early enough in the morning to have me a big breakfast in their tent with ever'one else, and whenever the miners and their women all went on back to work, me and ole Zeb set there in the tent and had us some more coffee.

"Kid," Zeb said, "what're you going to do about that there Morgan camp? We can't just set here in this camp forever."

"Well, hell, Zeb," I said, "I don't rightly know. I'm pretty damn good with my Colt, but I can't just ride on over there and take on that whole army what ole Morgan's got over there."

"Well, I know you can't do that," he said, "but we're going to have to come up with some kinda plan. We got to make something happen here."

"Well, I'm thinking on it," I said. "If you come up with any ideas on it, you let me in on them. You hear?"

I slurped the rest a the coffee outa my cup and set the cup down and got up and walked on outside. I didn't want ole Zeb a-pressing me no more about what I was a-planning, on account a I really didn't have no idea, and maybe I was a-thinking on it, but in my thinking, I hadn't managed to produce no worthwhile thoughts. I went walking kinda aimless around the camp, and I wound up

over on the north side a-looking towards Morgan's camp.
'Course, I couldn't actual see it from there, but I knowed
where it was at all right. I looked up into the high mountains around us, and I could see snow way up on their
tops. I really did like that.

Then come another one a them loud blasts, but it was
louder than the other'ns I had heared, and I figgered that it
musta been closer or else it was a bigger charge a powder
than them others. I weren't for sure which. But it did
make me jump whenever it went off, and I could hear
the critters in the camp behind me nickering and braying
and such and even stamping around some. Weaver and
Tucker come up and stood one on each side a me and
looked towards Morgan's along with me.

"The son of a bitch," Weaver said.

"How come that there blast to a been so loud?" I asked.

"He's moving closer to us," Weaver said.

"He'd best not come any closer than that last one," said
Tucker.

Weaver pointed ahead and off a little to his left.

"He's moving along that ridge," he said. "If he moves
much farther this direction, his blasting could send the
side of that mountain right down on our camp."

"Is there some way we can get ourselfs up yonder
where we can take a look and see just what the hell he's
a-doing?" I asked.

"We can get up there," Weaver said.

"Well, s'pose," I said, "me and a few men with guns
was to climb up there to take a look."

"Why with guns?" Tucker said. "Just to take a look."

"The guns would be just in case a something un-
expected," I said. "I don't like to get caught with my
britches down, if you get my meaning."

Tucker nodded.

"I get your meaning," he said.

"I'll go with you," Weaver said. "And I bet Charlie will too."

"You and Charlie got rifles?" I asked him.

"Yes," he said, "and we can both handle them too. When do you want to go?"

"Right now," I said.

It was just a few minutes later whenever ole Raspberry tuck the lead and me and Weaver was a-follering him. They both had their rifle guns all right, and I was a-packing my ole Colt as usual. I wasn't never no good rifle shot nohow. Anyhow, we clumb a long climb, and now and then the going got pretty tough all right, but final ole Raspberry stopped along a low ridge. Me and Weaver come up beside him, and he nodded.

"There they are," he said.

And they wasn't very far off from us. They was digging around in the side a the mountain, and even I could tell that what they was up to was they was digging holes to shove them dynamite sticks into.

"That's too close," Weaver said. "They're not even blasting for gold. They're trying to scare us off. If that doesn't work, my bet is that they'll move right on over here where we are and blast this ridge away."

"They'd rain a mountain down on us if they did that," Raspberry said.

"Well, whyn't we just discourage them somewhat?" I said.

I looked around us, and I seed where I could climb my ass up a little higher and then work my way over closer to them Morgan hands. It looked like to me as if I could get might near close enough thataway for some decent shots with my six-gun.

"I'll go over thataway," I said, a-pointing, "and when

I get to where I want to be, I'll wave back at you. Then you get ready with your rifles. I'll snap off a shot or two at them from over there, and then you two cut loose from over here."

"Do we shoot to kill?" Raspberry asked.

I looked at Weaver.

"That's up to you," I said. "I figger on just skeering them back on down into their camp. If we shoot at them from here, they might not come back thisaway, on account a they'll never know whuther or not we'll still be here a-waiting for them."

"I think that's good enough for now," Weaver said. "Let's just put some fear in them."

"All right," said Raspberry.

I went a-crawling on up the mountain. Now, I ain't no kin to no mountain goat, and once or twice I slipped some, and it skeered me so once that I like to a messed my britches but I never. I kept on a-going. Once I looked down, and I seed how far I'd fall if I was to take a tumble. I didn't look down no more after that. I final got to the place where I didn't want to climb no higher. I just wanted to work my way on a little closer to them bastards, and so I started into moving along on a kinda little ledge what was there, and then I had final made it all right. I slipped the Colt outa my holster, and I looked back at Weaver and Raspberry. I could see that they was a-watching me.

I waved my shooter in the air, and then I looked down on them Morgan men, and I tuck me a shot. It zinged into a rock just to the left a one a the bastards, and he did jump. He pulled a gun out, and he ducked behind that rock. I shot again, and he laid low. Just then Weaver and Raspberry cut loose on them with their rifles, and them Morgan men hopped and jumped around not knowing whichaway the bullets was a-coming at them from. They ducked behind something, and then whenever another bullet hit something, they'd move around to the other side a the rock or the ridge or whatever cover they thunk they had found.

Whenever I figgered we had sent enough lead their way, I waved at Weaver and Raspberry again, and we ceased our firing and just set quiet for a spell. I seed one a the Morgan men peek out kinda like he wanted to hunt for a target, but he never seed none a us, so he never did shoot.

"Let's get outa here," he said. I heared him clear enough from up there where I was at. Then he turned to run, and he run as far as he could before he went to sliding down the side a the mountain on his ass. His buddies all follered him, and they all slud too. It was pretty comical, and I did enjoy a-watching it. When I final seed that they was all gone, I started in to making my own way back towards where ole Weaver and ole Raspberry was at. But then I made my big-ass mistake. I looked down again, and it skeered me real bad. It put all kinds a fear into my very heart and soul, I can tell you. I went to shaking, but I tried to control it and keep myself a-going. Then I come to that there one place where I had slipped before, and of a sudden, I couldn't move. I was just stuck to the side a that mountain, and right then I had me a most dreadful vision of a godawful unpleasant death just a-waiting right ahead a me. Either that or a real long fall clean on down into China.

Chapter 8

"Oh, lordy Jesus God," I said, "please get my ass down safe offa this son-of-a-bitching mountain."

I hadn't never prayed to no one nor nothing before in my whole entire life, but I had heared about Jesus and them, and I knowed that some folks did pray like that, and I had even heared that now and then they got whatever it was they had prayed for, and I was so ske-ered to be froze on the side a that there mountain like that on account a the things that ole Zeb had told me about folks falling off and all, I just had to do some-thing, and I figgered that chancing a prayer couldn't do no harm, and, hell, it might even help. I even had me a vision just then of a great big hand a-reaching down outa the sky and taking aholt a me and lifting me offa there real gentle like and then setting me down safe on solid flat ground. But a course, it never happened like that. I heared Weaver a-calling to me though.

"Kid," he said, "what's wrong?"

"Come on, Kid," said Raspberry. "You're all right. You can make it easy."

"I can't make it atall," I said. "There ain't nothing easy about it neither. I'm friz solid here, damn it."

And I was too. My damned ole fingers was all ten dug deep into the side a that mountain, and my both feet was pressing down as hard as they could onto whatever toehold they had found. Then the rest a me from top to bottom was smashed hard right up flat against the side a the mountain, and that was including the right side a my face. I couldn't even move one finger, not if I'd a wanted to. I don't think I could blink my eyes, and I was only just barely able to draw a breath.

"What do you mean?" Weaver said. "You've got a good handhold just to your left. I can see it from here. Move your left hand over and you'll find it."

"I ain't moving nothing," I said. "I can't."

"Look, Kid," Raspberry said. "We'll talk you through it. One step at a time. I can see your whole way back from over here. Just move one hand. Then one foot. I'll bring you right along. I can see the way."

"Well, I can't see it, damn it," I said. "Talk all you want to. I ain't moving. I ain't moving nothing."

"What are we going to do?" I heared Weaver ask Raspberry. I could hear them talking to each other just like as if they'd been right there beside a me.

"I've seen it before, Willie," Raspberry said. "It happens to some men like that. He's right. It's like he's frozen there. He really can't move."

"Kid," Weaver said, raising his voice again, "can you move your left hand?"

"No," I said, "and I ain't going to try neither."

"All right then," Raspberry said. "It's all right, Kid. Just hang on. Hold on tight. I'm coming after you."

I wondered just what the hell that meant. If I couldn't move and was stuck to the side a the mountain like that, what the hell was he going to do whenever he come after me? I couldn't figger out any way he could do nothing for me. I figgered I was just a goner and that was that, unless a course old Jesus was to decide to do what it was I had asked him to do.

Now, you might be a-wondering just what kinda cowardly chicken shit am I after all, and I guess I couldn't really blame you none for that with what I'm a-telling you about and all, but remember that I had done faced me a good many bad-ass gunslingers whose clear and often stated intention was to blow my ass all the way to hell, and I had faced them with a cool head, and I had always come out clean and clear too. There weren't a man alive who could skeer me a-standing in front a me with a gun, long as I had my own Colt strapped on me. No sir.

But what all it just goes to show is that I don't keer who it is you want to talk about nor how big he is nor how many men has shot at him nor how many he has shot down and kilt and maybe had fistfights and all kinds a things like that a-happening to him all around and through the years, no matter how brave you think a man might be, nor how much you might look up to him or admire him or even be askeered of him, there is something somewhere that'll skeer the shit outa him, and if he tells you different, he's a ball-faced liar. Well, so what I'm a-telling you is just only that I had done come right smack up against what it is that skeers me, right there on the side a that mountain.

"Hang on, Kid," Weaver said. "Charlie's coming for you. It won't be long now. We'll get you out of there."

"How?" I said. "Is he going to carry me on his back? Can he fly or something?"

"Just hang on," Weaver said. "Don't panic. Try to think about something else."

Well, I commenced to thinking about Paw and Maw and even my poor ole dog Farty what had been shot dead by that bastard Joe Pigg what had set me off on my fugitive's trail when I was only a snot-nosed kid fourteen year old. And then I wondered if anyone would bother to let Maw and Paw know it whenever I was dead, and if they would tell them how it was I come to die.

I wondered, too, if I would go to heaven or hell and whichever one I was to wind up in, would I run into ole Farty there. I kinda hoped that I would and that we'd be able to go a-hunting for something together. I didn't know if Maw or Paw would really give a shit was they to hear that I had give up the ghost, even in such a horrible way, but I figgered at least my pardner ole Zeb would keer and so would Red. I sure did hate it that I would never see them again. Then I felt a hand on my left shoulder, and it kinda startled me somewhat, and damned if ole Raspberry weren't right there beside me and a-touching me.

"All right, Kid," he said. "Just relax. Let me take your left hand and move it. I'll put it right over here where you can get a good hold. Okay?"

"No," I said. "I ain't a-turning loose. I'll fall all the way down to China if I do. I got aholt a something here, and I mean to keep aholt of it."

Raspberry moved his hand to my left wrist, and I hollered like I had been burnt.

"Turn a loose a me, you son of a bitch," I said. "Leave me be."

"Charlie," I heared ole Weaver say from over there where he was at. "Charlie, there's a dirt ledge just down below you. Not too far down. It's plenty wide too. You can drop right down on it. Both of you."

"You hear that, Kid?" Raspberry said. "There's a ledge right under us. All we have to do is just drop down."

"I ain't dropping nowhere," I said. "I'll drop to China and get smashed to bits."

"Kid," Raspberry said, and he was trying to keep his

voice nice and calm and soothing. "You can't just stay
here like this. You've got to do something. You've got
to get off this mountain somehow. Let me help you."

"I ain't dropping and I ain't moving," I said.

"Your muscles will give out on you sooner or later,"
he said, "and then you'll fall for sure."

"I bet I can hang on here till I starve to death," I said.
"Then I won't know about it whenever I fall. I'll done
be dead."

"You'll get weak and fall before you die," he said.

"Well, then, just shoot me offa here," I said, "but
shoot to kill."

Then by God, that son of a bitch Raspberry, of a
sudden, without no kinda warning nor nothing, just tuck
right aholt a my left wrist and plucked it right offa the
side a that mountain, and I went to losing my balance
and hollering and flailing around, and then I felt myself
a-flying backward through midair, a-screaming all the
way, and I could feel it whenever my belly and all my
guts and even my private parts all went right up into my
chest and somewhat into my throat, and I felt like as if
I had been flying six hunnerd feet through the air, and
then I hit the ground, and I weren't broke to pieces atall.
I was sure all outa breath though, and I tried to suck in
some air.

I was laying flat on my back on that ledge they had
told me about. I looked up, and I could see ole Charlie
Raspberry just about six feet up from me where I was
at. He was still hanging on to the side a the mountain
there where I had been stuck, and I knowed then that
six foot or so was all the farther down I had actual fell.
I set up then, and I felt around on me for all a my parts
what had gone up into my chest and my throat, but they
was all already back down where they had original come

from. Then ole Raspberry, he dropped down onto the ledge beside me.

"You all right?" he said.

"I guess," I said. "I ain't dead."

"Well, look over there. Look ahead to where Willie's waiting for us," Raspberry said. "From here, we can stand up straight and just walk right back over there. Okay? You ready now?"

"No," I said. "You go on ahead."

"Now, Kid—"

"No, really, Charlie," I said. "I ain't like I was up there no more. I'm okay now. Really. I just want to wait a bit. That's all. Go on now."

"You sure?"

"Yeah, I'm sure," I said, kinda aggravated. "I wanta set here a spell and watch to make sure them Morgan bastards don't come back up here for no more blasting. I'll keep watch on the place for a spell. You go on back. Both of you. Tell ever'one what we done up here and that ever'thing's okay for now. I'll be along directly. I'm just fine now. Go on."

Final, I convinced them that I was for-real okay, and they tuck off and left me there, but what they didn't know, 'cause I hadn't told them, was the for-real reason I had run them off like that. You see, whenever I had went flying through the air like that, and my guts had all come loose the way they had did, well, I had made myself a real embarrassing mess what I didn't want to have to tell no one about, and I hadn't wanted them two hanging around long enough to catch the hint of it from their nostrils neither. I didn't know just what it was I was going to do about it, but I did know I was going to have to figger it out for myself.

Well, I unbuckled my gun belt and laid it aside a good stretching arm's length away. Then I pulled off my boots and set them over there too. The messy part come next when I slipped outa my ruint britches, and it like to a made me sick. The legs was mostly all right, though, and so I used them for rags to try to clean myself up the best way I could, and then I throwed them nasty britches off the side a the mountain.

So there I was, a-setting half nekkid, and that the bottom half a me too, on a ledge up on the side a the damned ole mountain. It was still daylight, and I knowed I couldn't just get up and walk back into the camp like that, with ever'thing I had a-hanging out like that and swinging loose. I didn't want no one to see me like that, but even more, I didn't want to have to tell no one how come me to be in that condition.

Well then, I thunk about ole Chastain nekkid in his jail cell, and I knowed better then just what a bad thing I had did to him, but then I figgered that after all he had been better off than what I was at that moment, on account a at least he could tell folks that he had been forced into that humiliating condition at gunpoint. Me, I didn't have no such good excuse as that.

Well, I just had to come to grips with the situation I was in. That was all there was for it. I had to figger out how to deal with it. That's what being a man is all about—figgering out how to deal with whatever situation you find yourself caught up in. I pondered my plight for a spell, and I decided that I would wait till nightfall right there on that ledge, and then I would go down and back into the camp. Thataway, there wouldn't be as many folks likely to see me come a-walking in. Maybe a few. But if I was to wait long enough, maybe no one would see me. The only problem with that was that if I was to wait till dark time, I would have to make the rest a that climb back down to the camp in the dark, and that could be a little bit dangerous.

That last part a the way back down weren't real dangerous. It was a gradual slope, but in the dark it might could be a little tricky. I figgered it'd be worth a skint knee or two and maybe even a scratched-up ass, though, to keep from being saw the way I was. I kept my thought that I would wait for dark.

Well, I set there with the pebbly ground a-digging into my bare ass and my knees drawed up against my chest, embarrassed even though I was setting there by my own self and no one nowhere around, and I sure was a-wishing the time would pass faster for me. I considered taking me a little nap to help the time to pass, but then I weren't at all sleepy, and besides that, I was askeered that if I was to actual go to sleep, someone might come along a-checking up on me to be sure was I all right. I figgered I'd just have to set there and be bored.

Now and then I looked back towards where them bastards a Morgan's had been blasting to see if any of them was coming back around, but they never. Most a the time I stared over there at where Raspberry and Weaver had been at. That was the direction I was really worried about. No one come around though.

I got boreder and boreder, and then I commenced to getting real hungry too. As the sun final got kinda low in the sky and I figgered I didn't have too much longer to set out there, I started into getting cold on account a my bare nekkid legs and ass being exposed to that cool night mountain air like that. I went to shivering some. I heared the noise a someone a-coming up the mountain. You know, they kick loose rocks and such, and you can hear it, and I got real nervous and panicky.

"Who's there?" I hollered out.

"It's me, ole Zeb."

"Don't come up here, Zeb," I yelled. "I'll be down directly. You go on back down right now."

"You all right, Kid?"

"I'm just fine," I said, "but you do like I say and get your ass on back down there."

Well, he did all right. He never even poked his head up over the edge, and I was grateful for that, I can tell you. But I still had to set there and wait for dark to fall. I considered praying to Jesus again, but then I reminded myself that he hadn't did nothing for me the other time, so I let that thought go. I tried thinking on something nice and pleasant, like the time I had just recent spent with ole Red, but that didn't work neither, 'cause all it done was make me worry that Red might somehow find out about this embarrassing fix I had got myself into. There just weren't nothing for it but only to set there and be miserable and wait.

The sun did final go down, and the precious darkness come. I pulled my boots back on and stood up. I picked up my gun belt and thunk for a minute about what to do with it. Then I put it back down, and I tuck off my shirt, and I tied it around my middle like a apron or something. It covered me up, but even so, anyone who might happen to see me would know that I had lost my britches. Then I picked up my gun belt again, and I strapped it on around me over the shirt where it was tied. I headed on back to the camp.

I done a little slipping and sliding going down that there trail, but I didn't scratch my ass up too bad. I was some surprised, though, at just how different it was going down it in the dark than it had been going up in daylight, and even then I'd had me someone to foller. I made it though, and then I stood still with my heart a-thumping looking into the camp to see was anyone out walking around. I seed ole Myrtle, but in a minute, she ducked into the big tent.

I tuck off at a run towards the little tent where me

and ole Zeb was a-staying, and then I seed a man come outa a shack, and I ducked real fast behind a barrel and crouched down there till he went on his way. Then I tuck up my run again, and this time I made it all the way. I went inside under the flap door as fast as I could, and there set ole Zeb and a lit lantern a-setting on the table and him looking square at me.

"What the hell happened to you?" he said.

"Zeb," I said, "don't ask no questions. Just fetch me a bath."

"But what the hell happened?" he said.

Then of a sudden the tears just come a-streaming outa my eyes like from a bawling baby, and they just run down the sides a my face like little rivers, and I didn't wanta say nothing about it, but I just couldn't help myself, and then before I knowed what I was a-doing or a-saying or had time to give it no thought atall, I just blurted out loud, "Charlie Raspberry throwed me offa the side a the mountain, and I shit my britches."

Ole Zeb, he never laughed at me. He never even said nothing. He stared at me for a minute or so kinda like he couldn't hardly believe what I had just tole him, and then he popped up and run for the door. He was a-going to fetch me my bath. He didn't say that, but it was what I had asked him to do, and I knowed he was a-doing it. But me, I just stood there a-waiting on account a I was askeered to sit down on anything, and I was shaking all over and still running them salty tears.

Chapter 9

Come morning, I was all cleaned up and dressed in fresh clothes, on account a ole Zeb, he had managed to get a bucket a hot water into the tent the night before, and even though it had tuck him a while to do it, I had managed to get my bath all right. Now, if you recall, I had got hungry a-setting on that ledge, and here it was the next morning, and I still hadn't had nothing to eat, so my belly was a-growling something fierce for food. I knowed I would have to go on over to the big tent and have myself some breakfast. They was just two problems.

Ole Zeb, he knowed about the terrible thing I had did. I thunk I had solved that problem, though, 'cause I had done told him that if he was ever to breathe out one little tiny word about that humiliating incident, that no matter where we was at nor how many witnesses there might be, I would just shoot him dead, even though he was my pardner and all that. I know he believed me what I said too, so I felt pretty safe that Zeb would keep his mouth shut about that.

The other thing worried me some more though, and that was that Weaver and Raspberry had been there to see me freeze up the way I done on that mountainside. Well, I'd just have to take my chances on that one. I

braced myself up and walked on over to the big tent
with ole Zeb, and whenever we went inside, there was
a big cheer went up, and folks come a-running and mob-
bing all around me and patting me on the back and
ever'thing like that, and then they practical carried me
over and set me down at the table, and someone come
a-fetching me a breakfast plate all piled up with flapjacks
and eggs and ham and such. Someone else fetched me
my coffee. They final kinda settled down.

I couldn't figger what that was all about, but I could
feel my face kinda heating up like as if I was a-blushing,
and I knowed that was on account a I found myself a-
setting right beside ole Willie Weaver and looking across
the table straight at ole Charlie Raspberry. I only looked
down at my plate and started in to eating.

"We told them about how you ran off that bunch with
the dynamite," Raspberry said.

"That's what the cheering was all about," Weaver
said.

I looked up then, and I looked right at Weaver and
then at Raspberry.

"But what about—"

"That's all there was to tell," Weaver said. "They appreciate what you did for them. We all do."

Well, I be damned if I didn't feel them tears a-coming
back into my eyes at that, but I done my best, and I fit
them back. I tuck me a big gulp a hot coffee. Then, even
though ole Weaver and ole Raspberry seemed as if they
had kept my embarrassment to just only theirselfs, and
so had ole Zeb on account a I had threatened his life, it
kinda come to me that I might had oughta take the conversation in a whole entire new direction away from the
events a the night before.

"Well, all that's well and good and all," I said, " 'cept
only for one little ole thing."

"What's that?" Weaver asked me.

"Since we went and shot at them fellers last night," I said, "and we driv them off from their meanness and all, I reckon we sorta declared open and all-out war on them, and since we went and done that, we gotta be watching our ass real keerful from here on. They ain't gonna set still. They'll be up to something. You can bet your ass on that."

"The Kid's right about that, Charlie," Weaver said. "They'll be planning some kind of retaliation. Probably soon."

"As far as I'm concerned," Raspberry said, "it's about time. I don't know about you, but I'm tired of this cat-and-mouse game we been playing with them."

"We have to do some planning of our own though," Weaver said. "We don't know just what they'll pull, and we have to be ready, whatever it is."

"We can put guards out all around," Raspberry said.

"That's a start," ole Weaver agreed.

I had just et the last bite a my breakfast and was slurping out the last a my coffee, and it was a good thing too, 'cause just then we heared a commotion outside. Ever'one in Weaver's gold camp et breakfast together in the big tent, so they wasn't no one a us out there. It had to be the damn men from Morgan's camp. I jumped up and headed for the front door and most a the men in there was right behind me. Some of them was wearing guns, but most of them went unarmed most a the time. They had rifles back in their own tents or shacks. We come out, and some of them went a-running for them rifles. One man dropped dead just almost right beside me from a gunshot. The women come out, too, a-running this way and that way and screaming and all and gethering up kids and hustling them off somewhere.

What it was it was some a Morgan's men all right,

maybe eight of them, and they was shooting in all directions and one of them rid up right close to the big tent and tossed a lit torch up on top a the canvas and set it to blazing right off. I whipped out my Colt right fast, and I dropped the man offa his horse what had throwed the torch. Then I just spun around to the next most convenient target, and I dropped me another'n. Some a the miners was in the doorways a their private tents or shacks by then, and they was popping away with their rifles and hitting their targets occasional. They was another couple a torches throwed, and a couple a smaller tents was on fire. It was a small war going on there, I can tell you.

They had caught us with our britches down, so to speak, what meant that initial they had the advantage on us, but we rallied in a hurry, and we fit back like hell and turned the situation around on them for damn sure and certain. Well, they was four a the bastards down and dead, and a couple more was bleeding in their saddles. One of them yelled out real loud.

"Let's get the hell outa here."

They turned their horses around almost all at once and lit out fast going north, back towards the Morgan camp. I snapped me off a quick shot at the one what was the fartherest behind, and I nicked him in the shoulder. I seed the blood fly and heared him holler. He was too far off by then for a second shot, so I let him go. I wondered, though, how come none a the miners with rifles didn't take no shots at the fleeing shits, but I guess they just wasn't used to killing and couldn't bring theirselfs to shoot a man in the back. Under circumstances like what we had just then experienced, I sure as hell wouldn't have no such qualms. Like I said, I had done shot one a the bastards, and I only nicked him on account a it was a long shot for a six-gun. I'd a shot him dead if I coulda.

Well, they was gone, and we was assessing the damage they had did. We had four men kilt and a few others wounded, no one real bad, and we had kilt four a them and shot up most all the rest of them. It looked to me like a broke-even deal 'cept for the fact that they had set them fires. Some a the men was busy tossing buckets a water on the blazes, and some a the women was crying and wailing, but most of them was at work patching up the wounded. It was a real mess, I can tell you that. I had said just before that we had declared war on the son of a bitches, and here we was a-standing in a fresh fit battle zone for sure. I knowed then what war was like. It didn't spare no one, not women nor kids. We was lucky on that score, though, 'cause none a the women nor kids was hurt, not direct. 'Course, each dead man had left behind him a widder and some orphans, and that there was sad, sure enough.

The deal that these folks all had with each other was that they was all equal partners in this mining adventure, and so whenever them poor fellers got theirselfs kilt, why, the rest would all see to it that their widders and orphans was tuck keer of. Whenever I learnt that, I was real proud a ole Weaver and them. After a while, things was kinda under control again. Me and ole Zeb was standing there looking at the ashes around us, and ole Weaver, he come over to stand there with us.

"Well," he said, "you had it straight, Kid."

"What's that?" I asked him.

"You said it was war."

"That's right," Zeb said. "You was right about that. We're in a war all right."

"We got to finish it," I said.

"How're we going to do that?" Weaver asked me.

"I been thinking on that one," I said. "We're going to go right back at them. Right now."

"Right now?" Weaver said.

"It's the best time," I said. "They'll be figgering that we're a-setting over here licking our wounds, but the truth a the matter is that they got theirselfs hurt most near as bad as they hurt us. I say hit them right now. It'll be the biggest surprise they ever had, I can tell you that."

Weaver kinda shuck his head a little, and then he scratched it some.

"Well, all right," he said. "How do we do it?"

"I ain't seed you all doing no blasting," I said, "but do you have any dynamite?"

"Sure," he said. "We don't like to use it, but we have some just in case we should need it."

"You know that there place where—well, where we was at last night?" I said.

"Yeah?"

"Could you and another man or two get yourselfs over a bit more farther up there where as you could drop some a them sticks right down on them?"

"I think we could," he said.

"Do you have some men what's good rifle shots?" I asked him.

"I can think of four that's pretty good," he said.

"Well, then," I said, "if you could take you and one more to drop them blow sticks and two more with rifles to pick off whoever they can from up there, I could take two more with rifles along with me and go into the camp from the road. I figger we could do a hell of a lot a damage thataway."

"Why just seven men?" Weaver asked me.

" 'Cause you done lost four," I said. "Got some others hurt. If we work this the way I say, I don't reckon none

a them Morgans'll get through the road to ride over in
here, but just in case, we don't want no women and kids
left in here all by theirselfs. Ever' able-bodied man what
don't go out on this raid has got to be here armed and
a-watching to pertect the women and kids."

"Okay," he said. "That makes sense."

"And here's another thing," I said. I was a-thinking
how none a the miners with rifles hadn't shot at them
bastards what was running away from us. "The men that
goes up yonder with you and the ones who rides over
the other way with me, they got to go into this thing
cold-blooded. When they get a target, they got to shoot
to kill. If they do like I say, we'll win this war this
morning. It'll all be over with and did."

"I'll get the men together," Weaver said.

Weaver tuck Raspberry with him and a bundle a dynamite sticks, and then two more men with rifles went
along. They'd all had a good talking-to by me and Weaver both. Then I had along with me ole Tucker, what
was too fat to be climbing up with Weaver, but they said
he was a hell of a shot with a rifle, and I had ole Zeb.
Zeb brung a rifle and that shotgun he had stoled from
Chastain's office whenever we broke outa there. I
weren't at all sure I wanted ole Zeb to come along, but
he wouldn't have it no other way.

Anyhow, me and Tucker and Zeb was all mounted
up and ready to go, but I knowed it would take Weaver
and them a little while to get up on that mountain, so I
said we'd wait a while to let them get in place up there.
We could see them most a the time too, so whenever I
seed that they was getting close, I told the others let's
go, and we rid outa camp on the road. Thataway, we
lost sight a Weaver and them for a while.

Whenever we come close to Morgan's camp, I slowed

us down. I didn't figger them to be expecting us along so soon, but I didn't want to take no chances that they might be laying in wait. What I wanted, was I wanted the first sign a trouble to them bastards to be the first stick a dynamite that Weaver and Raspberry dropped in on them. Then while they was running around on account a being bombed like that, me and my two pardners would come at them from the other direction. I knowed, too, that once we rounded a little bend in the road, Weaver and them would be able to see us from up there where they was at. We had talked about that. That was the signal for them to commence the battle, whenever they seed us come around that bend.

Well, we rounded it, and I couldn't see no Morgan soldiers in the road ahead nor along the sides a the road, but still I called a halt.

"Hold it up right here," I said.

We stopped and set there in our saddles a-waiting, and it seemed like a long wait, but it wasn't prob'ly no more than a minute, maybe not even that. All ole Weaver needed was he just only needed to spot us down there in position and then have time to get a match struck and to get a fuse lit and drop it on down. Then a course, there would be however long it tuck the fuse to burn on down. I told myself all a that while I set there a-waiting. I also thunk about how it was that I was a-going into a situation here where the plain and deliberate plan was to just go and kill a bunch a men dead what I didn't even know them atall. Oh, I had met Morgan and a couple a the others that time I had rid into his camp, but I didn't really know them. But I guessed that was the way it was in a war. I also knowed what they had been doing to our new friends, and I figgered they deserved whatever they got back on account a that meanness they had did to my new friends.

Then there was also two men what knowed just how I had acted on the side a that mountain the night before, and then there was my own pardner, ole Zeb, what knowed even the worst part a the whole mess, and I meant to do something to kinda erase them ugly memories outa their heads if I could. I needed to try to wipe them outa my own mind too, I was that embarrassed over it all. So here we was waiting to do some serious giving back to Morgan and them, and me, I was downright determined to do even more than my share a the giving.

Then Lord godamighty, the whole earth shuck with the blast. I hadn't never saw a dynamite blast that close up to it before in my whole entire life, and it was sure enough a sight, I can tell you. It roared and it thundered, and I could feel it hit me in the chest way off over there the way I was. Flames shot out and black smoke billowed. Clouds a dirt riz up high, and I seed boards a-flying through the air like sticks, and I even seed a man or pieces of a man a-flying. Well, me and Tucker and Zeb had a time controlling our horses, it was that bad. They whinnied and nickered and reared up and stamped their hoofs and danced around. We had a fight on our hands a-keeping them there where we wanted them and keeping our own ass in the saddles. I hadn't figgered on that part.

We did manage to keep them under control though, but I was sure glad that there weren't no one a-shooting at us at the time. We wouldn't a been able to shoot back nor to duck nor nothing, but I reckon that ole Morgan's men, they was busy enough trying to figger out who had blasted them and from where. Then another one hit, and this time it landed on a shack that I didn't know at the time but that ole Zeb told me later musta been where ole Morgan kept his supply a dynamite. I thought it was the end a the world.

It weren't just one big blast, although the one first one was big enough and loud enough, but then come another and another, and it seemed to me like as if it weren't ever going to stop. I never seed so much fire a-flashing and black smoke a-rolling and dust and trash and all a-flying through the sky in all and ever' direction. This time ole Tucker lost his seat. He landed hard on the road, and his horse tuck out for home.

Whenever the holy hell had stopped, I asked him was he all right, and he come up on his feet a-gasping for breath and said that he was, so I told him to just stay there where he was at and take cover behind a rock and pick off any Morgan men what might come close enough to him for it. He scrambled over and tuck his cover.

"Come on, Zeb," I said.

We lit out for what was left a that Morgan camp, and one more stick a dynamite went off. Our horses both went into their dance again, and we final fit them back under control and resumed our attack. As we was a-riding into the camp, the first thing what happened was a man come out from behind a shack and surprised the hell outa me, but ole Zeb raised up that scattergun and like to of tuck the bastard's head off. We kept a-going.

Another man come out from somewhere, and I was raising up my Colt when someone up there with Weaver picked him off with a rifle shot. I snapped off a shot and dropped one. Another one had managed to get onto a horse and headed out lickety-split towards the road over there where ole Tucker was a-waiting. That there was the stupidest way for him to go, but I figgered his brain musta been somewhat fuddled on account a all the blasting. Sure enough, Tucker brung him down with one shot.

I hauled back on the reins a my mount and jumped

down outa the saddle just as a couple a men come running out from a lane between two high walls a flames, and I whirled around and dropped them both in their tracks. I heared Zeb a-shooting back behind me too, but I was too busy to look back and see what was happening there. The riflemen up on the mountain was a-shooting down amongst us too. Then of a sudden, ever'thing was quiet. I couldn't think of nothing for it but only that we had done kilt them all. I weren't about to relax though. Not yet. I helt my shooter ready, and I was turning quick and looking around in all directions. I seed Zeb still a-setting in his saddle and holding his rifle and he was a-looking around too. Then he shouted at me and turned in his saddle and fired off a quick shot with his rifle all at once.

I turned fast toward whatever it was he was a-shooting at, and then I seed ole Morgan hisself along with the man whose thumb I had shot off, and they was a-riding as fast as ever they could make their horses go, a-heading north outa camp along that road what me and Zeb had wanted to take whenever Morgan and his men had stopped us from doing it that time. Well, Zeb's shot had missed its mark. I sure didn't want them two getting away. They was the mainest mean ones a the bunch. I run back over to where my horse was at and started into trying to mount up, but the dumb critter was still nervous and skittered up from all the noise and such and give me so much trouble that by the time I got up on his back it was too damn late. They was gone.

Oh, I rid out after them all right, but I never set eyes on them again. They had got well down that road before I had even got back in the saddle. I give it up and turned around and rid back to where Zeb was a-waiting for me. Me and him rid all around that waste of a camp a-checking here and there, and we final determined that there wasn't nothing left alive 'cept for a few horses. We gethered them up and rid back over to where Tucker was still a-waiting.

"Pick one and climb up," I said, and he mounted a horse. We all rid on back into Weaver's camp, and by the time we got on in there and offa our horses, Weaver and Raspberry and them was back down from offa the mountain. Me and Zeb had ever'one gethered up around us in quick order.

"We did it, Kid," Weaver said. "We won."

The cheers went up, and it was a while before it was quiet enough for me to give ole Weaver a answer to what he had said.

"I reckon we did all right," I said. "Me and ole Zeb here checked out the whole entire Morgan camp, and there ain't nothing alive over there. Not now since we brung out all the rest a his horses."

They all cheered again. I can tell you, it was a happy bunch a miners on that day. 'Course, they was still some sorrow amongst them on account a the men they had lost that morning, but the war was over at last, and they knowed then that they could get on with their work without no more mean interference from that Morgan bunch a would-be claim-jumpering outlaw bastards. When they final quieted down again, I looked over at Weaver.

"Only bad thing about it," I said, "ole Morgan hisself and that one-thumb bastard got away clean."

"Morgan and Shark got away?" Raspberry said.

"Yeah, Shark," I said. "That's his name."

"Damn," Weaver said. "If Morgan got away, he just might be back with another bunch and try again. I'm afraid he won't just give it up. Not like that. Not that easy. He'll be back all right."

"Well, he might," I said, "but I don't think it'll be anytime too soon after what we done here today. Besides, he'd have to go skeer hisself up a whole entire new army before he could make another run at you. And before he does try it, if he does, I might just run across his path again somewhere. I'd say that you all can just about almost relax. Oh, keep your eyes peeled just in case. But don't worry your heads none too much on account a ole Morgan. Leastways, not for a while yet."

"All right. But, say, we had us a deal, Kid," Weaver said. "Remember? It's payback time."

Well, my head was still a-swimming what with all that action we had just had ourselves, and I had to ask ole Weaver just what was it was he a-making reference to. It sure didn't ring no bells inside a my head.

"You help us solve our problem," he said, "and we'll help solve yours. Remember? So now that Morgan's out of our way, at least for a while, like you said, some of us can ride on down into Fosterville with you, and talk to that sheriff, and clear your name. That should settle your problems."

"Well," I said, "it sure as hell should, and I'm mighty anxious to get it did. All right, let's get your camp all straightened up real nice here first, and then we'll just go on ahead and do that."

Chapter 10

We was all on our way down the mountain on that narra trail meaning to do just exactly what ole Weaver had promised me he would do, and I was thinking how ever'thing was going to be straightened out between me and the law pretty soon now. We was maybe halfway down the trail whenever we seed the posse a-coming up at us. Now you might think that shoulda been all right, on account a I was wanting ole Weaver and them to have a good talk with Jim Chastain and convince him a the truth a the matter that me and Zeb and Paw couldn't no way a been the owlhoots he was after. But it didn't work out thataway. That seems to be the general way a life that things don't work out the way you mean for them to.

It didn't work out like that atall, 'cause me and ole Chastain, we seed each other right at the same exact instant a time, and he done just what ever'one had told me he would do whenever he would see me again. He pulled out his revolver and started in to shooting and shouting. He hollered out to the posse behind him, "There they are. Shoot to kill."

Well, I went tumbling offa my saddle and rolled over to the edge a the road and got my ass in behind a boulder what wouldn't a even been there if it hadn't a been for that there rock slide ole Zeb had caused us to do a while back, and I hauled out my own shooter right fast and commenced to firing back, but only I weren't shooting to kill. I was wanting to prove that I weren't no murderer, and killing a lawman sure didn't seem like the way to go about accomplishing that task. I didn't want ole Weaver nor no else a-getting kilt neither. I just only figgered that the way to make ole Jim and his posse set still and keep their heads down was to make like I was a-shooting back at them. It worked too. They knowed my reputation as a slick gunhand.

"Weaver," I called out. "Zeb. Get ever'one's ass back up the mountain."

"We can't leave you here like this," Weaver said from somewhere. I don't know just where he was at, but I kinda assumed that ever'one back behind me had did like what I had did and tuck cover whenever the shooting started. I could tell that Chastain and them had dismounted and hid down below on account a I was a-looking down on them.

"Zeb," I said, "can you hear me?"

"I hear you, Kid."

"Get them bastards all back up the mountain," I said.

"Come on, fellers," I heared Zeb say. "The Kid knows what he's a-doing."

I could hear them all scurrying their way back up the mountain then, and so I knowed that I was left there all by my lonesome a-facing a whole damn Chastain Fosterville posse what was determined as hell to kill me dead, but that there was the way I wanted it. Well, I didn't know exact what to do, and I figgered that I was a goner for sure, but still ever'time I seed one a them son of a bitches stick his damned ole head up, I pinged me a shot off somewhat close to him to make him duck his ass back down again.

I got to thinking that since I had done made up my mind not to kill no one, I could real easy shoot all my bullets up in just a little while, and then I'd be in a sure-fire hell of a fix, so I went and looked all around me, and I seed right off that they was a bunch a loose fist-sized rocks laying around within easy reach, and being up high the way I was and them being down below me, I was in a real good position to take advantage a that source a ammunition. I went to picking up good throwing rocks and chunking them down thataway, and now and then, I got me in a good hit.

My first toss, I was pretty sure I beaned one of them, 'cause I heared him holler. I rained down a few more rocks kinda in general, and then I tuck to waiting a bit and watching for targets, and whenever I done that, why, I did hit me a few more of them for sure. Then it come to me what me and ole Zeb had did the last time, and we was in damn near the same place where we had been back then. I decided to send a whole rock slide down at them, and since they was so many loose rocks from the last time, it didn't take too much effort to cause another one. I miscalculated on one thing though.

When them rocks went to rumbling down the trail, ole Chastain having been out in the front a the posse, he was up some higher on the trail than anyone else, and them rocks tumbled right on past him, but the rest a the posse seed it coming and jumped up and skeedaddled on down the mountain to get away from the slide. Chastain was separated from his bunch. I had got rid a the posse all right, but I still had ole Jim to deal with. Whenever the rocks quit rumbling, I could hear their voices from way down there most near on the flat.

"What do we do now?"

"We can't get through there."

"Let's head on back."

"What about Chastain?"

"He can take care of himself."

So they by God mounted right on up and rid off lickety-split and just abandoned the poor son of a bitch to his fate, which was a-going to be they didn't have no idea what. I didn't neither just yet. I knowed for sure, though, that if I was to just go down there and face ole Jim, he would sure enough try to kill me dead for what I had did to him, and I wouldn't have but two choices, neither one a which I liked. One was to just go right on ahead and kill him, what you already know I didn't want to do that, and the other'n was to let him kill me. I didn't want that neither. I guess I coulda follered Zeb and Weaver and them back up to the gold camp, but I didn't want to bring no more trouble on them folks, and I figgered that if ole Chastain was to eventual dig that there trail out and get his ass on up to the camp, why, if I was to be there he'd spot me right off, but ole Zeb, he might could just sorta blend in, being a crusty old prospector and all.

I wanted to talk to Jim anyhow, and if he just absolute refused to listen to the voice a reason and all, why, I wanted to get on to the serious business a running them three real outlaws down. Now me and ole Jim was on opposite ends a all them rocks I had sent down the trail. There weren't no way a getting up or down with a horse, but I figgered a man could climb around all right, long as he was to stay offa them loose rocks, so I eased myself back farther away from what had been the trail and commenced to working my way over rocks and boulders and such on down toward where I figgered Chastain was still a-lurking.

'Course, far as I knowed, he coulda been a-doing the same thing as what I was a-doing, but 'cept he coulda been trying to work his way down to his horse in order to hightail it back toward Fosterville like his posse had did, or he coulda been a-working his way up to try to come on me by surprise. To tell you the truth, I don't know which a them things he was a-doing if either one, but I had the advantage on him, me being up higher than what he was, and I did final spot him hunkered down behind a rock with his six-gun in his hand. I come up behind him though. I sneaked in on him, and I leveled my shooter right square between his shoulder blades. There ain't no way on this whole entire earth or the history of it that I coulda missed him.

"Don't move a muscle, Jim," I said, and he didn't. He friz stiff instant. I said, "Drop that shooter."

He didn't drop it though, and I knowed that he was a-thinking could he spin around right quick like and snap off a lucky shot and get me without me getting him at the same time or even first.

"Jim," I said, "drop it. You know I can kill you."

"Yeah," he said. "They say you're a regular Billy the Kid."

Well, that was the last thing I wanted to hear, and I snapped off a shot what blowed a hole in his Stetson and knocked it offa his head. He flinched and dropped his revolver and stuck his both hands up in the air.

"You going to kill me?" he asked.

"Damn it, Jim," I said, "once I thunk that we was friends. I sure did believe that you knowed me better than that. I ain't never shot no one what wasn't shooting at me to kill me. Well, I did shoot off Paw's left ear a while back on account a he pissed me off real bad, but if I'd a wanted to kill you, you'd done be dead."

"What do you mean to do then?" he asked me.

"I want you to move on down the way a little more farther," I said, and he had to climb over some rocks to do that, but he done it, and I done the same thing till I was just right there where he had been, and I picked up his shooter and tucked it in my belt. "I was on my way into Fosterville," I said, "with some witnesses what coulda proved to you that me and Zeb and Paw ain't the ones what you want, but whenever you seed me you went to shooting first, so I sent them off. I didn't want no one kilt over this here misunderstanding what you got stuck so firm in your stubborn muley head."

Jim, he didn't say nothing to that, and I hoped that he was a-thinking a the pure wisdom a my words. He knowed damn well that I was a-telling the truth about one thing. If I'd a wanted him dead, he'd a done been kilt. I was that good, and I knowed it, and he did too, and I'd had me a couple a good chances, if that had a been my intention.

"Jim," I said, "I didn't rob that stagecoach, and I didn't rob your bank, and I didn't kill none a them innocent folks what got kilt. Neither did Paw and Zeb."

"Damn it, Kid," he said, "if you're telling me the truth, the best thing you could have done was to stay put in my jail."

"Hell, you was ready to string us all up," I said.

"If you'd been locked up in my jail, and if you're telling the truth, you'd have had a perfect alibi when the bank was robbed," he said.

Well, I hadn't never thunk about it thataway, but whenever he said it, I sure couldn't argue none with it. The only thing is, that there thought didn't do me no good then.

"Well," I said, "I ain't going back and set on my ass in your jail cell and wait for the bastards to come and rob your bank again. What's did is did. Start in a-stripping off your clothes."

"Oh, now wait a minute, Kid," he said. "You're not going to do that to me again."

"It's either that or I commence to shooting off your ears and such," I said.

"What makes you want to do such a mean thing?" he said.

"It's the best way I know of to slow you down without actual shooting you in a kneecap or something," I said. "Now peel them off."

Well, he done it, and I made him toss them clothes over to me, and I gethered them up in a bundle. Now, my horse was up above that rock slide, and there weren't no quick way to get it down, and Jim's horse had went down the trail with the rest a the posse horses whenever the men had got off their backs to take cover, so it was on down there below. I was a-wanting to be down there, too, and a-riding off somewheres, so I come up with a quick plan.

"Now, Jim," I said, "I'm a-fixing to climb over these here rocks till I get all the way down yonder, and then I'm a-taking your horse, and I don't want you to go charging me with no horse-stealing neither. What I'm doing is I'm swapping with you. You can work your way up there where I left my critter. The fastest way for you to get down from here then will be for you to ride on up to the end a the trail to the mountain road and then turn north. You'll come onto a little gold camp run by a feller named Weaver. Him and his people is good folks. While you're there, ask them where the hell me and old Zeb was at whenever your bank got robbed."

"I can't ride into a gold camp stark nekkid," he said.

"Why not?" I said.

"Kid!" he said. "Damn you all the way to hell."

Then I recollected the way I had come down offa the mountain whenever I had found it necessary to toss away my soiled britches, and so I rolled up his shirt and throwed it back to him.

"There you go," I said. "Be seeing you, Jim."

I went to crawling over them rocks a-heading down to the bottom, and I heared ole Jim yell out at me, "I'll get you for this, Kid," and I figgered that one way or another, he likely would, but I meant to put off the getting a me for as long as I possible could.

So there I was all by my lonesome again. Zeb was up in the camp with Weaver and them, or leastways he would be pretty soon, and Paw was on his way back to Texas. Now, it's true that ole Zeb was my pardner and all, but at just that there time, I was glad I had got myself separated from him. I hoped that he'd be safe up there with Weaver, and I figgered I could move around a little more freer by myself than if he was to be a-tagging along with me. The other thing was that too often whenever I got me a idea, ole Zeb, he'd come up with a different one and commence into telling me what all was wrong with my own. I figgered that just then I didn't need none a that kinda confusion in my head.

I made it on down to the bottom a the foothills there and found ole Jim's horse just a-grazing away real contented like and not giving a shit what the hell was a-going on around it. I caught it up real easy and mounted and tuck out headed north. I didn't really have no definite plans. I still figgered them outlaws was up thataway somewheres, and that I might could run across them if I was to wander around up there. Judging from the recent bank robbery in Fosterville, they wasn't getting too far away in their depradating.

That evening found me back in that there grove a trees off east a Fosterville a-studying on the notion a going back in there for another visit with ole Red. I was a-trying to figger out should I sneak on in like I done the last time or just ride on in all bold as hell. 'Course, I knowed that ole Jim wouldn't be back in town for a spell. What I was a-asking myself was did anyone else in town besides just Red know me all that well and if anyone else was to get a look at me, would they think anything special about me without me being in the company a two old codgers. Well, I never really answered the question, but I was kinda tired a sneaking, so I decided to just ride on in.

I found ole Red in the big main room a the saloon, and they was quite a few men in there drinking and having a good ole time. Whenever Red seed me, she come a-running, and glommed onto my left arm, she knowed better than to take and encumber my main shooting arm, and she dragged me off into a corner and set me down in a chair and set down close beside me.

"Kid," she said, "are you crazy?"

"You done asked me that once before," I said.

"Everyone's looking for you," she said.

"They're looking for a skinny kid with two old men," I said. "Hell, they won't notice me just all by my lonesome. Besides, ole Chastain's up on the mountain nekkid. He won't be back for a spell yet."

"You didn't," she said. "Not again."

I grinned real big and nodded my head.

"Kid, he'll kill you for sure."

"He likely will if he ever gets him a chance," I said, agreeing absolute with just what she had said.

"Well, what're you doing?" she said. "What're you doing here?"

"I'm just sorta riding north," I told her. "Sorta looking for them three outlaws. I just figgered it'd be kinda nice to stop here and pay you a little visit along the way. Hell, Red, I can't hardly ride past this town without stopping in to see you. You know that, don't you?"

"Well, let's get out of here before someone recognizes you," she said.

"Get out to where?" I asked her.

"Oh, we'll go to my room," she said.

Now that there is exact what I wanted to hear, and I give her a smile, and I said, "Okay." I stood up, and so did she, and she started in to steering me toward the back door. We was almost there, but we had to pass by one more table what had a cowhand-looking feller a-setting at it and a-drinking whiskey just all by his lone-some. He weren't no big man, 'bout medium built, I guess, but then, medium is big to me, since I'm so scrawny. I didn't pay him too much mind as we walked past him, but then I heared his chair a-being pushed back, and then I heared his voice.

"Kid Parmlee?" he said. "Is that you?"

I stopped and turned around to face him, and then is when I seed that there was something kinda vague like familiar about his ugly features. I couldn't place him though. I didn't think that I had ever saw him before. He was wearing a low-slung gun on his left hip, and he was dirty and unshaved. I kinda squinted at him, and I give ole Red a sorta gentle shove away from me, on account a he didn't look to me like he was wanting no friendly talk. She moved on over to the bar.

"Do you know me?" I said.

"I know who you are," he said.

"You got business with me?" I said.

"I been looking for you for quite a spell," he said. "I mean to kill you."

"You might try," I said, "but before one of us is final kilt, and likely it'll be you, do you mind a-telling me what it's all about?"

"You kilt a whole mess a my cousins," he said. "You son of a bitch."

"What's your name?" I said.

"It's Henry," he said. "Henry Pigg."

Then he went for his shooter in a flash without no
further warning, but I was expecting it all right. I been
shot at enough that I got a kinda feel for it, you know.
And he weren't too bad, but then, me, I'm real fast.
That's how come them to keep on a-calling me a regular
Billy the Kid, as much as I don't like to hear it said.
Anyhow, I beat him, a course. I jerked out my big Colt
and thumbed back the hammer and fired all in one motion and well before he even had his hammer cocked.
There was a hell of a roar, us being inside the way we
was, and my bullet tore a big hole in his chest. Blood
went all over the place, and he done a little dance all
staggering around and trying to hold up his shooter and
get off a shot at me, but he never, and final he just fell
over right onto his face so flat and hard, I bet he busted
his nose. Only thing is, he didn't keer at that point,
'cause I'm pretty sure he was done dead before he ever
hit the floor.

I kept my gun in my hand and looked around the
room kinda furtive like to see if they was anyone in there
looking bold enough to come after me. They all just set
still, while the stinking smoke from my gunshot kinda
drifted around and filled the room, and I commenced to
backing slow towards the back door. Red, she never
made no move away from the bar. She just stared at me,
and I reckon she had done changed her mind about taking me on up to her room. I guess her mood was way
changed on accounta what I had just did. I didn't have
no choice in the matter though, and I wondered couldn't
she see it thataway? Why, if I hadn't a kilt him, he'd a
kilt me for sure. It was his stated out loud intention.
Anyhow, if I had me any doubts left in my head regarding what was in ole Red's mind, she cleared them right
up by what she said next.

"Kid," she said, "get out of town. Hurry."

I didn't argue with her none. I got to the door. My back was a-pressing on it. I tuck me one last look around the room.

"Ain't there no end to them goddamned Piggses?" I said.

I got to my ole horse and mounted up, and I rid outa town near as fast as I could make him go. I was blind fool mad too, I can tell you. Here I had planned me a whomping good night with ole Red, and it had to go and get spoilt by a damn fool on accounta something what had happened way back yonder in time when I was only fourteen year old. You know, sometimes the world just don't seem fair.

Chapter 11

Well, if I had gone into Fosterville a-thinking that
I could kinda slip around and not be noticed, that there
last Pigg had tuck keer a that for sure. I lit outa there in
a hurry, I can tell you, and you mighta noticed that I got
me a long history for such a young feller a hitting the
trail without I first got myself well prepared for it. I
didn't have myself no food nor no camping stuff. I had
me a blanket roll across the saddle, but that's all. Oh, I
did have a canteen a water. So anyhow, there I was a-
riding the cold, hard trail again without I was really
ready for it.

I did have me some money in my pockets, thanks to
ole Zeb what always managed to keep us pretty well
fixed from panning gold dust here and there, so whenever I come onto the next town down the road, and me
being real hungry and all, I stopped in and went to a
eating place on the main street a the town. The place
was called "Harry's," but the funny thing about it was
that it weren't run by no Harry. It was run by a woman
name a Gertie.

Ole Gertie was all right too. She was older than my
own old maw, and she weren't nothing like no other
woman I ever seen or knowed before or since then. She
was a tough ole gal, that's for sure. She was damn near

as short as me, but I bet you she weighed three times as much, and her hair was gray and kinda stringy like. Her old dress was greasy from cooking, and she was dusted all over with flour. I never seed her without she had a stump of a ceegar in the left corner a her mouth, and her just a-chomping on it.

And she sure could cook. She whomped me up a steak and taters and gravy and biscuits and other stuff and fed me two plates full. I had lots a her good strong coffee too. I was in there at a odd time, and she didn't have no other customers just then, so me and her got to talking, and we got good acquainted. I hadn't give away no information on myself though. Then she got to talking about a bank robbery what had tuck place in their little town just a week or so before, and then I really kinda perked up to listen to that.

"It was three of them," she said. "One little squirt 'bout your size."

I didn't let that bother me none. Hell, I knowed I was a little squirt. That was how come me to get so damn good with my Colt shooter. You know, they called that Colt the equalizer, and I come to find out how come. I figgered that my own ole equalizer equaled me up with any man. Anyhow, she went on.

"Then they was two old farts with him. I was in here a-cooking just like now whenever I first heard the ruckus out in the street. Someone was hollering, "They robbed the bank," and then they was some gunshots. I grabbed my greener from behind the counter and went out the front door. I seen a man laying dead in the street, and I seen them three a-heading for their horses. The squirt, he was just right over there a-coming outa the bank. It's just two doors down. And his back was turned toward me, so I leveled my greener on him and cut loose. I dusted his britches good. He yelped out something fierce and managed to get into his saddle, but I g'arantee you, he weren't none too comfy a-setting on all them pellets I put in his backside."

"Gertie," I said, "if someone was to pull down his britches and give him a close look, would they see that his hind end had been peppered?"

She let out a raucous laugh, and then she said, "For damn sure, sonny. They was blood in his saddle all right."

"Well, now, Gertie," I said, "I am sure happy that you told me that there tale. Now I'm fixing to tell you one. First off, I'm knowed as Kid Parmlee."

"Glad to know you, Kid," she said. "You already got my handle."

"Yes, ma'am," I said. "Now here's the tale. While back I was running with my ole pard, Zeb Pike, and my ole paw had hitched up with us. We had been up in the mountains for a spell and hadn't heared no news, and we come down to water, you know, and we went into Fosterville back down south a here where we knowed the sheriff, ole Jim Chastain. Well, ole Jim, he throwed down on us before we knowed what was what, and he throwed us into his damned ole jail cell. Seems like three men what sounded like us had robbed a stagecoach up this direction and kilt a man in the doing of it. Ole Jim, he figgered it was us. Anyhow, I broke us outa his jail, and so now he's after us and I'm after them real outlaws so I can to prove to ole Jim and ever'one else that it never was us in the first place."

"Well, I'll be damned," Gertie said. "So it's them three what robbed our bank here that you're after."

"It sure sounds like it to me," I admitted. "But now that you've butt-shot the kid, maybe I can prove that it never was me on account a they can pull down his britches and look for them buckshot marks."

"By damn," she said. "And not only that, Kid, but I got me a good look at that little snot, and I can tell them for sure that he ain't you."

Well, right then and there I tuck ole Gertie for a angel a mercy come down from the gates a heaven to rescue me from a horrible fate a either getting my ass blowed all to hell by ole Jim Chastain or else getting hung up by my neck to stretch to death. Hell, I jumped up outa my chair and give her a big hug. I hadn't never even hugged my own maw the way I hugged ole Gertie.

"Gertie," I said, "I think you have just saved my life."

"You just ride back down to Fosterville," she said, "and fetch that sheriff up here. I'll set him straight."

"I don't reckon it'll be quite that easy," I said, "on account a whenever he sees me again, he won't wait for me to tell him nothing. He'll just commence to shooting at me with a full intent to kill me dead."

Then I went and told her how come me to say that. I told her how I had left poor ole Jim nekkid in his jail and then done it to him again up on the mountain. She just looked real serious and kinda shuck her head slow.

"Hell, Kid, any man would want to kill you dead for doing that to him," she said, "not once but twice. That was a bad thing you done."

Then of a sudden she went to laughing. After a while her laughing sent her to coughing, and final whenever she got control a herself again, she tuck a deep breath, and she said, "The picture of it just come into my mind a the nekkid sheriff. It was a mean thing you done, all right, but it was a pretty funny one at the same time."

"I kinda wish I hadn't did it now though," I said, " 'cause, ole Jim, he sure is mad at me."

"Well now," she said, "if you can't go talk to him to straighten this all out, what are you going to do?"

"I guess I'll just keep on a-riding around these parts

and hope to blunder into them outlaws," I said, " 'special that kid with the speckled butt. Meantime, if ole Jim or any other lawman comes along thisaway, maybe you could tell them that you've saw me, and you know that I ain't him."

"I'll do that," Gertie said. "You ain't fixing to head on out today, are you?"

"I was," I said.

"You wouldn't get far down the road before dark set in," she said. "Why don't you stay here tonight? I'll give you a place to sleep the night and fix you a good breakfast in the morning. What's more, there won't be no charge for none of it. It'll be on the house."

Well, that sounded just fine to me, and so I thanked her kindly and tuck her up on her offer. After a while, she locked up her front door and led me through the back door, and I'll be damned if that there eating place weren't just the front room a the place where she lived. The back rooms was all her house. She set me down on a comfy couch and fetched out a bottle a good whiskey and two glasses and poured us each a drink and set down beside me. I rolled myself a cigareet and lit it. We had us a good time a-visiting and drinking whiskey and smoking and all. She sure was a grand ole gal, I can tell you. But then, I didn't know the half of it.

It come on late evening and I was a-thinking that it was might near time to hit the hay and wondering where the hell she was a-going to put me, when of a sudden, the ole gal reached a hand over and put it right down there between my legs and went to rubbing on me. That sure surprised me, but it didn't surprise me near as much as the fact that I went and tuck to it, if you get my meaning. Why, here was this ole gal what was older than my own maw, and her a-acting like that on me, and me not running for my life.

Well, I ain't going into no more details, on account a I ain't that kind, but I'll just say that ole Gertie tuck me right into her own bed with her, and we didn't get right off to sleep neither. We was some time before either one of us thought about sleeping. We woke up in the night a time or two and done it again each time too, and then we done one more in the morning. Ole Gertie, she was a live one.

Come time for her to open up her place a business, though, and we got our ass up and got dressed and went on into the business part a her place there, and she unlocked the front door and went to cooking my breakfast. Right away she had some more customers come in, and me and her just acted like we wasn't nothing to each other atall. When I had et my full, I got up to leave, and just then a man come in with a badge on his chest. He give me a look as he walked by me. Gertie come up to me then, and she handed me a bagful a food for the trail.

"I'll see you later, Kid," she said. "I'll give you time to get outa town, just in case, and then I'll tell the sheriff here your story—and mine. Maybe that'll be a start toward convincing your Chastain."

"Thanks, Gertie," I said. "I'll be back."

Riding north along the road what I thunk would eventual take me on into Denver if I was to keep a-riding on it long enough, I was thinking about ole Gertie and what a streak a luck it had been, me a-coming across her. Now if I could only just get my hands on that other kid, what now had his ass shot full a Gertie's buckshot, I could damn sure prove that me and Paw and Zeb was innocent a them robberies and killings. I was also thinking about ole Chastain and how if I was to come across him again I wouldn't have no chance to talk about nothing. I was hoping that he would ride all the way up the road to ole

Gertie's town so that she could tell him the truth a the matter before I would have to actual face him again.

'Course, that weren't all I was a-thinking on. I was thinking on the kinda night I had just spent with ole Gertie and how no one would ever a believed it. I couldn't hardly believe it my own self. And the mainest thing I couldn't hardly believe about it was that I was not just only willing, but I had actual enjoyed it. I come to the reality about life just then that young and pretty ain't ever'thing.

Well, long about noon, I stopped and opened that sack ole Gertie had give me, and I found me some biscuits and some dried meat and some tins a beans. I didn't want to build a fire and make a for-real camp, so I just et some dried meat and biscuit, is all. I washed it all down with water and got back to moving along. Like before, I didn't have no special destination in mind. I was just kinda wandering, but only I was wandering in the general area in which them owlhoots had been doing their operating. I knowed I was right about that, on account a ole Gertie telling me how they had robbed the bank recent there in her town. They was still around all right. I figgered if I was to do much wandering without getting my own ass caught or kilt first, I was bound to run across them sooner or later.

I rid on till late evening with the sun a-getting low in the west and coloring up the horizon over thataway real pretty like, and I hadn't seed no sign of a town a-coming up any time soon, so I figgered that I had best be a-looking for myself a place to make me a camp for the night. They was plenty a water in that country on account a the snow way on up in the mountains, and so it weren't long before I was able to pick me out a nice enough spot.

I unsaddled my ole horse and set him a good place

by the crick which run by, and there was aplenty a grass there too. Then I built me up a good little fire and rolled out my blanket on the ground. I fetched me some water from the crick and set it on to boil so I could have me some coffee. Ole Gertie had put ever'thing I needed in that there sack. I went and het up a tin a beans too, and I had myself a good enough meal. It weren't nothing as good as ole Zeb's camp cooking, but it satisfied me all right.

I poured myself a last cup a coffee for the night and was just a-setting there by my little fire and a-sipping my coffee, and then I heared the sound a horses a-coming along the road. I set still and listened for a space, and I figgered they was coming up my back trail, coming from the south. They was moving slow and easy though, and they weren't too many of them. It didn't sound like no posse to me, but I weren't about to make no dumb mistakes. I put down my cup and backed away from the fire out into the dark and waited.

By and by three riders, a-leading one horse without no rider, come into view, and I got all excited thinking that they might be just exact who it was I was a-looking for, but then they come closer into my fire, and I seed right away by the firelight that it weren't. It was three cowhand-looking fellers. They stayed in their saddles.

"Anyone to home in the camp?" one of them called out.

"Who wants to know?" I said, and I seed them kinda stiffen in their saddles.

"Just some travelers looking for some hospitality," the man said.

"You lawmen?" I said. "You on anyone's trail?"

"Not us," the man said. "We're just outa-work cowhands, is all."

"Climb on down," I said, "and welcome."

I come on back into the light a my fire then, and I told them boys where to put their horses over yonder where I had put mine. They done that, and then they come a-walking back over towards the fire.

"You boys hungry?" I asked them.

"We sure are," one of them said. He weren't the same one what had talked before, and I tuck him to be the youngest one a the bunch by the look of him.

"I done et and drunk up alla my coffee," I said, "but I'll put on some more. I got aplenty."

"That's right neighborly of you," said the first one. They all went and set around the fire, and I dug down into my sack a stuff from ole Gertie again. Before long I had them all fed, and we was all of us setting around with coffee a-sipping and making small talk about how there weren't no ranches around with jobs for outa-work cowhands. I lied just a little bit by telling them that I was in the same fix what they was in, and I was doing mainly the same thing what they was doing. I didn't see no harm in it, 'cause if I hadn't a been on the trail a them owlhoots, likely I woulda been looking for me some cow-punching job.

"Which way you riding?" one a the men asked me.

"I was headed south," I said, a-lying again.

"You might just as well turn north and ride along with us," he said. "We done checked all the ranches behind us, and there ain't no work to be had."

"I reckon you just saved me some trouble," I said. "But I been up north, and I didn't find nothing there neither."

"It's hard times," the young'un a the bunch said.

"Enough to make a man turn to bank-robbing or stage-robbing or something," I said, saying it kinda casual like, as if I mighta really meant it or I might nota.

"No profit in that," said the older one. "Not around

these parts. We had some cousins what got into that line a work, and they're mostly dead now."

"Besides," the younger one said, "there's three bad ones running around this here area doing all the dirty work. They ain't leaving nothing for no one else. You want to get into the robbing line, you best go to some other part a the country."

"Yeah," I said. "I heared about them three. You fellers ever think about taking up gold-hunting?"

The older one shuck his head.

"Naw," he said. "That ain't no kinda work for cowhands."

Well, a powerful need come on me just then, I had drunk so much coffee, so I got up and walked out away from the fire into the dark to take keer a that little necessary, and I could hear them three a-talking back there, but only I couldn't make out anything they was a-saying. When I had finished up with my business, I headed back over thataway kinda slow, staying ready for anything. I still didn't have no idea just who the hell them three was. You mighta noticed that we hadn't bothered to exchange no names nor nothing like that. That made me figger that they was kinda like me, meaning they didn't want to give out their names to no stranger. There's got to be a reason a feller is like that.

Just as I come back into the flickering campfire light, all three a them men stood up a-facing me. I stopped still, seeing that move as just a little bit threatening.

"It come to us just now," said the older one, "that you might be the one they call Kid Parmlee. They say you're a regular Billy the Kid."

"So what if I am?" I said. "I ain't the one what's been doing all that robberying, and you done said you ain't no lawmen."

"We ain't no lawmen," said the younger one.

"And we know you ain't the bank-robbing kid," the older one said. "Back down the road in the last little town, we heard about how that old woman at Harry's told the sheriff there all about you. She seen the other kid, and she seen you. She shot that other one in the ass too. She told the sheriff there that them that was looking for you was on the wrong trail."

Well, that come to me as a big relief, as I guess you would know. Now all it needed was for the sheriff what Gertie had told all that to in her town to get his ass on down to Fosterville and tell it to ole Chastain. But then, if they knowed I weren't the outlaw, I wondered what the hell they was up to taking that there menacing stance in front a me.

"Well?" I said.

"Do they call you Kid Parmlee?"

"That's right," I said, "They do. And there's some that calls me that other thing you said too, only I don't like that one too much. What of it? Just what is it that you fellers are a-getting at here?"

Standing there a-yakking like that, I give them three a good looking over, and I seed something about their ugly faces that was somehow vague familiar. I couldn't put a finger on it though. I was pretty sure that I hadn't never saw none of them before. Then the third one a the bunch, the one what hadn't said not one word up till then, he spoke up, and he kindly talked outa the side a his mouth.

"You know them outlaw cousins of ours that was made mention of while ago?" he said. "The ones that's all been killed? You're the one that killed them. And just for that, we mean to kill you."

"Your names ain't Pigg, is it?" I said.

"No," he said. "My name's Elza Hook."

"I'm Clarence Hook," the next one said.

Then the oldest one, he hitched his britches up and give me a sneer, and he said, "I'm Jason Pigg."

Chapter 12

"Oh shit," I said, and I whopped my forehead with the palm a my left hand. "I can't hardly believe this here thing is really a-happening to me."

"Skeered, are you?" Elza said. "You'd oughta be. You're the one person in the whole world all of my family wants to see dead."

"Naw," I said, "it ain't that. I ain't skeered none. It's just that whenever I went and kilt ole Henry Pigg back yonder in Fosterville, I asked myself, 'Ain't there no end to them Piggses?' And I was hoping they was, and that maybe he was the last one, but it looks to me now like there really ain't no end to you bastards."

"We got a lot of kinfolk," Jason said.

"Only thing is some of us is Hooks, not Piggs," said Elza.

"Nobody alive in the wide world knows all that more than me," I said. "How many more a you worthless shit-eating son of a bitches has I got to kill before the rest a you leave me alone?"

"We can't never leave you alone, Kid," Elza said. "Not till you're dead and stinking. You done killed too many of our kinfolks for us to do that. We got to kill you. If we don't, we're shamed. We got to kill you."

"They's been aplenty of you try it before," I said.

"They're all dead and burried. Is that there what you want for your own selfs?"

"They's three of us here right now," said Clarence. "You think you can take us all three and us all coming at you at once?"

"It's been did before," I said. "I've tuck three at a time. You know what they say about me. They say—"

"That you're a regular Billy the Kid," said Elza.

"That's right," I said. "Maybe you'd oughta think somewhat about that before you get yourselfs kilt over nothing."

"It ain't over nothing," Jason said. "It's over a matter of family honor. It's over revenging our kinfolks."

"Besides, I don't think you can take all three of us," Clarence said.

"Maybe not," I said, "but two of you at least will go on along to hell with me. Y'all maybe wondering which two it might could turn out to be?"

"Naw," Elza said. "One of us maybe. The other two'll drop you for sure."

I was about to tell them that I didn't really want to kill no more Hookses nor Piggses on account a I felt like I had did me enough a that, but I never did get a chance. I had just only tuck me a breath in order to start in a-talking, whenever a voice come right outa the dark out there around us and surprised the hell outa all four of us. I stood still, but them others all looked around in all directions.

"It looks to me like you'll all three be dead before the first body hits the ground," that there mysterious voice said. It was a smooth and clear voice, and it sounded like as if it come from someone who was a-standing right in there in the midst of us.

"Who the hell is that?" said Clarence.

"Never mind," the mystery voice said. "Just get your

horses and ride out of here. That way you'll live a while longer."

"I got him pegged now," Elza said, his voice real low. "I know where he's at. I'll take him. You two get the kid. Now."

Whenever he said that last word, he jerked out his shooter and whirled around to fire, but before he could even pull his trigger, a flash come outa the darkness back there behind them, and ole Elza spinned again, hit in the high left chest by that stranger's bullet. I yanked my Colt out and shot ole Clarence right smack in the nose, and just about the same time a second shot come outa the dark and hit Jason in the back a the head. I tell you, they was blood and brains all over the place. Them three would-be killers was a-laying there deader'n shit. I stood there with my shooter in my hand, and the stranger, he come walking into the light a-putting his own gun away. He was a medium-height feller with long hair a-hanging down all over his both shoulders, and he was grinning real wide.

"You don't need to worry about me," he said. "I'm not named Hook or Pigg, and I'm no lawman nor bounty hunter. None of my relatives have been killed in gunfights."

"I'm obliged to you, mister," I said.

"I was after those three anyway," he said. "They stole my horse. Made me walk quite a ways."

"Then I reckon it might be just over yonder with their three and my own," I said. "They come riding in here a-leading one extry horse."

"It's mine," he said. "I saw them ride in."

"You been a-watching all that time?"

"And listening," he said. "Is there any of that coffee left?"

"There sure enough is," I said. "Here. I'll pour you a cup."

I done that and handed it to him, and then I tuck me another look at the feller with him a-settling down by the fire there in a little bit a light. He was a young feller, maybe some older than me, and he was dressed real fine, but the thing what really kinda tuck me offa my guard was that his skin was dark like, and his features, they was, well, different.

"Say," I said, "are you a redskin?"

"You mean am I an American Indian?"

"Yeah," I said, "a Injun."

"I'm a Cherokee," he said.

"Churkee," I said. "I heared that name before. Well, I'm ole Kid Parmlee."

I stuck out my hand and he tuck it and shuck it.

"What can I call you?" I asked him.

"Cherokee will do," he said.

"All right, Churkee," I said. "You can just call me Kid. Ever'one else does. Is your village around here somewheres?"

"I come from Sacramento, California," ole Churkee said. "My parents went out there in 1850. A good many Cherokees went out with the forty-niners looking for gold. My folks didn't find any, but they stayed in California anyway. So I was born out there."

"Well, I be damned," I said. "I just thunk that all Injuns lived in villages out on the plains and—"

"Lived in tipis with totem poles out front and ran the rivers in birchbark canoes," Churkee said. "Well, it's just not true, Kid."

"You got yourself a little lip whisker there too," I said. "Injuns ain't s'posed to have no whiskers."

"Really?" he said. "No one ever told me. If I'd known, I wouldn't have let them grow."

Well, I figgered he was putting me on then, and I could feel the skin a my face a-burning somewhat. I was glad it was after dark so he couldn't see it none too good by just only the light from the little campfire.

"I reckon I'm kinda ignernt," I said. "I ain't hardly got no book learning, and I for sure ain't never met a Injun before. I heared people talk, is all. 'Course, I know that folks says all kinds a things, and it don't pay to believe it all."

"Oh, it's not your fault, Kid," he said, "and if you did have some 'book learning,' you wouldn't have read the truth."

"No?"

"No way," he said. "What few books there are about American Indians are all full of shit. Let me tell you about my own people. The Cherokees used to live back East where the states of North and South Carolina, Kentucky, Tennessee, Virginia, West Virginia, Georgia, and Alabama are now."

"I ain't never seed them places," I said, "but it sounds like a whole lot a land."

"Well, it is," he said, "and we owned it all, but then the white man came, and he started in taking a little bit here and a little bit there and then finally he wanted it all. They decided to move us all out west, and when we put up a kind of a passive resistance, you might call it, they sent the army to round us up and move us out. They marched us all out to some land west of Arkansas, north of Texas. They call that forced march the Trail of Tears. We lost many of our people on that move."

"You mean, they just prodded all the Churkees outa there all at once on account a they wanted to get your land for theirself?"

"That's right," he said. "Anyhow, we built a new Cherokee Nation out there. We have a brick capitol building, schools, stores, roads, our own newspaper. We have everything the white man has, only ours is usually better."

"Well, I be damned," I said. "I ain't never heared a that. I didn't know Injuns went and hunted gold neither."

"Many Cherokees did," he said. "Like I told you, my parents didn't find any gold, but they stayed in California anyway. My father became a merchant in Sacramento. I was born out there."

"My pardner, ole Zeb Pike," I said, "he's a goldhunting man. He learnt me a little bit about hunting gold."

"Where is he?" Churkee asked me.

"I left him up in the mountains with some folks," I said, and I toyed around in my head with telling ole Churkee the whole tale, but only I managed to keep myself from doing it. After all, I didn't hardly know the feller, and he was a Injun. He sure did look good and talk smart though, and he had maybe saved my worthless ole life. 'Course, he mighta only did that on account a his horse.

"What're you doing out thisaway?" I asked him.

He sipped on his coffee and didn't say nothing, not for a while. I figgered that maybe he was a-doing like me and a-wondering if he should oughta tell me much of anything on account a he didn't really know me atall. Final, he went on ahead and spoke up though, and what he had to say sure enough did surprise me right smart.

"I'm looking for a man," he said. "A white man. I mean to kill him."

"Well," I said, "do you mean a perticular white man or will just any ole white man do for you?"

"This is a particular white man," he said. "His name is Randall Morgan."

Well, I reckon my jaw musta dropped on down and

my ole eyeballs popped wide open or something, 'cause the very next thing he said was he said, "Do you know him?"

"I know him," I said.

"Friend of yours?"

"Not hardly," I said. With what he had just told me, I reckoned then that it would be okay for me to just go on ahead and tell ole Churkee my whole sad tale, so I done just that, commencing with the day me and Paw and ole Zeb rid down into Fosterville and got our ass throwed in jail. I went on from there up to where we run into Weaver and them and then how ole Morgan was a-giving them so much shit. I told him how we had wiped out Morgan's place up there but ole Morgan and his henchman Shark had rid off and got away from us. Well, then, he knowed it all. The whole story. He sure knowed that old Morgan weren't no friend a mine. He just set there a-thinking for a spell. By and by, he spoke up again.

"Morgan was my father's business partner," he said. "It's a long story, and even I don't know or understand all the details, but Morgan robbed my father blind. He got away with all the money and left Father broke and ruined. The business is gone. I won't let Morgan get away with that. We Cherokees have been robbed enough by white men. If it takes the rest of my life, I'll find Morgan. I'll kill him."

"You mean, your old folks is out there in Californy without no way to make a living?" I said.

"My father found a job," Churkee said. "He's working for another store owner, so at least he's not starving. I wouldn't have left them destitute."

I didn't know what that there word meant, but I didn't ask. I had a kinda idea what he meant by it. I was just setting kinda stunned on account a him being after that same damn Morgan what I had been at war with, and I was feeling kinda bad on account a white people being so mean and bad, but then, I had knowed some pretty bad ones my own self.

"Which way you going from here?" I asked him.

"I really didn't have any idea," he said, "until just now."

"Just now?"

"You just now told me that you and your friends ran Morgan down out of the mountains," he said. "I didn't even know he was around these parts for sure. You've ridden up here from down south, and you didn't come across him on the way. That probably means I've got to look north or east in order to find him. I don't know what he'd be doing east of here, so I guess I'll look north."

Well, I liked the sound a that, on account a I was headed north my own self a-looking for them three outlaws, so now I figgered that maybe I could have myself some company along the way in my search. I didn't really too much like being all by my lonesome like I was and trouble ahead, and a feller like ole Churkee what seemed to be most as handy with his shooter as I was my own self with my Colt seemed like he'd make a hell of a good pardner if I was to run across them tough nuts. The other thing was that if they was still any lawmen a-looking for me and Zeb and Paw, they wouldn't look near as hard at scrawny little ole me if they seed me in the company of ole Churkee, a Injun, instead a two old fart white men. I thunk that all over in my head right quick like, and I come to a decision.

"Churkee," I said, "I'm a-riding north a-hunting them three owlhoots what folks tuck for me and my paw and ole Zeb. You're fixing to look north for ole Morgan. You wanta ride along with me for a spell?"

"I don't mind if I do," he said, and that was the commencement of a good friendship and worthwhile joining up between two men. I'll tell you right now, I never was sorry I hooked up with ole Churkee. He become my faithful Injun companion for a spell. Well, we come right off to a agreement a mutual benefit for our future pardnering, and that was that if we was to come onto ole Morgan and Shark, why, I would help him in his getting-even business for his daddy, and if we was to come across them three outlaws what me and Zeb and Paw had been mistook for, then Churkee would help me in getting them three rounded up. It was a good deal for the both of us, and then we final decided that it was time for us to get some sleep, but only them three dead avenging Piggses and Hookses was a-laying just a few feet away and some splattered brains and blood around too.

We talked about dragging the bodies off, but we final decided to move the camp instead. Churkee said he seed another good place just a little ways down the road, so we fetched up the horses and loaded up my cooking stuff and put out the fire and moved on down there. We picketed the horses, fixed us up a new fire for the night, and made our beds. Then we went on to sleep that night feeling pretty good about the whole situation. Least, I know that I did, and I believe he did too. And ole Churkee, just before I dropped off to sleep, he said one last thing to me.

"Kid," he said, "our partnership deal includes any Piggs or Hooks we might come across along the way."

I slept real good on that thought.

In the morning, we had us some biscuit and beans and coffee, and then we put out the fire and cleaned the place up. We saddled up all a the horses, packed up our stuff, and mounted up. We was both mounted, and we was leading along three extry saddle horses with their saddles. We figgered we'd just sell them extry horses and saddles somewheres along the way. It was long about noon that day when we final come to a little town. It was called Nugget. We rid on in there and tied our horses to the rail out front of a place called the Miner's Saloon. We went inside and went right up to the bar. I ordered us up a glass a whiskey each, and while we was waiting for the barkeep to fetch it on over, I rolled me a cigareet and offered the makings to ole Churkee. He tuck them and rolled him one real easy. I dug out a match and we lit up, and the barkeep brung our drinks. I paid him.

A big feller at a table was giving us a hard look. I could see him in the mirrer behind the bar. Churkee seed him too. We finished our whiskeys, and just then the big feller got up and come a-walking our way. He pushed his way right in between me and Churkee, and then he give ole Churkee a real hard look.

"You look like a goddamn redskin to me," he said.

Churkee looked him right back in the eye.

"I don't see that who or what I am is any of your business," he said.

"Injuns ain't allowed in this saloon," the man said. "Matter of fact, Injuns ain't allowed to buy booze."

"I reckon I paid for that, mister," I said. Well, he turned on me then.

"It's against the law to buy booze for a redskin," he said.

"You a lawman?" I asked him.

"No," he said, "but—"

"Excuse me," said Churkee. "I'm about to do you a favor. You probably don't realize it, but that man you're talking to is Kid Parmlee. You know they say he's—"

"A regular Billy the Kid," the man said. "Hell, Kid,

I didn't know who you was. I'm sorry. If the Injun's with you—"

"His name is Churkee," I said.

"Oh. Yeah. Well, if Churkee there is with you, then ever'thing's all right." He turned away from the bar then to look out over all the customers a-setting around at tables. "Ain't that right, boys?" he said. "Anyone Kid Parmlee wants to bring in here is okay."

He got hisself some nods and muttered agreements, and then he looked back to me.

"Okay?" he said. "No hard feelings?"

"I ain't got no hard feelings," I said. "Anyhow, I just kilt me two men last night, and I ain't really in no mood to do no more killing just now. Churkee, you got you any hard feelings on anyone here?"

"Naw," Churkee said. "I quit taking offense at ignorant statements a couple of months ago. I just hear too many of them."

"Hey, Sam," the dumb bastard yelled out at the barkeep. "Bring a bottle of your good stuff over here for these two. I'm paying." He looked at me again. "Okay?"

"Okay," I said, "and by the way, mister, just for your information. Ole Churkee here is a whole lot more deadlier rattlesnake than what I am. Count yourself lucky, friend. Hell, you could be a-laying dead on the floor right this very minute, if ole Churkee had been in a different mood."

Chapter 13

Well, they was hotel rooms attached to that there Miner's Saloon, and so while ever'one was proper respectful a me and ole Churkee, I went on over there to the desk where a clerk was a-lounging and got us a room for the night. No one balked none about it neither. I reckoned they knowed better than that. I tuck the key from the desk clerk and went on back over to where Churkee was a-waiting for me at the bar. We tuck the bottle and our two glasses and went on upstairs. No one made no moves against us. We went into our room and put the bottle and glasses down, and then we went on back downstairs. We walked outa that place and went and tuck keer of our horses down to the stable where I asked the man if he might be interested in buying them extry three, and he was, so we sold them and got us a pretty fair price too. We split the cash even betwixt the two of us, tuck up our saddlebags and blanket rolls, and went on back over to our room. I shut the door and locked it and then went for that whiskey bottle. Then ole Churkee, he pulled a little notebook outa his saddle-bag, and he set down and commenced to making some marks in it. I seed them.

Now, I'm sure you know already that I ain't had much learning, but I do know how to read and write. I read slow, and I don't know all them big words, but they ain't no use nohow, and I print mostly, but I can write my own name good if I have to. So anyhow, I knowed that Churkee weren't writing reg'lar writing.

"What's that there?" I asked him. "Is them some kinda witching marks you're a-making?"

"It's Cherokee," he said. "I'm just keeping some notes, a journal, you might say."

I wouldn't a said no such thing, 'cause I don't know what the hell that there "journal" means, but I never let on.

"You mean, you're a writing in Churkee?" I said.

"That's right." ·

"I ain't never heared a no Injun writing," I said.

"Most Cherokees are literate in their own language," he said. I was sorry to hear that, but I didn't say nothing more about it. I figgered that maybe it was something a Churkee wouldn't want to be a-talking too much about. You know, sometimes folks likes to keep their miseries to theirselfs, so I kinda changed the subject real delicate like. "Well, read some a that out loud," I said.

"It wouldn't mean anything to you," he said.

"That's all right," I said. "I just wanta see can you really read it. I wanta hear what it sounds like—them marks you make."

"All right," he said. "I'll write something you might be able to remember."

He made four a them marks off by their self, and then he read them out loud. "Uk san," he said. "Say it."

"Ook san?" I said.

"That's good," he said.

"That's what you read from them marks there?" I asked him.

"That's right," he said.

"What's it mean?" I said.

"Asshole. Feel free to use it any time you feel it's appropriate."

"Ook san," I said. "Ook san. Hey, I'm going to remember that one. Am I for real talking in Churkee? Ook san."

"You certainly are," he said. "You have a limited vocabulary, but you're talking Cherokee."

"Ook san," I said. "Ook san."

Churkee finished up his notes and put his little book away. It was still a little early in the day for more whiskey drinking, and I was a-getting hungry, so I suggested to ole Churkee that we go on out and hunt us up a place somewhere to eat something besides beans and biscuit. He agreed with me on that there, and we went on outa the room and locked the door and started on down the hallway. We was a-coming up on the landing there whenever Churkee put out a arm to stop me and stuck his finger up to his lips to shush me. I stopped still and listened. It didn't take me long to reckanize the voice a that bully what had backed down whenever he heared my name called.

"We ought to run them two out of town," he was a-telling someone. "He's a cold-blooded killer. They call him a regular Billy the Kid. Why, he's worse than Billy the Kid. And then having the gall to bring that damn Injun in here like that. Why, hell, he's just rubbing it in our face. What do you say, boys?"

"Ah, I don't know, Roscoe," someone said.

"Listen," Roscoe said. "We got laws, ain't we? What the hell good does it do to have laws if we let someone like that come in here and ignore them?"

"They ain't hurting no one."

"Naw, it ain't like they killed someone or something."

"But if we let it go by, it'll just get worse," Roscoe

said. "You want to wait till they do kill someone? Give them a inch, they'll take a mile."

"What do you mean, Roscoe? Next time Kid Parmlee'll come in here with two Injuns? Long as they can pay for their drinks, I don't see no problem. Leave them be before you get yourself into some real trouble."

"Well, I do see a problem," someone said. It was a new voice. "I agree with Roscoe. Something damn sure ought to be done about it. A killer and an Injun in our town. In our saloon."

"Sit down, Sherm," said another.

"What do you want us to do? Shoot them?"

"Someone go get the sheriff," Sherm said. "He can throw them in jail."

"For what?"

"It's against the law to be selling liquor to an Injun."

"Then they'd have to throw me in jail," the barkeep said. "It was me what sold it."

"We wouldn't need the sheriff if you'd all get behind us," Roscoe said. "There's enough of us to take them."

Well, now, that there was enough a that shit for me. I stepped on out onto the top step, and Churkee, he stepped out right alongside a me, and the whole bunch a them bastards down there shut up all in a minute. It was that quiet you coulda heared a mouse fart. I started in to walking down the stairs kinda slow and steady and Churkee moving along right beside me. No one a them sniveling cowards said nothing, and ever'one of them was a-looking right smack at us as we was a-coming down towards them. We final come to the bottom a the stairs, and we walked right over to ole Roscoe and his new pard that there Sherm. I stood there in front a Roscoe a-looking him in the eye with my coldest and meanest look. Churkee was doing the same thing to that Sherm.

"What was it you was a-wanting to do?" I asked Roscoe.

"Nothing, Kid," he said, and his tone a voice had sure enough changed. He was some nervous, I can tell you that much. "Me and the boys here was just talking. That's all. Just talk. Nothing to it."

"I heared you saying something about me breaking a law," I said.

"Oh, that," he said, and he tried to give out a laugh but it choked up on him. His face had kinda paled some, and he had commenced to sweating on his brow. "It's an old law," he said. "You know, one of them they don't take off the books when they should, you know? It don't mean nothing. No one pays attention to it these days."

"From where I stood," I said, "it sounded to me like you was paying it some serious attention all right."

"You got it all wrong, Kid," Roscoe said.

"Uk san," said Churkee.

I nodded. "I reckon you're right about that," I said.

Just then they was shots fired out in the street, and ever'one looked thataway. Sherm and Roscoe was visible relieved by that interruption. A man come a-running in from outside. His face was pale, and he was a-sweating and waving his arms around like crazy.

"They're robbing the bank," he said.

Someone at a table close to the door jumped up and pulled out a shooter.

"Let's go, men," he said.

Well, we all follered him a-pulling out guns, and then I seed them out there in the street. A skinny, scrawny kid and two old farts. They had just clumb up onto their horses and was skeedaddling outa town a-headed east. The kid turned in his saddle and fired a last shot, and a man on the street fell down dead. There weren't no reason for it. Another man on the street turned back towards us what had just come outa the saloon, and then I seed the badge on his chest.

"Get your horses and guns," he yelled out. "You're all a posse. Come with me."

I looked at Churkee.

"It's them," I said. "I seed them. Come on. Our damn horses is in the stable."

We headed for the stable at a run, but just as we was a-running past the sheriff, I heared him tell a man to gether up food and water and foller on behind. Men was already mounting up and ready to go. By the time me and Churkee had got our saddles on our nags and rid outa the stable, the rest a the posse was already disappearing outa town. We hurried on to catch up with them. They was a-riding hard, and so did we at first, but then ole Churkee, he looked over and hollered at me.

"Slow down," he said.

"But they're a-moving on," I said.

"They'll have to slow down soon," he said, "unless they want to kill their horses and wind up on foot. When they slow down, we'll catch up."

Well, a course, I seed that he was a-making good sense, I knowed better my own self, but only I just hadn't been a-thinking, I guess, so I slowed down the pace and rid kinda easy alongside him.

"What about them outlaws?" I asked him. "Ain't they likely to get away if we don't move a little more faster?"

"They'll have to slow down too," he said. "We'll get them. Just be patient."

I knowed that he was right. I was just awful anxious to get that damn kid in my gunsights, him and his two old pards, on account a, a course, they had been making ole Chastain and some others believe that me and my pard and my paw was killers and thieves. That had been going on for so long that my anxious was just a-getting

the best a me. I wanted them real bad, and the sooner
the better. Anyhow we rid along easy like for a spell,
and then we speeded up for a while, and on like that,
and sure enough, we eventual catched up with that damn
posse. Their horses was a-panting too. I figgered they
had rid them so hard that final they had been forced to
slow down. Churkee was right.

"Any sign a them bastards?" I asked.

"Just their tracks," the sheriff said. "We're on the
right trail."

"Did you get a look at them, Sheriff?" I asked. "Back
yonder in town?"

"I sure did," he said. "It's that same bunch that's been
terrorizing the whole countryside around these parts."

"Well, I'm sure glad a that," I said, "on account a
you know then that it ain't me up there we're a-chasing."

He give me a funny look, and I said, "I been mistook
for that skinny kid before, and I got on his trail in order
to prove that I ain't him and he ain't me. Now I got me
a witness, and it's you. Even if we don't catch them."

"We'll catch them, all right," he said. "No matter how
long it takes. I've got supplies coming after us, so we
won't have to turn back."

I recalled then hearing him tell that feller to get the
supplies and foller along, and I had to hand it to that
sheriff for that fast thinking. If this here chase was to
wind up taking some days, we'd have food and water
and plenty a bullets and bandages and such, and we'd
be able to keep on a-keeping on. That was plenty smart
a him to think a that in the heat a the situation back
there in town.

Well, we lollygagged along the trail for so long that
I begun to get impatient again, and I tuck me a look at
ole Churkee, and he was just looking relaxed in the saddle like as if there weren't nothing at all wrong or to

worry about in the whole entire world, so I tried my best to act the same exact way he was a-acting, but the truth was that I weren't near so calm on the inside. That damn kid and his buddies was up there somewhere ahead of us, and I was powerful anxious to get him. Final the sheriff decided that him and the rest a the posse had eased up on their mounts long enough.

"Come on," he said, and he kicked his horse into a good lope. The rest of us done the same. Then I could see up ahead that we was headed into some green hills, and since I couldn't see no sign a them three owlhoots, I figgered they musta gone up in there already. If we was a-going to have to go into the hills after them, they'd have theirselfs a chance to lay a ambush on us, maybe more than one chance. I was a-going to say something about that to the sheriff, but before I had a chance to open my yap, he done it. He held up a hand to slow us down.

"Watch it, boys," he said. "They went into them hills up ahead. They could be waiting for us."

Of a sudden, ever'one got kinda tensed up like. It was one thing for a whole gang a posse to ride down on three men out in the open a-blasting away like hell, but it was a whole different deal if them three might be hid and waiting to pick us off one at a time. Ole Roscoe, he was the first one to speak out and let his chicken shitness show.

"I don't think it's a good idea to just ride on up in there," he said.

"We got them outnumbered," the sheriff said.

"I know that," Roscoe said, "but that won't make no difference to the first few they pick off from their hidey-holes."

"They might not've stopped," said another guy in the

posse. "They might be riding like hell to get away from us."

"But they might not too," said that Sherm. "They might just be laying in wait up there like Potter said. They could pick a few of us off for sure, and I don't aim to be one."

Well, then, I figgered that Potter was that there sheriff's name. Me personal, I didn't have no idea what was the likeliest possible about that there situation. Them three bastards could be riding like hell or they could be laying up in ambush. There was just only one way to find out that I could tell, and that was to just keep on a-riding on their trail. If they was to take some shots at us, why, then we'd know. I weren't a-skeered to take that chance.

"I'm riding on ahead," the sheriff said. "Who's going with me?"

A few a the men opined as how they'd go along, and they headed on into the hills right behind ole Potter. That Potter, he showed some guts all right. If there really was a ambush up there, he'd likely be the first one to get dropped. Roscoe and Sherm hung behind though, and so did me and Churkee, on account a Churkee give me a sign to hang back. I didn't know what for, and I weren't about to ask him with them two a-setting there. Then Roscoe tuck a look over at us, and he kinda puffed up some.

"Well, I ain't a goddamned coward," he said. "Come on, Sherm. Let's go get the bastards."

Them two kicked their horses in the sides then and headed off after the rest a the posse. 'Course, they was pretty safe, on account a if the shooting did start, they would be way back in the back a the crowd. I'm sure that's what ole Roscoe was a-thinking too. He didn't fool me none. What I didn't have no idea about was what ole Churkee was a-thinking. I knowed he weren't a-skeered. I give him a look and seed that he was just a-setting and watching that posse ride into them hills and Roscoe and Sherm a-taking up the rear at a safe distance. Final he nudged his horse into motion.

"Come on," he said.

I didn't like to think that he was more a scaredy cat than what them two was, but I didn't know what else to think, 'cause I didn't know where the hell he was a-headed, till he turned off to our left and led me toward them hills at a angle. Then it come to me what he was for real up to. If them outlaws had for sure laid down a ambush, they would be a-watching the posse come at them. Me and ole Churkee, we could get in behind them maybe. 'Course I didn't know them hills, so I didn't know how hard or easy it was a-going to be to do that, but Churkee was acting like he knowed what he was a-doing, so I just rid along with him. I didn't say nothing, and he didn't neither.

We rid up into them hills for a space, and then Churkee stopped and clumb down outa the saddle and lopped the reins around a small tree there. I done the same thing what he had did. I was trying to act like I knowed what he was up to, like I was smart enough to a figgered it out or maybe even thunk a the same thing my own self, but really I was just a-watching him real close and follering along in total and complete ignernce. He started in to making his way on foot up the side a the hill through some thick, scratchy bushes and trees, and I follered him right along.

It was rough going too, I can tell you, but it weren't nothing like being on the side a that mountain where I had shit my pants, so I kept up with him pretty good. I got tired a having to brush the bushes outa my face and push my way through all that tangled bramble and stuff, but I didn't say nothing, not even whenever it scratched me up something fierce. Ole Churkee, he sure did act like he knowed just what it was he was a-doing. Final we come to some big rocks and outa all the brush, and that was some relief, but then it was a little harder climbing up over them smooth round slippery boulders. But then I thunk that I had final figgered him out, on account a I could see that them boulders went on up kinda high. Maybe if we was to get our ass on up there to the top, we would be able to look right down on where the ambush was laid out, that is, if it for real was.

And then of a sudden, there weren't no doubt about it no more, on account a we heared gunshots. The posse had for real rid into the ambush. We climbed a little harder and faster then, I can tell you.

Hell, a well-laid ambush can make all the difference in the whole world. It don't matter none atall how good a shot a feller is if a man picks him off from a hidey-hole beside the road before he even knows there's a man a-waiting there. He could be the best gunfighter in the world, and he'd still be dead and maybe even not know about it. And if all three a them outlaws was laid up real good, and if they had ketched ole Potter and them total and complete by surprise, why, they could conceivable kill the lot of them.

Chapter 14

Well, ole Churkee got way up ahead a me. He sure could climb. I was a-trying to make my way up a big round slippery-ass boulder, and I tuck to sliding, and I slud all the way back down to the bottom of it.

"Shit," I said.

I looked up, and I seed Churkee whip out his six-gun and commence to shooting at something. I tackled that rock again, and it was slow going, but I managed to get on up to the top of it the second try. I still had one more to go to catch up to Churkee, and I tuck on that one. Churkee was reloading by then. When I final got my ass up there alongside a him, he was a-shooting again, and I looked down to see could I tell what he had found to shoot at. I seed one a them two old farts what rid with the kid.

Obvious, he had been a-shooting down at the posse, but whenever Churkee shot at him, he had turned on around to defend hisself against this here attack from behind. I couldn't hardly see the posse on farther down, and I didn't see no one else but 'cept just that one old man.

"Where's the other two?" I asked Churkee.

"I don't know," he said. "Keep this one busy."

Well, I didn't ask no questions. I figgered that Injun

was up to something, so I just done like what he said. I hauled out my shooter and commenced to firing down at the old bastard down there, and he sent some shots back up my way too. To tell you the truth a the matter, we was too far away from each other to do any damn good with just only six-guns, but that didn't keep us from a-trying. 'Course, I didn't really want to kill the old son of a bitch neither. I was just only trying to do what Churkee had told me to do which was to keep the old shit busy. I really wanted to catch him and the other two alive and take them in for trial on account a it seemed to me that would be the best way a clearing me and Paw and Zeb.

Then I seed ole Churkee a-skulking up on the old man's blind side. I tuck me another shot just to keep the owlhoot's full attention on me. Well, sure enough, he ducked down behind a rock, but I could see his hat and his gunhand, and I was pretty nigh well sure that he was looking up in my direction. Ole Churkee, he made a move to get in closer, and so I zinged me another shot offa that rock just kinda in front a the ole man. He hunkered down a little more. I don't know what the damn posse was a-doing all this while. Likely they was just glad that the ambushing on them had come to a close.

Then it come on me, if the ambushing on them had come to a close on account a me and Churkee getting all the old man's attention, where was them other two at? Well, that got me to worrying, I can tell you. Anyhow, before I could spend too much time a-worrying, ole Churkee stood up down there kinda behind the ole man and showed hisself.

"Throw down the gun or die," he said.

The old man musta been trying to figger which a them things he'd ruther do, 'cause he didn't do nothing but just set still for a bit. Then with his both hands kinda up in the air, he stood up real slow like, but he never turned to take a look at Churkee. He stood up for a few seconds, I guess, and then he dropped the gun.

"Come on down, Kid," Churkee called up to me, and so I went to hunting me a way down there. I found one, but it was kinda slow going. I was I guess about halfway down to where they was at, and then something brung them other two back into the front a my brain. I stopped and yelled down at Churkee.

"Hey," I said, "what about them other two?"

I was kinda worried lest one a them two would see me all exposed like that a-climbing down to where Churkee and his prisoner was at and pop up and pick me off.

"There's no sign of them," Churkee said. "Come on."

Well, I made it on down there, and I looked over the edge, and I seed that it was just as far down again to where the posse was at, but whenever I peeked over the edge someone down there tuck a shot at me. I jumped back right quick.

"Hey, down there," I hollered out. "Stop your damn shooting. This here is Kid Parmlee. Me and Churkee has got your bushwhacker."

"Come on down then." I think it was ole Sheriff Potter a-talking. Well, we made it down there, and it weren't easy, but we done it. At the bottom, we walked that old man ahead of us and went on over to the posse. I seed that one man was down and dead, and then that there Ook san Sherm, he was hit in the thigh and bleeding something fierce. One a the other men was a-tying a rag around his leg, but ole Sherm was a-crying and a-howling like a baby. I remember thinking that it was kinda funny. Sherm and Roscoe had rid along behind, a-thinking that they'd be the least likely to get hit. Hell, even I thunk that Potter'd get it first before anyone else.

Me and Churkee marched the old man right over to ole Potter.

"Where're the other two?" Potter asked us.

"We never seed them," I said.

"I think they left this one behind to slow us down," Churkee said. "There's no sign of them up there, and when we drew his attention away from you, there was no more shooting down at you."

"That's right," Potter said. He looked at the old man. "How about it?" he said. "Is that how it was? Did they leave you behind to slow us down?"

"Go fuck yourselfs," the old man said.

"Let's string the old bastard up," said Roscoe.

"He's my prisoner," Potter said. "There ain't going to be no lynching here. He's going to jail, and he'll have a trial."

"Then he'll hang," said someone.

The old man looked over his shoulder at Churkee. "I shoulda let you shoot me," he said.

"What's your name, old man?" Potter asked.

"You figger it out," the old man said. "I ain't giving you no help on nothing."

"Where's the money from the bank?" said Potter.

"Find it," said the old man.

Potter looked at me then. "Where at's his horse?" he asked me.

"I never seed it," I said.

"Wagon's coming," one a the posse men said.

Potter looked back the way we had came.

"That's our supply wagon," he said. "Tie this man's hands, and when the wagon gets here, toss him in the back. Couple of you stay with him and meet the wagon. The rest of us are going to look for his horse."

Well, it was Churkee what found out about the horse.

Whenever we all gethered back up down there where we had been, he went over to Potter.

"The horse is gone," he said. "Two men rode on out leading a third horse."

"You seen the tracks of three horses?" Potter asked him.

"That's right," said Churkee.

"How do you know one was empty?"

Churkee shrugged. "I could tell you that I'm a fair hand at tracking," he said, "but why don't I just say that we know there were three men on horseback. We caught one man, and three horses rode out of here."

"The double-crossing bastards," the old man shouted from the back a the wagon.

Potter walked over to the wagon.

"How's that?" he said.

"We was all three of us s'posed to ambush you," the old man said. "They not only sneaked off a-leaving it all to me, they even went and stole my horse and tuck all the money. Damn them both to hell. All the way down to hell."

"What's your name, old man?" Potter asked again.

"Ben Wright," the old man said.

"Who're the other two?"

"Old Charley Coy," Wright said. "The kid's name is Jerry Gish."

I thunk that was a hell of a dumb name for a killing outlaw. My own name weren't too good neither, but then, that was how come me to never use it and threaten to kill my own old paw if he ever breathed a word of it to anyone. Anyhow, I felt pretty good about it all on account a now at least Sheriff Potter and ever'one in his posse knowed that the outlaws was Jerry Gish, Ben Wright, and Charley Coy and not Kid Parmlee, my paw and ole Zeb. We was cleared for sure. I needed to figger a way to get Potter to talking face to face with ole Chastain so that Chastain wouldn't try to kill me no more, but that shouldn't a been too tough to do, I figgered.

Well, Potter had ole Sherm tuck a little bit better keer of since we had supplies, and he loaded Sherm up in the wagon along with that there Ben Wright. Then he had us all mount up again and head out. Me and Churkee had to go back around and fetch our horses from where we had left them, and so we was once again hurrying along to catch up with the others. We done it though, 'cause this time they wasn't running like crazy. We rid on up behind the supply wagon and on past it to catch up with ole Potter. He was a-doing okay though, 'cause them tracks was right plain at that point.

"You two did real good back there," he said as I come up alongside him. "Thanks."

"I got me a stake in this too," I said.

We rid on without no more talking for a spell, and final we come down on the other side a them hills, and we was on flat ground again. Right after that, ole Potter lost sight a them tracks. We slowed way down and waited for Churkee to ride ahead and scout out the trail, and then as he moved on ahead, we follered. Churkee was some good tracker, I can tell you. I figgered that maybe Injuns was made thataway so that they could do it natural like.

The going was slow, and we never laid eyes on them two outlaws all the rest a that day. Whenever the light was might near gone, Potter called a halt, and we made us a camp for the night. We built us up some cooking fires and cooked up a meal outa the supplies that had been brung in on the wagon. By and by, we all bedded down.

*   *   *

We was up early when morning come, and we had us a good breakfast and some coffee, broke our camp, saddled and mounted up. Churkee picked right up on the trail, and we rest of us follered him along like we done before. I noticed that we was headed kindly northeast. We was moving along like that whenever ole Roscoe hollered out, "Potter, you sure that damn Injun knows what he's doing?"

"You want to see if you can a better job, Roscoe?" Potter said.

"I think we're wasting our time," Roscoe said. "I think they're long gone. I think we oughta turn around and go back. That's what I think. Any a the rest a you boys agree with me?"

"I do," said Sherm from back in the wagon. "I'm hurting here. I need a real doc to look at my leg."

"All right, Roscoe," Potter said. "Put Sherm on Harry's horse. Harry, you get in the wagon. Roscoe, you and Sherm can head on back. I won't hold it against you."

"Wait a minute," Roscoe said. "We ain't headed back like that. Just the two of us and him hurt. What if we was to run into them two outlaws?"

"They're out in front of us," I said.

"How do I know that?" said Roscoe. "I don't trust your damn redskin up there."

"You're just a chicken shit," I said. "There's two a them and two a you. I'd call that even."

"Sherm's hurt," Roscoe said.

"His hands and arms is both okay," I said. "He don't shoot with his leg, does he?"

"Hey," Roscoe hollered out. "Who else wants to head back? Well, come on. Am I the only one here who's got any sense? At least a couple of you ride on back with me and Sherm. Come on."

"Looks like it's just only the two of you," I said. "Why don't you go on ahead and get going. I'm just about fed up with you anyhow."

"Potter?" Roscoe kinda whined.

"It's your choice, Roscoe," said Potter. "Take Harry's horse and ride on back, or else shut up about it. The rest of us are going ahead."

Well, all that there fussing had went on long enough that ole Churkee had got out a little ways ahead of us, so Potter kinda kicked his horse into a trot and the rest of us done too, and we rid on to catch up. Churkee was still a-moving slow like, on account a having to look hard for them tracks. I looked on up ahead, but I couldn't see no sign of no riders up there.

"Cherokee," Potter said. "You sure we're still on their trail?"

Well, he tuck the thoughts right outa my head, and I was glad that it was him what said it.

"We're after them, all right," Churkee said.

"That's good enough for me," said Potter.

We rid the rest a that day and spent another night out there on the prairie. At breakfast the next morning, ole Roscoe and Sherm had picked up a couple a allies.

"It's just too far out, Potter," one feller was a-saying. "I rode on with you after Roscoe wanted to head back, but I figured we'd have caught them by now. Hell, we've probably ridden out of your jurisdiction anyhow."

"I know damn well we're outside of my jurisdiction," Potter said, "but I ain't letting that stop me. Did you forget they have the bank's money? Our money?"

"I didn't have no money in that damn bank," the man said. "It takes everything I make just to earn a living. I can't save a dime. And I'm losing money the longer I stay out here on this wild-goose chase."

"Go on then," Potter said.

Well, Sherm and Roscoe and two others rid out then. We still had a fair-sized posse though. More than enough to take that damn kid and old man we was after. Hell, I'd a rid after them two all by my lonesome if I'd a had to. I kinda tuck a liking to ole Potter, even if he was a lawman. I liked him for standing up to Roscoe and them the way he done, and I liked him for ignoring the problem a his jurisdiction. Besides, I had already tuck to two other lawmen in my time, so I figgered it weren't no shame to take to another one. Potter watched them ride for a bit, and then he said, "Anyone else want to quit on me?" No one said nothing.

Once them four had rid on out a-headed back for home like dogs with their tails between their legs, the rest of us cleaned up and packed up and headed out on the trail just like before, moving slow along behind ole Churkee as he scouted the trail. It was long about midday, and I was a-riding alongside a Potter, and I seed ole Churkee top a rise up ahead and then of a sudden come to a stop, turn and ride back down to join us.

"I saw them," he said. "Not far beyond that rise."

Potter set and thunk, but not for long.

"Men," he said, "spread out in a line. We'll ride slow up to the top of the rise. When I yell 'charge,' we'll go after them. Hit them with everything you've got, but if they throw down their guns and surrender, stop shooting. I'd rather take them in for trial. Is that clear?"

Ever'one opined as how it was, and so we all spread ourselfs and rid up in a line to the rise, and we seed them out there all right. They wasn't too far away from us. Potter drawed his six-gun, and so did the rest of us. Then he hollered, "Charge," and by God, we rid hard. Them two outlaws seed us a-coming, and they lit out. We commenced to shooting, and that kid, he turned around in his saddle and shot back at us, but it's awful hard to hit something thataway, and he never. We kept after them, and off to my right, I seed one a the posse's horse go down and throw his rider off over his head. I never slowed down, though, to see did the man get back up. I just kept on a-riding and a-shooting, and so did all the rest.

Then someone's bullet hit the old man's horse up ahead. It were that Charley Coy, and old Coy, he went down hard. He didn't get right back up, I can tell you that. Potter yelled at someone to stop and take charge a the prisoner. The rest of us kept a-going, and the kid up ahead was still a-trying to hit someone or something with his wild shots. Then he musta run outa bullets, 'cause he never looked back again. He just rid hard as he could. I knowed that someone was fixing to kill a horse or two if this here chase didn't quit soon, but I reckon ever'one else felt like what I did, and they didn't want to take no chances on slowing down to save their horse and let the little shit get away in case his horse had the more staminer than did ours.

Then ole Churkee, he started in to pulling out ahead a the rest of us, and he was a-riding hard. I could see that he was slow closing the gap betwixt hisself and the kid, that Jerry Gish. Gish was a-slapping at his horse something fierce with a little quirt, but Churkee kept on a-closing in. Gish looked over his shoulder and seed Churkee closing in, and he slapped harder and faster with his little piss-ant quirt. Churkee closed in some more.

I kept on a-riding fast, but I did ease up on my horse just a little on account a I knowed that I couldn't catch Churkee, and if he didn't catch that Gish, well then, I sure as hell weren't a-going to do it. I think ole Potter seed the same thing and figgered the same thing, 'cause me and him was a-riding most neck and neck. Churkee come up almost right alongside a Gish then.

I was a-watching close. That nigh onto him, most men woulda tuck a shot and blowed ole Gish outa the saddle, but that ain't what Churkee done. No sir. What Churkee done was he rid up as close as he could get, and then he leaned across and stretched his arm and tuck hold a Gish's shirt collar and lifted that little shit right outa the saddle and then just let him drop to the ground while his ole horse kept a-pounding hoofs and riding away. When that little runt landed on his ass on that hard prairie ground, why, I mean to tell you, I never seed nothing like it before or since then. He bounced straight up again real high and turned hisself a flip-flop like and lit down and bounced again two or three more times at least before he quit bouncing and went to rolling. Ole Churkee was a-going so fast that he rid right on past him, but by the time ole Gish final quit a-rolling, me and Potter was right there beside him a-looking down on him with our shooters in our hand. Then ole Gish, he final managed to set up and suck in some air, and then he looked up right square into my face, and he said, "You son of a bitches, I'll kill ever' damn one a you if I ever get a-loose."

Well, I give him my most iciest stare, and whenever I spoke up, I done it in my most coldest and meanest-sounding tone a voice.

"You'll have to shoot me in the back," I said, " 'cause there ain't no way you could take the likes a me to my face."

"I'll kill you," he said. "One way or the other. And I won't stop there. When you're dead, I'll stomp your whole head into brain mush."

Chapter 15

Well, ole Churkee final managed to get his horse
slowed on down and turned back around, and he come
a-riding back real slow and easy like, a-taking pity on
the poor horse what had just did him a hell of a job, and
the rest a the posse come riding on up to where we was
at. Two a the men already had that second old man, ole
Coy, with his hands tied behind his back, and a couple
more of them jerked ole Gish on up to his feet and went
to hog-tying him. He kept up a steady string a cussing
at us, I can tell you, and for some reason, he was a-
spitting most a his venom right at me. I wondered how
come.

Anyhow, the supply wagon come a-rolling on up to
us then, a-rattling and a-clattering, and they throwed Coy
and Gish on up in there with ole Wright. They was all
trussed up good. Sheriff Potter got down offa his horse,
tuck the hat offa his head and swiped at his forehead
with the sleeve a his shirt.

"We'll move back into those hills for a little shade,"
he said. "We'll make us a camp and rest up overnight.
Head back early in the morning. Couple a you boys
catch up the kid's horse. Ed, go get the saddlebags off
the old man's horse."

I didn't really like it, them to keep on a-calling ole

Gish "the kid," on account a that was what I was called, and it was the fact that he was about my size and age and all and running with two old men what had got me in all that trouble in the first place. But I didn't say nothing about it. I didn't want to start no fuss. I figgered my troubles was all over and did with now that we had them three all roped up like that. Wouldn't no one be accusing me and Zeb and Paw a-doing their dirty deeds no more.

The mainest thing what I had left for me to do was to just get the word on down to ole Sheriff Jim Chastain back down in Fosterville. I weren't quite sure how to go about that, on account a I knowed that if I was to ride into his sight, he would just start in a-shooting at me without giving me no chance to tell him nothing. I'd have to figger out how to get it did though. Then I could go on back up in the mountains to ole Weaver's gold camp and fetch ole Zeb back down outa there—that is, if he'd be a-wanting to leave. Me and Zeb would be free again. We could go right on back to hunting gold for oursels, a-looking for ole Zeb's mother lode or bananzy or whatever he called it. Or if he was to want to stay with Weaver and them for some unknowed reason, well, hell, I could go hunting me up another cowboying job, which was what I liked doing best anyhow.

"You smart-ass little shit face," I heared Gish say, and I looked over toward the wagon where he was at, and he was a-looking real mean and right at me again. "You're the first one I'll be a-coming for."

"Sheriff Potter," I said, "why don't you turn that little shit a-loose and give him a gun? He's a-wanting to kill me real bad, and I'm developing the same kinda sentiment towards him. Me and him can go at it right here and now. Save yourself a lota trouble and save your town some money."

"I can't do that, Kid," Potter said. "I got to take him on in. You know that."

Me and that other kid just stared at each other then, and it come to me that he was just about my size all right, but he was a hell of a lot uglier than what I was. It kindly pissed me off that folks had mistook him for me. I just couldn't figger how in the world they could think I was that ugly. I wished real bad then that ole Potter hadn't a been such a stickler, 'cause I would dearly loved to of shot that kid dead, or even not dead but just only hurt him real good.

Well, we all mounted on up and rid back into the hills like ole Potter had said and made us a camp for the night. Some a the posse men had rounded up the saddlebags offa all three a the outlaws' horses, the two live ones and the one dead'n, and ole Potter had gone through them bags hisself, and he had come up with all the bank's money all right. So it looked like we had been right successful in our chasing down a the outlaws and the loot. We all settled in feeling right smug. A chill come into the air that night, and me and Churkee was a-setting by a fire and drinking coffee. It was done dark. We was some tired out, but we wasn't yet what you'd call sleepy.

"What now, Kid?" Churkee asked me.

I kindly give a shrug, you know, like as if I didn't really know or hadn't give it all that much thought.

"I got to make for damn sure that ole Jim Chastain, the sheriff over to Fosterville, knows the whole truth about all this here matter," I said. "Once I get that little chore tuck keer of, I reckon I'll be free to do whatever I take into my head to do. I'll go back and find my ole pardner, Zeb, I guess. See if he's got anything pertikler in his old head. What about you, Churkee?"

"I still have to find Randall Morgan," he said.

Well, I tell you what, what with chasing down old Gish and them, I had just about forgot all about ole Morgan and the fact that Churkee was on his trail. I felt plumb bad about that too. Here Churkee had done gone way off outa his way to help me out with my running down a Gish and them two old men, and he had even gone and caught up with ole Gish all by his own self there in the end, and there I had went and put his own personal manhunting job most nearly outa my head.

"You know, Churkee," I said, "I just now give it all a second thought. I think that if it's all just the same with you, well, hell, I might just tag on along with you for a spell. If that's all right."

He tuck a sip a his coffee and then lowered the cup down and looked right across that fire at me. The fire-light was kindly bouncing on his dark face. Then he grinned.

"I think that would be all right," he said.

Well, it tuck us a couple a more days in the doing, and we was all sure enough glad that ole Potter had thunk about bringing along that there supply wagon, but we all got back all right into Potter's town, what, if you recall, was named Nugget, and Potter got them three owlhoots all locked up safe and sound in his jail. That damn Gish was still a-cussing and a-threatening. I wished again that Potter had went and let me and him shoot it out back out there on the prairie. I'd a shut the little shit up once and for all.

Me and Churkee tuck keer of our horses over to the stable, and then we went back over there where I had rented us a room. Sherm and Roscoe was in the saloon part a the place whenever we walked through, and I seed that they was giving us hard looks. Some a the other men what had rid with the posse was in there too, and they was telling the tale how me and Churkee had did most a the ketching. I figgered that was going down hard with them two cowards. You know, they hadn't tuck to me and Churkee right off the bat whenever we first rid into Nugget.

I knowed that I still had me a bottle and a couple a glasses up in the room, so me and ole Churkee coulda just went right straight on up there and poured us each a big drink a whiskey and set our ass down to drink it there in the room a-saving the expense a buying more drinks bat the bar, but the only thing was I figgered it would be some fun to stay around in the saloon a while and kindly rub it in. Churkee musta figgered the same thing, 'cause he never argued with me none about it. I ordered us each a glass, and me and Churkee set down at a table. Them fellers from the posse kept on a-bragging on us, and them other two, Roscoe and Sherm, just kept on a-glaring. By and by, Potter come in and ordered hisself a drink. He set down with me and Churkee.

"You boys doing all right?" he asked.

"Yes, sir," I said. "We're doing just fine."

"I sent a wire down to Fosterville," he said. "I told Chastain that I have the real outlaws in custody, and that you were with me in the posse, Kid. Invited him to come up and take a look if he feels the need. That ought to straighten things out for you."

"I'm obliged to you, Sheriff," I said.

"It's the least I could do," he said. "You two did a lot for me, for this town, hell, for the whole damn territory. Oh, we'd have caught them sooner or later, but thanks to you, it was sooner."

"Glad to be of assistance," Churkee said.

"Hey, Potter," ole Roscoe hollered out from over yonder where he was at. "Ain't there a law against selling whiskey to Injuns?"

"Don't start anything, Roscoe," Potter said.

"I want to make a complaint," Roscoe said. "I got a right. I'm a citizen. I want to make a complaint on that damn Injun setting there a-drinking whiskey bigger'n shit in our saloon when it's clear against the law. And you just setting there with him too, and you the sheriff. Well? What're you going to do about it?"

Potter looked kindly tired, and he give Churkee a straight-in-the-face look.

"What is your nationality, my friend?" he said.

"I'm a Mongolian," Churkee said, and I don't know what that meant, but whatever it was, he said it with a straight face and never blinked no eye.

"See there?" said Potter. "He's Mongolian. So relax, Roscoe."

"My ancestors came here a thousand years ago across the Bering Strait," Churkee said. He tuck a sip a his drink. "They wandered all the way down to North Carolina where they settled and evolved into contemporary Cherokees."

"What's that mean?" Roscoe said.

Well, hell, I didn't know what ole Churkee was a-talking about neither, so I never said nothing. I just kept out of it. If there was to be any shooting over it, I'd a been in it right off, but I couldn't get into it with them fancy words and all.

"It just means that he's Mongolian," Potter said. "That's all. And I don't know of any liquor laws pertaining to Mongolians. Do you?"

"Well, no," Roscoe admitted.

"Then just keep quiet and mind your own business."

"I don't know. I just think it's a sad thing," Roscoe said, "that we got us a paid killer and a damned Injun or a mongoo—whatever he is—come right into our town, a-drinking our whiskey, and our own sheriff is a-buddying up with them when he had oughta be arresting them or running them outa town. That's all."

Well, I kicked my chair over backward and stood up fast a-looking right at that Roscoe. I understood what he said all right, and I didn't like it none. I had my snake-eyes look on him too.

"I ain't no paid killer, you son of a bitch," I said. "And I'll kill you dead right here and now for nothing just to prove it."

Roscoe shut up and set still. It got real quiet there for a space. I was ready for just about anything, I can tell you.

"Sit down, Kid," Potter said.

I didn't set right away, and so he said it again.

"Sit down."

I set, but I kept my snake-eyes on that goddamned Roscoe. Then ole Potter stood up slow like and walked on over there to where Roscoe was a-setting. Potter just stood there a-looking down on Roscoe.

"Go on home, Roscoe," he said. "You're out looking for trouble, and I'm tired. I don't want any trouble in town tonight."

"You can't make me go home," Roscoe said. "I ain't done nothing. I got a right to set here as much as you or any man. More right than them two."

Well, ole Potter, he heaved a heavy sigh and started to walk on off. He headed right for the door just like as if he had done give up on trying to talk any sense into that damn Roscoe's thick skull, but soon as he got on over to the backside of ole Roscoe, he whipped out his shooter damn quick and whirled around and brung the barrel a the gun down hard smack on top a Roscoe's dull bean. It made me wince to see it and to hear it, I can tell you. It didn't hurt Roscoe none, though, on account a he just slumped dead away. He didn't even make no whimper. I reckoned it would hurt aplenty, though, whenever he come around awake again and had his feelings back. Well, ole Potter put away his shooter and looked at a couple a men who was just a-setting there.

"Drag his ass on over to the jail," he said. "Tell ole Lick Skillet over there to lock him up for the night."

Them two men got right up all right, and they went to dragging Roscoe's limp body outa the saloon by his feet. It weren't no easy chore neither. Roscoe was a big man. Potter come on back over and set down with us again.

"Maybe now we can have us a quiet visit," he said.

Well, I poured me another glass. I had done had a couple, and I was commencing to feel some woozy, but ole Churkee, he had just been a-sipping on that first glass a his. He was still clearheaded enough, I'm sure. And ole Potter, he gulped his down, and it didn't seem to have no effect on him atall. I was a-wishing that I could drink whiskey like that. It's fun to drink whiskey when you got good company, but only in my case it makes me get drunk pretty damn quick and so the evening's over for me just when it starts in to getting real good. We made some small talk, and I finished my drink and poured me one more, but I recollect a-thinking that was likely a big mistake. 'Course, ole Roscoe was outa the way, and I didn't figger that I had no special reason to keep myself all alert and ever'thing, what with Potter and Churkee both right there, and Gish and them in jail.

Then I heared a shot. Then there was another one and another one. Potter was up and out the door before I knowed what the hell was a-going on. Churkee follered him, and so did most ever'one else in the place. I got up kindly slow and unsteady and staggered for the door.

On my way over, I heared more shots and all kinda yelling and horses stamping around. I made it to the door and pushed my way through them batwings, and just then a bullet smashed into the wall just right over to my left side. I pulled out my Colt, but I was slow, and I couldn't tell what was going on nohow, so I just fell on over on the sidewalk and snugged myself up against the wall real tight.

A couple a men went running past me, and a man on horseback went riding fast down the road, but the real action was off to my left and down the street a ways. I kindly thunk that the jailhouse was down there, but my thinking weren't none too clear. I tried to set up then and see could I tell what was a-happening, but the most I could tell in my fuzziness was that there was some kinda ruckus all right. Pretty soon it all come to a stop. At least the shooting and the stomping horses quit. It got quiet 'cept for some hollering around.

Churkee come back then, and he seed me there and give me a hand up to my feet. My head was some dizzy, and my legs was wobbly, I can tell you, and for once in my life I really did wish that I hadn't a drunk so damn much whiskey. With Churkee a-holding me up, I made it back inside and back over to where I had been a-setting before, and I dropped my bony ass down heavy into the chair.

"What's going on?" I said, and my speech was real blurry. Even I noticed it.

"Someone broke those outlaws out of jail," he said.

"Before they even spent a night?" I said.

"That's right," he said. "The deputy, the two men that took Roscoe over there, and Roscoe have all been shot and killed."

"Damn," I said.

"Potter's talking to some of the men who were in the

posse," he said. "He wants to gather it up again and go after them first thing in the morning. He says it won't do any good to go after them tonight."

"You going?" I asked him.

"I'm thinking about it," he said.

"Well, me too," I said. "Hell, it's like we done all that work for nothing."

"There'll be more of them this time," Churkee said. "The three we brought back and however many there were who broke them out. They can't seem to get a handle on that. It could turn out to be a big fight."

"I been in big fights before," I said. "I ain't a-skeered."

"You're pretty drunk, Kid," he said.

"I'll be sober in the morning."

Just about then ole Potter come on back in, and he was follered by some more men. I sorta reckanized some of them from the posse. Potter stood with his back to the bar, and the rest tuck seats a-facing him.

"It was five or six men who did the job," Potter said. "We're not sure exactly. That means we'll be after either eight or nine. I'll need a good-sized posse in the morning, and I'll want to get an early start."

"Who done it, Sheriff?" someone asked.

"We don't know."

"They was a man over to the Watering Hole earlier," someone said. "He was a-hiring gunfighters."

"What was his name?"

"I never did catch it."

"Go on back over there and see if he's still around," Potter said, and the other man hurried out the door.

"You think that's who done the jailbreak?" someone asked.

"I don't know," said Potter. "Now, listen. I want everyone here to quit drinking for tonight. I want you all to go home and get a good night's sleep." He looked over at me and ole Churkee. "Will you boys be riding with us again?" he asked.

"I will," I said.

And then ole Churkee, he went and said, "Yes. We will."

That other feller come back in then what had run over to the other saloon in Nugget, that there Watering Hole.

"They're gone, Sheriff," he said. "Ole Joby said that he left out with six men hired on."

"They must be the ones then," Potter said. "If someone was over there recruiting gunfighters, and he's gone, then it must have been them who broke Gish and his gang out of jail. It's one way to recruit outlaws."

"What're you going to do, Sheriff?"

"We'll go after them, of course," Potter said. "First thing in the morning. We'll have those three back in jail before they know it, and we'll have them some fresh company too."

"Wonder who that fresh company is."

"Oh, I know who it is. I got his name over there at the Watering Hole too," said the feller what had made that run. "Joby heard it said. And he told it to me.

"All right then," Potter said. "Who the hell was it?"

"It was Randall Morgan," the man said. "That's what Joby told me. Randall Morgan."

Chapter 16

Drunk as I was, I seed ole Churkee's ears prick right up at that news. I knowed that he was all-fire excited about it too, on account a he was at long last hot on the trail a the very bastard what had brung financial ruin onto the head a his old paw. I still didn't quite know how no Injun coulda been in business in Californy, but if that's the way that Churkee said it was, well, that's just how it was, I guess. Anyhow, Churkee got me up to my feet again, and he commenced to walking somewheres with me.

"Where we going?" I said.

"Upstairs to bed," he said. "That's where I'm taking you. Then I'm going after that bunch of outlaws."

"At night?" I said. "In the dark?"

"I can track them all right," he said.

He had me to the foot a the stairs by that time, and I was a-trying to lift my feet one at a time to put them on the steps.

"But ole Potter, he said we was to wait till morning," I said.

"I know what Potter said, but I'm not obliged to follow his orders. This way, I can stay close to them and keep track of them. I'll leave you and the posse some signs along the way so you'll know you're on the right track. Can you remember what I'm telling you?"

"Yeah, I can remember. What do you think? I'm drunk or something? You're a-fixing to head on out and foller them bastards all night long, and you'll be a-leaving us some sign along the way so we'll know that we ain't lost."

Just then I stumbled and woulda fell on my nose if ole Churkee hadn't a been a-holding onto me. He catched me up, and I reached for another step with one a my feet. I don't recollect just which one it was.

"Did I get it all right?" I asked him.

"Yes," he said. "I wonder if you'll remember by morning."

"I will," I said. "I will. Don't you worry your head none about that. I can handle myself a little whiskey all right."

"A little. Yes," he said.

It sounded to me like there was a dig somewheres in that, but I couldn't figger out just what it was, so I let it go. We was up on the landing by then, and so we wobbled on over to the room. It tuck me a while to dig the key outa my pocket, and then I couldn't poke it in the hole, so ole Churkee, he tuck it away from me and opened the door. He staggered me on in and throwed me on the bed.

"I'll see you on down the trail, Kid," he said.

Then he was gone. I was a-laying on the bed still all in my clothes, and I know that I was a-laying still, but the whole damn room commenced to spinning around and leaning thisaway and that. I opened up my eyes and stared them on the winder, 'cause that was all I could see there in the dark, and I focused them on that winder, and the room kinder settled down then, but whenever I let them close again, well, the damn room would start in again. I tried my best to keep my eyes open and a-looking right straight at that winder. I thought about taking off my gun belt and my boots, but I knowed I didn't have it in me to do that, so I just let it go. By and by, in spite a all my efforts, my eyes closed and I went on off to sleep.

Now if I'd a been sober that night, a whole lota different things mighta happened. In the first place, I mighta been able to be a some help whenever them owlhoots busted Gish and them outa jail. I mighta been able to nail me one or two a the bastards. But in the second and mainest place, I wouldn't never a let ole Churkee ride outa there all by his lonesome the way I done. I'd a tried to talk him into waiting till morning and riding out with the rest a the posse, but if he turned out to be just too damn stubborn for me, why, I'd a rid out with him. But then, I weren't sober.

You know, it don't hardly pay to think on things like that. It don't make no matter what I mighta did if I'd a been sober or if I'd a been thinking better or if anything else, on account a what's did is did, and that's all they is to it. All the thinking in the world won't make it no different. And then, too, sometimes you does something without thinking about it before you do it, and then ever'thing works out just fine and dandy. There just ain't hardly no way you can figger out nothing about this here life.

Well, in spite a ever'thing, I was up early in the morning. I had been good and drunk all right, but then, it hadn't been all that late neither. My head didn't feel none too good, but I went out and found myself a big breakfast and et it and drank lots a coffee, and that made me feel a whole lot better. Food and coffee does wonders for a feller's body. I figgered that one out all right. Whenever I finished up with my last cup a coffee, I rolled myself a cigareet and smoked it, and then I went on down to the stable and saddled up my ole horse. I clumb on his back and rid on over to the sheriff's office.

I was the first one there, so I rolled me another smoke. I set in the saddle and puffed on it. By the time it was gone, I was needing to take me a leak real bad. I was still the only one around, so I just rid ole horse around the corner, slud off his back, and wetted the ground there. Then I clumb back on and went back around to the front. Then I seed ole Potter a-coming.

"Howdy, Sheriff," I said.

"Morning, Kid," he said. "Where's your pardner?"

"You mean ole Churkee?" I said. Nobody hadn't called ole Churkee my pardner before, and up till then, whenever I thunk that word, why, I thunk about ole Zeb, but whenever ole Potter said it the way he done, why, it come to me that ole Churkee sure enough was my pard. That didn't take nothing away from ole Zeb. He was still my pard, and he always would be, but I reckoned that I could have two pardners. I didn't see nothing wrong with that.

"Churkee tuck on off last night," I told Potter. "Said he didn't want them bastards to get on too far ahead of us. He's going to leave Injun sign along the way so as to make it easier for us to foller along."

Potter kindly scratched his head on that, and then he said, "It might work better that way. Okay."

'Bout then some a the others come riding up, and pretty soon we sure enough had us a posse a men. It was bigger'n the last one. That shooting in town just the night before along with the killing of a couple a their citizens, one not so much a leading one, had riled folks up. There musta been twenty or maybe even twenty-four. The supply wagon all loaded up come along too. Ole Potter, he give a speech about how we was all to foller orders and all that, and then he turned his horse and headed us all outa town.

We rid on out a ways a-follering tracks, and then the tracks begun to fade. We kept on a-riding in the same direction anyhow, on account a there wasn't no reason not to, and then I seed a pile a rocks up ahead. I pointed over thataway. Potter nodded. He seed it too. We rid on. In another couple a miles, we come across another pile a rocks, and we slowed down to look at it, 'cause it had a stick stuck in it.

"It looks to me like ole Churkee is a-telling us to foller where that there stick is pointing," I said.

The stick was pointing east.

"That's the way I read it too," Potter said. "Let's go."

We turned and headed east. Churkee's next sign pointed us north, and we went up thataway for a spell. We wound up riding off in ever' damn direction they is. We'd go off one way for a few miles and then turn again. I was about to get dizzy from it all. When we come to the next sign, Potter stopped us all.

"What the hell's going on, Sheriff?" one a the men hollered.

"I think they're just riding in circles to throw us off the track," Potter said. "I don't know what we can do but just keep following the signs."

"Sheriff," I said, "I got me a idee where they might be a-headed."

"Let's hear it," he said.

"Well, sir," I said, "it was ole Morgan what was rounding up gunslingers back there in Gooseneck, and it was him what broke them three outa your jailhouse. Right?"

"That's right."

I went on then and told ole Potter the whole story about Morgan and his gold camp a-trying to run off

Weaver and his bunch up in the mountains, and how me
and ole Zeb and Weaver's boys had turned the tables on
them. We had wiped out the whole bunch, all 'cept for
Morgan hisself and ole Shark. I figgered that Morgan
and Shark was together still, and that they was meaning
to go on back up there and get even with Weaver for
what we done, and then get back to his original plan a
taking over the whole damn area. That was how come
them to be rounding up new gunhands over in Gooseneck, and that's how come them to bust Gish and them
outa jail. They meant to use them too.

"Anyhow," I said, "that's what it looks like to me."

"So you think they're trying to throw us off the trail
and then ride back up to that gold camp?" Potter said.

"That there'd be my guess," I said.

"Well, Kid, you may be right," he said. "But I don't
want to take a chance on losing their trail in case you're
wrong. Come on, men. Everyone gather around."

He got down offa his horse, and so did the rest of us,
and we all cluttered around him to hear what he was a-
fixing to say. He told the rest of them what I had told
him, and then he told them what he had told me.

"Now here's what we're going to do," he said. "I'm
going to divide this posse right down the middle. Half of
you will ride with me. I'm taking my half up the mountain. I'm putting Mac London in charge of the other half,
and, Mac, I want you and your bunch to keep following
these signs. If you should come across them, don't try
anything foolish. You'll still outnumber them, but not
by much."

"They won't get nothing past us," that London said.

"If the Kid's right," Potter said, "you'll eventually
follow the signs right up the mountain and catch up with
us."

"I got you," London said.

"Kid," Potter said, "you're coming with me, and you lead the way. All right. Let's ride."

Well, I headed us back toward that main road what run north and south and alongside a the bottom a the mountains there. I knowed they was two ways up. One would take us up into Weaver's camp, but what I didn't know was whether or not anyone had ever cleaned off that part what me and ole Zeb had messed up with rock slides. The other way would take us through the wreck a Morgan's camp, and if I was right with my idee, ole Morgan and them might all be back in that very camp. I told that to Potter as we was riding along.

"Let's try the southern way," he said. "Up to Weaver's camp."

We kept on a-riding till it was nigh dark, and we hadn't come to the road yet. Potter called a halt, and we made us a camp. We had tuck along some supplies with us, but the wagon and the most a the supplies was riding along with the other bunch. So we had us some supper and some coffee and rolled out our beds. I slept good that night.

In the morning, we tuck out early again after we had et some breakfast and drunk us some coffee. We was at the road by mid-morning. We stopped there.

"If we keep going," Potter asked me, "where will we be by noon?"

"I'd say 'bout halfway up that son of a bitch with no place to stop and set down," I said.

"All right, then," he said, "let's make camp and have some food."

While some a the others was busy a-building fires and getting the food and coffee ready to cook, ole Potter said to me, "I don't see any sign that your pardner left for us here."

"I didn't see none neither," I admitted.

"Then we might have us a problem," he said. "If he hasn't been here before us, that means the outlaws didn't go up there. They're still out there leading the rest of the posse around in circles."

"I got me another idee," I said. "You wait right here till I come back."

I mounted up on ole horse, and I hit the road headed north. I still felt like I was right about what I said on my first idee. If the outlaws hadn't gone up that road back there, and Potter was right in what he said, that if they hada, ole Churkee woulda follered them and left us a sign, but if they hadn't gone up there, then I figgered they had gone up on the northest trail so as to come right into the old Morgan camp. I meant to find out. It was a fair ride up thataway, and I knowed that Potter and them would be getting anxious concerning my return, so I moved ole horse along as fast as I dared to. He done good. When I final reached the place where the trail went up into the mountains, I seed it.

Ole Churkee had been there all right. They was a white stick jobbed into a neat little pile a fist-sized rocks, and it was a-pointing up. The bastards had gone up thataway, and Churkee was behind them. He was all by his lonesome too, and I hoped that he didn't try to take them on thataway. I figgered that he was too smart for that, but I knowed, too, that he was awful anxious to get that damned Morgan. Well, there weren't nothing I could do for it but to just only get my ass back to Potter and them, and then get all of us back up to the road on top what would take us on over to Weaver's camp. I turned around and lit out.

I made it back to the camp all right, but even before I rid in, I could see ole Potter a-pacing. I pulled up kindly close to him and jumped offa ole horse.

"Well?" he said.

"I found Churkee's Injun sign," I said. "They went up on the road to Morgan's camp all right. Churkee went up behind them."

"Eddie," Potter called out, and a man come a-running. "Ride back out there on the prairie and find the rest of the boys. Bring them back here. We'll be headed up that mountain trail there. Follow us along."

"Yes, sir," Eddie said, and he went and mounted up his horse and tuck out.

"Well," I said, "we heading on up?"

"You get yourself something to eat first," Potter said. "Drink some coffee."

"Hell," I said, "I'm all right."

"I want you to stay that way," he said.

I went over to the clostest fire and found some beans in a pan and a coffeepot on the fire. I got me a plate and filled it up and got me a cup and poured it full, and I set down on the ground to eat. I had my face down in the plate a-shoveling, when I seed four boots a-coming in my direction, and then I heared ole Potter's voice.

"I got someone here who wants to see you, Kid," he said. "Says he's an old friend."

I looked up, and I be damned if it weren't ole Jim Chastain. He was looking down at me right stern like, but I noticed right off that there weren't no gun in his hand.

"Hello, Kid," he said.

"Howdy, Jim," I said. "Did Sheriff Potter here tell you about them three outlaws?"

"He told me," Chastain said.

I give a nervous laugh then.

"Well, then," I said, "you know that it was all a mistake whenever you locked up me and Zeb and Paw."

"I did the right thing, Kid," he said. "If you had

stayed put, we'd have found out we had the wrong men in jail and let you out."

"You'd a had us on a trial, wouldn't you?" I said.

"It could have happened," he admitted.

"And if no one had done caught up with them other three," I said, "we mighta been found guilty on account a I'm skinny and I was riding with two old men, and then you'd a stretched all our necks and we'd be dead and them three would still be riding loose."

"It wouldn't have happened that way, Kid," Chastain said.

"Well, anyhow," I said, "you know it wasn't me and Zeb and Paw."

He nodded.

"I know that," he said. "Sheriff Potter tells me you helped capture those men once. Then someone broke them out of jail, and you're riding with the posse again. He also said that you're the one who figured out where they were going. You seem to be conducting yourself pretty well. What about Zeb and your paw?"

"I sent Paw back to Texas and Maw," I told him. "Zeb's up yonder with them miners."

"Well, Kid," he said, "I'm glad to know that it wasn't you after all. I kind of liked you."

"It's all over and did, then," I said. "I'm sure enough glad a that my own self. I sure didn't want to kill me no lawmen, special not you, but I didn't want to get all hanged up for something what I never done neither. I'd a fought you, Jim, if I'd a had to. And I reckon I'd a likely kilt you too."

"I know you would have, Kid," he said. "That's why I came at you with a shotgun."

"Yeah, well, I'm glad it's all over."

"Kid," Chastain said.

I looked up at him.

"Yeah?"

"It's not over," he said. "I know that you're not guilty of the stage robbery and the bank jobs and the killings. I know that. But there's the matter of jailbreaking, and then there's another matter. A personal one. I'm willing to let the jailbreaking go. I'm not unreasonable. But the other thing, well—just as soon as we get this business at hand under control, you and me are going to settle that personal matter, one way or another."

I looked up at Jim, and I wanted to say something to him, but only I just couldn't think a nothing hardly to say. He had done said that he was willing to forget the jailbreaking, and I thunk that was pretty good of him. But that there personal matter, well, 'course I knowed what it was he was a-talking about. When I first done it to him, well even when I done it a second time, it seemed like a real good joke on ole Jim. But then, I had suffered me some embarrassing times since then my own self and I begun to take a different kind a look at what I had did to ole Jim. While I set there a-staring at him like that, he seemed as cold as ever he coulda been.

Chapter 17

Well, by God, ole Jim, he just turned right away from me without no other word and started in to walking off, and damned if ole Potter, he didn't turn his back on me, too, and walk off alongside of him. I heared Jim say, as they was moving off, "Potter, I'd like to ride along with you and see this thing through."

"Glad to have you, Chastain," Potter said. "I'll take all the help I can get. Besides, we'll be outside my jurisdiction before we're through here."

"Well," Jim said, "we're outside of mine already, so I'll just go on and follow your lead. You're in charge. But to hell with jurisdictions. We need to stop that bunch."

Their talking kindly faded away then, they had got so far away from me, and, well, me, I just set there not quite a-knowing what to think about it all. It really for sure was a relief offa my head to of heared old Jim say it out loud and all by hisself that he knowed now total and for sure that me and Zeb and Paw wasn't the outlaws he had once thunk we was. That much was over with and did. Paw and ole Zeb was safe enough, and for sure now I wouldn't get my own ass all hung out on no tree branch to dry. At least not for them crimes. I had did what I had set out to do by the clearing a our good names.

But then, I sure knowed what ole Jim was a-talking about whenever he said that there business about the personal matter betwixt me and him. I knowed that he was a-meaning them two times I had left him plumb, stark nekkid and no way to get hisself covered up. I had embarrassed him real good, and there weren't no way that he was a-going to let me get away with that. He couldn't beat me in a gunfight. I knowed that. And him being a lawman and all, I didn't think that he would do no cold-blooded murder, like shooting me in the back or taking a shotgun to me or something like that. But he had something in his head to get back at me for what I done. I knowed that much.

Well, I et them beans real fast and drunk me a couple a cups a coffee, and then I got myself ready to ride. I was the last one, and ever'one else was a-waiting for me. Whenever ole Potter seed that I was ready to go, he yelled out for us all to mount up. Then he called me up alongside of him.

"Lead the way, Kid," he said.

I tuck out on that trail headed up the mountain, and it weren't too bad. I knowed it pretty good by then all right. Even whenever we come to the place where I had last seed ole Jim a-standing nekkid, there where I had made the rock slide for the second time, it looked like as if someone had done been back around and cleared it out there. I figgered that maybe some a Weaver's boys had did it so they could get their own supply wagons up and down. Now for sure the posse supply wagon ought to be able to make it whenever it come along. The going was slow though.

We made it on up to the top a that trail without no real trouble, and then we rid along the mostly flat road

a few more miles before we had to stop for the night.
We still had us a fair amount a supplies with us, and so
we was able to get ourselfs a good meal and some coffee
and all. For just a minute there I thought that I'd surely
like to have myself a glass a good whiskey, but then I
brung back to mind the last time I'd slurped down too
much a that stuff and what it had caused. I figgered then
that I was just as well off without it. At least for the
time being.

It was kindly cold in that camp that night. Well, what
I mean is, it had begun to cool off up in them mountains
all right, special at nighttime, but that ain't what I mean.
What I mean is that ole Jim Chastain was a-hanging
around ole Potter some close, I reckon on account a them
both being sheriffs and all, and since ole Jim weren't
talking no more to me since he told me what he told me,
that meant that neither did ole Potter on account a he
was over there with Jim. So it was kindly cold in the
camp for me.

Next morning we had ourselfs a breakfast and more
coffee, and then we all mounted up and headed on towards Weaver's gold camp. Weaver and Raspberry and
some others come out to meet us whenever we final
come into the camp, and I interduced both sheriffs to
them guys.

"Has Morgan showed back up yet?" I asked.

"He's back," Weaver said, "and with some more
men."

"We know about them men all right," I said. "Say,
where's ole Zeb?"

Weaver looked around in all directions.

"Why, I don't know," he said. "He was standing right
here beside me when we saw you coming."

"Well, I need to find him," I said. "I got news."

I left Weaver and Raspberry with the two sheriffs to

learn all about just what the hell was a-going on what with ole Morgan and them back over yonder at the site a their burned-out camp and the other half a the posse a-coming along the road behind us and ole Churkee over there on the other side a Morgan and all. I weren't too much worried about nothing by then on account a we had done whipped that first Morgan bunch, and this time we had us a whole lot more men, and ole Morgan, he didn't have nigh as many as what he'd had before. It didn't promise to be none too exciting.

I wandered all around that camp a-hunting ole Zeb, but he weren't nowhere to be found. I looked in the tent where I knowed he should be a-staying, and sure 'nough his things was still inside there. I looked over where some a the miners was a-digging. There weren't no sign a Zeb. Then I went inside the big tent, and I seed ole Myrtle just a-covered in a fine layer a flour, and she smiled real broad and genuine at me.

"Howdy, Kid," she said. "Welcome back."

"How do, Myrtle," I said. "It's a most pleasure to see you again. Say, Myrtle, have you saw ole Zeb anywheres? I been looking all over for him."

She give me a knowing kinda wink and pointed over to the kitchen part what was partitioned off from the mainest part a the big tent, and so I went on back there. I looked around, but I never seed ole Zeb nor no one else. I turned around and was a-fixing to leave, but Myrtle come into the doorway just then, and she pointed across the room to a pickle barrel what was a-standing there. I give her a curious look, and she just only jobbed her finger in the air still a-pointing at that barrel. I walked over to the barrel, and then I give a look back at Myrtle, and she pointed again and nodded her head kinda vigorous. I tuck hold a the lid and pulled it off, and there he was, all scrunched down in that pickle barrel, and the smell a pickles come a-whuffing out at me.

"Zeb," I said, "you old son of a bitch, what the hell are you a-doing in there? That there's a pickle barrel."

Well, he stood up, but he was slow, like as if he'd been wadded up too long, and he groaned and moaned something fierce, but final he was a-standing.

"I know what the hell it is. You don't have to tell me. I'm hiding out," he said. "You'd best get your own self hid too, and quick about it."

"How come?" I asked him.

"That Chastain is out there," Zeb said. "I seen him come a-riding in all bigger'n shit with a whole damn posse behind him."

"Hell, Zeb," I said, "didn't you see me? I was riding in with them."

"What?"

"I come in with the posse, Zeb. That's what I wanted to tell you about. I was down yonder in Nugget whenever the damn gang what Chastain thunk was us come and robbed the bank and kilt another man. Ole Potter, the sheriff there, he seed me, and he seed them, and he knows that we ain't them, and they ain't us, and he tole ole Jim Chastain what he seed. We ain't wanted no more, Zeb. It's all been done cleared up."

"You sure?" he said.

"Damn right," I said.

"Well, I mighta seen you," he said, "if you wasn't so damn little tiny."

"Shut up, you old fart," I said. "Climb back outa that damn barrel and come on out and meet ole Potter."

He wriggled a little bit and shoved, and then he said, "I can't get out. Give me a hand, Kid."

I tried but I couldn't pull him out neither, so I just went and pushed the barrel right on over and him in it, and ole Zeb, he hollered like I'd pulled his nose or something. Then he come crawling out on his hands and knees like a babe, and he stood up and commenced to yelling at me.

"You snot-nosed brat," he said. "I oughta lay you over my knees and whip your skinny ass. You'd oughta learn more respect for your elders, you wet-behind-the-ears little shit. Push a old man over like that. Baby-faced little bastard. Even if you ain't got no respect, I'm your own ole pard. Hell, that oughta mean something to you. Kids these days got no sense a what's right and what's wrong. Hell, just ain't got no sense."

"Zeb," I said, whenever he slowed down to ketch his breath again, "go take yourself a bath. Will you? You got a powerful odor a pickles about you."

Back outside, I come up on Potter and Chastain still a-talking with Weaver and Raspberry. I was some curious about any plans they might have for attacking ole Morgan's camp, since I had set my mind at ease about ole Zeb. I was kindly wondering and worrying about ole Churkee too, knowing that he was somewheres over on the other side a Morgan and them. I had found ole Zeb and set my mind at ease on him, and freed up like that, it got to pondering on Churkee.

"Potter," I said, "when we hitting that Morgan camp?"

"We'll wait for Eddie and rest of the posse to show up," he said. "It shouldn't be too much longer."

"We ain't got no way a knowing how much longer it'll be," I said. "We can't just sit here and wait for them. Hell, ole Churkee's over there somewheres all by his lonesome. We got us plenty enough men here to do the job with. Let's us just go on and get the no-good bastards and get it over with and did."

"Better to be safe than sorry," he said. "We'll wait."

Well, him quoting fancy sayings like that didn't impress me none, I can tell you that. I didn't like his decision one damn bit. I was a-thinking that ole Churkee might get impatient over yonder way all by hisself, a-wanting to kill Morgan as bad as he did, and he might just go on ahead and try to do something about it by hisself if we was to take too long in the doing a something. Even if he did manage to keep ahold a his patience, one a them Morgan men might could come across him over there accidental like. He wouldn't have no help, and so he wouldn't have a chance. I didn't like that a damn bit, like I said.

"What about Churkee?" I said.

"I have an idea he's smart enough to keep his head down," said Potter.

Well, that pissed me off complete and total, but I didn't have nothing else to say to a damn stubborn-headed lawman, and so I just kept my yap shut after that, and I turned and walked on off kindly stomping as I went so they'd know what I thunk about it. I went on over to the tent what Weaver had give to me and Zeb to live in while we was up there, and I found ole Zeb inside, nekkid in a tub a water, all sudsied up and a-scrubbing at hisself with a long-handled brush.

"Getting the pickle off?" I said.

"Shut up, Kid," he said.

"Zeb," I said, "I got me some serious talking to do. Them two damn sheriffs out there went and split their posse up. That what you seed out yonder is just only half a the whole entire mob."

"The rest coming along?" he asked.

"Yeah," I said, "but—"

"Good," he said. "The more the merrier, I always say."

I was tired a them fancy sayings like that, but I just

only gritted my teeth at it and just kept on with my serious talking.

"What ain't good," I said, "is that they ain't going to make no move on ole Morgan till the other half a the posse shows up, and who the hell knows when that'll be? Now, I got me a pardner over yonder on the other side a Morgan's camp, and he's all by his lonesome over there."

Ole Zeb, he looked up sharp at me whenever I said that what I said, and he was a-scowling something fierce.

"You got yourself another pardner?" Zeb said. "What about ole Zeb? Huh? You just planning to abandon me to myself up here in these cold and hostile mountains? Leave poor ole Zeb to die up here alone? Maybe get et up by mountain lions or something? Is that the way you do your old pard?"

"No, Zeb," I said. "It ain't like that. Pardners ain't like wives, is they? Can't a feller have more than one pard?"

Then I had to go and tell ole Zeb how come me to know Churkee, and how ole Churkee had pulled me outa a bad spot and then had stuck by me while we run down them three outlaws.

"Why, if it wasn't for ole Churkee," I said, "Chastain would still be a-looking to hang us."

"What did you call this here new pard a yours?" Zeb said.

"Churkee," I said. "It ain't his for-real name, I guess. He told me he's a Churkee Injun, and whenever I asked him what I could call him, he said just Churkee would do. 'Course, once I heared him tell someone else that he was mongo-lid or something like that. Hell, I don't know."

"Churkee," said Zeb, kindly musing like. "Churkee Injun. Hell, Kid, you got yourself a for-real Cherokee

Indi'n for a new pard. That's good enough for ole Zeb. Yes, sir. Them Cherokees is good people. Damn gov'ment done them real dirty too."

"Yeah," I said. "He told me about that moving of them across the country the way they done."

"The Trail a Tears," Zeb said. "The Trail a Tears. Yes, sir. Done them dirty."

"Zeb?" I said.

"Yeah?"

"What's that there mongo-lid?"

Well, he went and laughed out loud at me for so long that he damn near made me mad at him, but final he shut up and wiped his eyes.

"What's so funny?" I said. "I just asked a question, is all."

"Don't take offense, Kid," he said. "Mongolians lives over in Asia across the ocean. Some folks believes that's where our Indi'ns comes from. They say long ago some Mongolians come across the Bering Strait down into this land, and they become the Indi'ns."

"Where's that bearin straight?" I asked him. "Ole Churkee, he said something about that too."

"Ole Cherokee was a-putting someone on," Zeb said. "He don't believe that tale. Anyhow, it's a way up north a here, up where it's real cold."

"Colder'n these mountains in the winter?" I asked.

"Way colder."

Well, I figgered if Churkee's mongo-whatever ancestors come from a place colder'n that, why, I didn't blame them none for coming on down south and turning into Injuns, but I had let myself get kindly distracted from my main and only purpose for a spell there, so I forced my mind back on the track what it shoulda been on all along, if only ole Zeb hadn't a derailed it back there.

"Zeb," I said, "I can't wait for the rest a the posse to

show up. I got to do something about ole Churkee over there."

"Don't you reckon he can take keer a hisself?" Zeb said.

"At least as good as me," I said, "but I still don't like it."

I told Zeb how I'd been a-worrying that Morgan and them might come across him by accident or how Churkee hisself might lose his patience and go after Morgan, and I told him how come Churkee to be after Morgan in the first place.

"If it was you over yonder, Zeb," I said, "I'd be a-feeling the same way. How would you be a-feeling if it was me over there?"

"I'm beginning to get your meaning, Kid," Zeb said. "Fetch me that towel over yonder."

I fetched it and held it out to him, and he stood up in his nekkidness and tuck it and commenced to drying off his old wrinkled skin and his bristly old gray whiskers and hair.

"What you got in your old bald head?" I said.

"We got to go over there," he said.

"Well, how the hell can we do that?" I said. "If we try to ride through Morgan's camp, they'll spot us sure."

"We ain't riding through his shitty camp," Zeb said.

"We can't go back down the mountain and then over to the other road and back up again," I said. "That'd take way too long."

"You're right about that," he said.

"Well, damn it, Zeb," I said, "there ain't no other way but 'cept—"

I stopped before I said it on account a I didn't really want to say it. I didn't want to even think it.

"You're right, Kid," Zeb said. "It's the only way over."

"I can't do it, Zeb," I said.

"Sure you can."

"You know what happened the last time," I said. "And I'll still kill you if you ever breathe a word of it. You know what happened, and so you know I can't do it."

"Kid," he said, "a man can do anything if he puts his whole mind to it."

"Zeb, I ain't going up on that again."

He tossed away the towel and went to pulling his britches on.

"Well," he said, "I won't argue no more with you. I said what I believe, but you won't listen to me, old as I am. And me your old pardner. I listened to all your whining and all your lofty damn statements about pards and all that, but I reckon you never meant none a that stuff. If it was me over there, you said. I reckon if it was me over there right now this very minute, and you knowed that I'd get myself kilt lessen you got right on over there, you'd just kick back and say, well, there's only one way acrost fast enough, and I'm just afraid I can't do that. It's too bad about ole Zeb, but I can't climb that mountain without I mess my britches."

Well, that done it. I whipped out my Colt and cocked it and pointed the barrel right square betwixt ole Zeb's two beady eyes.

Chapter 18

So there I was, a-clinging for my very life to the same side a that straight-up-and-down side a that same goddamn mountain just in that same exact damn spot what had brung on me the single worst most humiliating experience a my whole entire young life, a thing what I hoped to forget about entire, but this here situation was bringing it all back to my mind in ever' little detail just as clear as anything could ever be. There I was again a-pinching the hell outa them damn slick rocks with all a my desperate fingers till I knowed full well that my whole both hands was clear pale white with all the blood squeezed out of them, and I could feel my poor ole guts a-loosening up too, but I squinched my asshole up as tight shut as I ever could, and I gritted my teeth till I could hear them grinding. 'Course, really and truly, I had me two damn good reasons how come I hadn't oughta been near as skeered as what I had been that other awful time. One was that I knowed from experience about that there ledge what I had fell down on before, or ruther, what that damned ole Raspberry had throwed me off on, so really, I knowed that I wouldn't be kilt if I was to fall, at least not there in that very exact same spot where I had already fell to. I mean, I knowed it in my head, but that didn't seem to help me none.

The other comfort what I shoulda had was that ole
Zeb, he was a-going along right ahead a me, see, and he
had went and tied a rope around his own waist and then
tied the other end a the same rope to me in the same
exact way. That there was s'posed to make me feel more
safer, you know, but I didn't rightly see it quite thataway. It looked to me more like if I was to fall, why,
I'd just go on a-falling and then I'd pull ole Zeb right
along with me 'stead a him a-holding me up. Even if
his idee woulda worked, which I didn't have no faith in,
not even a little bit, I just couldn't hardly see my ass a-
dangling and a-swinging out over next to nothing on the
end of a rope tied on to nothing else but just a crazy old
man up there a-hanging on to the side of a cliff. I reckon
you can somewhat understand my line a reasoning here.

"That's the way mountain climbers does it, Kid," was
what ole Zeb had said to me whenever I expressed my
doubts regarding his method, and I was s'posed to take
them words for a full and total explanation a how come
him to do it thataway.

So there we was, the two of us, me and my old pard,
two damn fools, it seemed to me, and me the worstest
a the two, just inching our slow and painful way over
the hard way to the Morgan side a the mountain pass. I
was a-thinking that I mighta could made it through that
den a outlaws after all. Or maybe I coulda made my way
down the south road and over to the north road and back
up to the cross the mountain road all in good time. But
it was too late for them kinda thoughts.

Well, I knowed it would happen, and it sure enough
did. I friz up again. Total. Complete. I just couldn't
move. I couldn't move even a finger. I was most skeered
to breathe on account a that made my chest to heave. If
a snake had a crawled outa one a them cracks in the
rocks right in front a my nose, I wouldn't a been able

to move a single muscle on my whole entire body to defend myself. I'd a just had to a let him bite my nose, is all, and let it swell up on me. I felt the rope pull tight against me, and it skeered me that it was going to pull me off.

"Zeb," I hollered. "Cut it out."

"Come on, Kid," Zeb said.

"I'm stuck," I said.

"No you ain't," he said. "Come on."

"I can't move, Zeb," I said. "I oughta know when I'm stuck."

"You going to shit in your pants?" he said.

"Goddamn you, Zeb," I said.

"Feel over thisaway with your right foot," he said. "There's a good stepping-on rock right there."

"I can't move."

"Feel for it."

"No. I can't."

"You little chicken shit," he said. "I'm downright ashamed a you. It's a good thing you done found your-self a new pardner, 'cause I'm dumping you. I can't have no little chicken shit for a pardner. Not ole Zeb Pike. Me with a mountain named after me. I got my reputation to think about."

Then I felt that rope drop from the other end, and it sure felt heavy when it stopped falling too. Ole Zeb, he had went and untied the damn thing off from around his own waist and just throwed it on down, and so there it was, just a-dangling off from me then and doing no good for no one.

"Zeb," I said, "what're you doing?"

"I'm going on," he said. "I'll find that Cherokee my-self and give him a hand, since you're just stuck here on the side a this mountain. I'll have to tell him that you couldn't make it."

"Zeb, don't leave me here like this."

"Chicken shit."

"Zeb, wait for me."

It tuck all the willpower I had in my skinny little chicken-shit frame, but I went to inching my right foot over the way ole Zeb had told me to, and damned if I didn't find that there rock he said was there.

"Zeb," I hollered out. "Zeb. I found it."

"All right, Kid," he said. "Now turn a loose with your right hand and reach over thisaway."

I done it, and I was sure a-trembling, I can tell you. I slapped at the side a that mountain, and I couldn't feel nothing but smooth. I was most near in a for-real panic. I didn't know if I'd be able to move my hand back where it come from even. My one hand was floundering around useless.

"A little higher, Kid," said Zeb. "You're just under it. Reach up just a little."

I felt up a little, and then I come to the handholt. Well, ole Zeb, he talked me on across the flat side a that mountain just in that way, all the way across till we come to a place where the mountain sloped again, and it was a steep slope, but it sure did seem like a gentle one to me after that there flat place. I looked back over where I had just come from, and I seed that I had come right on over that ledge what I had fell down on before and then on across a place where the ledge wasn't there no more, and if I'd a fell, I'd a fell plumb down to China for sure. I just couldn't hardly believe what I had just did. Ole Zeb, he was resting there on that slope, and I set beside him to rest myself up some too. I looked over at him, and he was just a-smiling real big.

"You done it, Kid," he said.

"I couldn't a did it without you, Zeb," I said.

"All I done was talk," he said. "You done it."

And I had did it. I knowed that I had. I had just gone
and did the one thing that in my whole entire life I was
the skeerdest a doing. I figgered that I would never be
able to tell ole Zeb just how much it meant to me what
he had helped me to do, but then, I kindly figgered he
already knowed. Then he proved it to me that he
knowed.

"How's your britches, Kid?" he said.

I looked at him, and I grinned. I was so happy with
myself what I had did that I almost laughed out loud.

"They're dry," I said.

"Let's go find our new pard," Zeb said. "You ready?"

Zeb knowed them mountains all right. Where we was,
we was right up over the top a Morgan's camp, and I
even looked down in there a time or two, and I could
see that Morgan and them was down there all right. I
couldn't set and study on them long enough to make out
what was they up to, but they was there.

Me and Zeb crawled along that slope for a considerable time, and then we went down in a kinda groove,
and I couldn't see down into the camp no more, but it
was a sorta relief to be in there, on account a we could
stand up and walk. No one from down in the camp
coulda seed us neither, so it was safe for us to do that.
I couldn't tell where we was a-going. I didn't even know
whether we was going north or south or up or down, but
ole Zeb, he knowed. I follered him.

Final we come on to a place where ole Zeb started
right up the side a that groove we was in. I follered him.
It was steep, but it weren't so steep you couldn't climb
it all right. We clumb for a while, 'cause we had gone
down kindly deep into that groove. When we come to
the top a that thing we was a-climbing, we was up high
again, and then I seed that we had got plumb to the other
side a ole Morgan's camp. I couldn't hardly believe it

what we had did. I was real full a all kinds a new ad-
miration for my ole pard, ole Zeb Pike. From where we
stood, I could see Morgan's camp, but just only enough
to see where it was at. I couldn't tell nothing more about
it nor anyone in it than just only what I said. It was there
and we was past it. That meant, a course, that we was
safe from their prying eyeballs too. I could also see the
mountain road a way off down there.

"What're we going to do now, Zeb?" I asked.

"I thought you was the one was going to come over
here without me and do ever'thing by your own self,"
he said.

Well, I let that pass. After all, he had just done a-
helping me come across that there cliff face what had
humiliated me before, and I couldn't never forget that.
I give it a real hard thinking about before I even tried
to answer him that one.

"Well, I woulda, Zeb," I said, "on account a ole Churkee, you know, but since you're here with me, I figger
maybe you got a better head for it than what I do."

"Well, I reckon you're learning something, Kid," he
said. Then he stood there a-looking around and a-
studying things, you know. He kindly scratched his nasty
old whiskers underneath his chin. "If it was to be me
down there," he said, "and I was a-wanting to keep a
eye on them outlawyers but not get saw by them, and
wait it out for the posse to get here, well, I reckon I'd
plant myself somewheres right down yonder."

He pointed down and to our right, a little betwixt us
and the Morgan camp. They was a ridge down there
alongside a the road. Whenever ole Zeb pointed it out
to me, why, it become plumb obvious. I wondered how
come me not to a come up with it my own self.

"Yeah," I said. "That looks good, Zeb. That there'd
be the place all right. Let's go on down and find him."

"Hold on now just a minute," he said. "First off, we gotta study on the best way to get down there. Then we got to figger about where to slow down and be real keerful so that he won't hear us coming up behind him and kill us dead before we can tell him that we're his pardners a-coming. And it's got to be you what he sees first on account a he don't know me from a smelly skunk, and he might shoot me in the head, if he's as good as you say he is."

"He's that good all right," I said, and I shoulda added that I'd a never thunk about all them things what he had just said. I was sure glad ole Zeb had come along with me. I had learnt a whole lot from ole Zeb in the time me and him had been pardners, but I hadn't never before felt like I was so lucky to have him on my side. Well, he done his figgering, 'cause of a sudden, without no leading in to it, he just said, "Foller me."

He tuck out at a fair clip down that steep mountainside, and he looked for all to me like as if he had one short leg. He was a-walking kindly sideways, you know, going down the side there, but only he didn't hardly bob up and down atall. That old man was like a damn mountain goat, a thing what I had never in my life seed before he had pointed one out to me once. I follered him, and I tried to manage the slope the same like he was a-doing, but I couldn't do it. I staggered along and slud now and then, and where he walked smooth like, I did bob up and down like the way a damn chicken walks.

We went on down like that for a space, and then the ground leveled off, and we walked more or less normal and straight ahead till we come on to a sudden and right abrupt drop-off, and then I figgered that ole Zeb, he had done miscalculated somewhat after all. He stopped right at the edge of that thing. I waited a minute or so for him to say something about our new situation, and when he never, I said, "Well, what now, Zeb?"

"Well," he said, "I know how I can go on down. I'm just a-trying to figger can you handle it thataway."

That burned me a little bit, but then I figgered that after the way he'd had to work so to get my ass on across that there sheer mountain face just a little while earlier, I couldn't really blame him for thinking like that the way he done.

"You just show me where to go, old man," I said, "and I'll foller you."

I figgered that "old man" would burn him some, and I'd just get me a little even with him thataway. He give me a look, but he never said nothing about it. He just motioned me on over to his side, and I walked over by him and looked on down over the edge there.

"It ain't too long a drop," he said. "We kindly slip our ass off over the edge, and then we turn a loose and let go. When your feet hits the ground, bend your knees and roll. You'll roll on down the slope yonder for a ways, and then you'll stop there where it starts to level off again. You got it?"

"Sure," I said, but I really couldn't recollect even the first thing what he had just said. "You go first. I'll watch you and I'll foller you. I'll do it just the way you do."

Well, ole Zeb, he got down on his hands and knees with his ass pointed toward the edge, and then he went to backing off. Whenever his legs got to dangling off in the air, he got his belly down on the ground, and he just kept on a-wriggling backward. Pretty soon there wasn't nothing of him a-showing up over the edge but just only his face and his arms. He kept on a-backing, and then he was just a-holding on by his fingertips. He turned a-loose. I looked over the edge right quick, and I seed him hit down there, and I felt a real funny feeling way down deep in the pit a my gut, most nearly clean down into my balls, and I seed his legs buckle and then him start in to rolling. He rolled over and over, and then he come to that leveling-off place what he had mentioned to me. He stopped rolling then, and he stood right up and waved at me. What could I do?

I was skeered most to death, but I had said it, and I had to do it. I tried my best to do just exact what I had saw ole Zeb do. I got down on my hands and knees and then clean down on my belly, and I crawfished backwards over the edge a that drop-off. I can tell you, though, that whenever my legs went out in space, I got real wriggly-bellied. I kept on a-going though, and then I kindly fell down over the edge just a-hanging on with my hands. I tried to look back over my shoulder, but I couldn't do it. My neck wouldn't twist far enough. I weren't sure atall what was down there underneath me. I didn't know what the hell I was a-going to land on. It come into my head that there might be a big rock down there what I hadn't noticed before. Then my hands commenced to getting real tired, almost sore, and I turned a-loose.

Good God A'mighty damn! I thunk that all a me except for my belly went a-dropping. And then whenever I hit bottom, it surprised the hell outa me. I had the presence a mind, though, to do just exact what ole Zeb had tole me to do, and I relaxed my legs just in time, and they doubled up underneath me, and I went down, and I went to rolling over and over so fast it like to made me dizzy with it. I thunk I would roll clean to China.

Of a sudden, I stopped. I was on that flat part. It had all happened just like ole Zeb said it would and just like it done for him. All 'cept for just one only thing. My belly hadn't ketched up with the rest a me yet. I set up and waited for it to come on and get back in there where it belonged. Zeb come a-walking over beside a me, and he looked down at me with a kinda concerned look on his old face.

"You ain't hurt, are you?" he said.

"I'm mostly all right," I said. "I'm a-waiting on my belly, is all."

Well, it come back, and I got up, and we started into walking upright again, and I was sure grateful for that. I tried to recall what this way down had looked like from up above so that I'd know what else there was a-coming up ahead a me and what else I might have to go through to get on past it, but I just couldn't recall nothing about it. Not a damn thing, so I just follered ole Zeb along. We come to a long ridge then, and we was walking along on it, and ole Zeb, he turned and looked at me and give me a shoosh sign, and I figgered that meant that we was a-getting close. I walked easy, keeping as quiet as I knowed how to. Eventual ole Zeb stopped again, and he peeked over the edge a that ridge we was on. I come up beside of him and peeked over too. Down below us was another ridge and below that was the road. Zeb didn't say nothing. He just pointed down to that next ridge. I nodded like as if I understood his meaning.

Zeb set down on his ass and slud off the edge, and he landed down on that lower ridge on his feet just as neat as a shot glass a good whiskey. I done the same but only when I hit, I fell over on my face. I was okay, but only it embarrassed me some, but at least I was a-keeping up with him. I guess I made a little noise, though, the way I landed, and he looked at me and shooshed me again. I stood up real easy and checked to make sure I hadn't lost my Colt in the falling down, but it was okay. Zeb started walking ahead. I follered him.

I tried to see over ole Zeb's shoulder to make out

where we was headed, and of a sudden it looked to me
like as if we was about to walk right offa the edge a the
world, but it weren't really so. What it was was there was
a kindly sharp curve there a-going to our right. Zeb come
to that curve, and he walked on around it and disappeared
from my sight line. I wanted to holler out to him, but he
had done shooshed me earlier, so I kept myself quiet. I
just moved on ahead easy like. Then I heared a voice.

"Hold it right there, old man, or I'll drop you in your
tracks."

I slipped out my shooter and held it ready but only I
didn't cock it yet on account a the noise it makes whenever you do that. I eased myself toward that curve.

"Don't shoot, sonny," I heared Zeb say. "I ain't one
a them owlhooters."

"There's two old men with them," the other voice
said. "You could be one of them."

That there voice was kindly familiar to me. I was
hoping, but I couldn't take no chance. I moved myself
on ahead slow and easy, and I was thinking that if that
ridge line was too tight up there around the curve, I
mightn't be able to shoot real good over ole Zeb's shoulder nor past him on either side. I was some nervous
about that. I didn't want to put Zeb in no danger. Then
I eased my ass on around the curve and right up almost
smack against ole Zeb's backside, and I could see over
his shoulder all right, but just barely on account a my
height, you know, but I could see good enough, I reckon,
and I was some relieved, I can tell you.

"Hey, Churkee," I said, "lower your gun. This here
is my ole pard, Zeb Pike."

Chapter 19

Well, ole Churkee shuck hands with Zeb, and then he looked back at me and said, "What are you doing over here?"

I told him how the posse had been divvied up and how I had follered his trail over to the south road so I knowed where he was at, but that one half a the posse was over at Weaver's and the other'n was on the way, and ole Potter, he was a-waiting for the rest in spite a the fact that I had told him that we was enough already to take that there bunch a Morgans. Then I tole him that I was a-worrying over him being off by hisself like that, and so I made to come over and join him, but ole Zeb, he was worried about me making my way across by my own self, and with good reason too, so he had come along. Well, whenever I got through with all a that, ole Churkee kindly shuck his head like as if it needed clearing out. I don't know how come.

"So what are you doing?" I asked him.

"I'm just watching this road in case anyone else tries to go in there or anyone tries to come out," he said. "If the posse attacks them from the other side and they try to make their escape, I'll be here."

"We'll be here," I said, correcting him what he said.

"How soon do you think the rest of the posse will arrive?" Churkee asked me.

"Ain't no way a knowing," I said. "We left them a-chasing after all that sign you left out on the prairie. Then we sent someone to fetch them on back."

"They shouldn't be too much longer then," he said. "I think we'd best get ready. I've been studying the situation here. Now that you two have joined me, I think two of us should stay right here, and a third should go over that way up on the mountainside."

I looked over where he was a-pointing at, and it was the side a the mountain all right, kindly looking down onto Morgan's camp. Way down at the bottom where it come down to the camp it was a straight drop-off of maybe twenty foot or so. I ain't too good a judge a them kinda things. But on up the side above that drop-off it was all a kinda gentle slope. They was boulders spotted here and there along the side. It looked to me like as if a feller could make his way along that there mountainside from one boulder till the next one till he got into a good position for looking down into the camp. The on-liest problem would be the getting from one big rock to the next one right out in the open. Anyhow, I was feeling kinda smug after what I done earlier on that ole mountain, and this here looked to be plumb easy.

"I can do her," I said, and I seed Zeb give me a look, but he never said nothing.

"Okay," Churkee said.

"Well," I said, "I'll just go on ahead and get started."

I made my way up and over to the first big boulder easy enough, and I hid down behind it and looked over into the camp. I seed some a them outlaws all right, and they wasn't none of them what seemed to be a-looking in my direction, so I crouched down kinda low and made a run for the next boulder. Soon as I went to running, I got me a surprise, on account a I was running on that slope, and it was kinda awkward, but I adjusted to it quick enough, and I made it on over to that next hidey spot without no one taking no shots at me. They hadn't saw me. I hunkered down there and waited a bit, and then I snuck me another look.

Well, it still looked to be safe enough, and I wanted to get my ass over one more time to the next big rock a-sticking outa the side a that mountain where I would have me a real good look down over most a that camp, so I tuck out again, and I was just about halfway across there whenever I seed that Shark. He was right down under me a-looking up at me, and he had out his shooter and, bang, he fired just as I seed him. I stopped as quick as I ever could, and his bullet kicked up dirt just in front a me. It startled me some, and my feet both slud right out from under me.

I went to sliding down that slope on the seat a my britches, and there weren't no way I could stop it. I seemed to go faster and faster, and then I come to the end a that gentle slope, what had turned out to be not so gentle after all, and I just flewed out into space over the edge a that drop-off there, and I was moving pretty damn fast. I could see down below me where I was a-headed, and I seed that ole Shark looking up with his mouth open and his eyes wide, and then I hit him. I come down a-straddle a his face like as if I was a-jumping into a saddle from offa something, and I heared his neck snap whenever I hit.

Well, hitting old Shark like that kindly broke my fall somewhat, and my feet dug into the ground and my ass whomped into his chest. He never moved. He was deader'n hell, I can tell you. But the commotion he and me had made drawed the rest a them outlaws right on out and put their all attention right on me. There weren't

no one else. I sure did feel lonesome, but I whipped out
my Colt, and I dropped the one what was clostest to me.

If you recall, me and Weaver and them had burnded
ole Morgan's camp clean down to just ashes, and the
place there where it had been builded was flat, so there
weren't no place to hide, not anywhere near me. Morgan
and them had put up a couple a new tents for temporary,
but they was off some little distance from where I had
landed my ass on poor ole Shark. I don't know just
where they come from, but I seed a half dozen a them
bastards coming at me, and they all had their guns out
and was a-firing wild. I figgered I was fixing to go out
in a blaze a glory right then, but I also figgered to take
a few a them shit heads along with me.

Well, I knowed the range of a six-gun, all right, and
even though they was a-shooting wild at me, they was
still too far off to do any good lessen one of them just
got hisself a lucky shot. Now you know, whenever a
bunch a men get to running together like that all ganged
up, one of them's bound to come out ahead a the rest,
so I watched for that, and whenever one did get out in
front, I waited just a bit longer, and then I fired me a
bullet right into his belly, and he went down hard. The
rest kinda spread out then. Like I said, there wasn't no
cover down there a no kind.

Then I seed some more a the bastards come on outa
them new tents, and then I heared some shots come from
back behind them. It was Churkee and ole Zeb what had
heared the shots and knowed that I was in some kinda
trouble. Maybe they had even seed me slide. I ain't sure,
but they did draw some a that unwanted attention away
from just only me. So some a the outlaws turned to face
Zeb and Churkee, and some of them kept after me. Well,
I was up on my feet by this, and I was a-running and a-
dodging thisaway and that and shooting whenever I got

me a good target. A few a their shots come awful close for comfort, but I never did get hit, and I tuck out a couple more of the turds.

Then the real uproar commenced, 'cause just then Potter and them come in from the direction a Weaver's camp, and they come in a-shooting and a-hollering. It was almost like another a them war fights but only this time there weren't no explosions happening around like what there had been before. Them owlhooters was in a real bind, I can tell you. They had the big bunch a the posse and miners a-coming at them from one direction, ole Zeb and Churkee from another direction, and just me by myself off over in yet a third. Some more a them fellers dropped dead from bullet shots, and then the ones what wasn't kilt final went and throwed down their guns and up their arms and give up the fight.

Potter set some men to tying the hands a the standing-up outlaws behind their backs, and Zeb and Churkee come a-running over to where I was at.

"Are you all right?" Churkee asked.

"I ain't hurt," I said.

"I never seen nothing like the way you tackled that there Shark," said Zeb. "Whatever put a thing like that into your head?"

I give a shrug.

"Well," I said, "it just kindly popped up there. I seed where he was at and where I was at, and I figgered I could take him thataway. That's all."

"Damn, damn, damn," Zeb said. "That was really something to behold."

I looked at Churkee then, and I said, "Did you get Morgan?"

"I never set eyes on him," Churkee said. "Let's take a look around."

We started walking over toward the tents, and whenever we walked past one a the bodies what I was responsible for, we tuck us a good look at it, but I already knowed that none a them was ole Morgan, nor neither one a the old men nor that damn kid Gish. We strolled on over to where the live ones was all rounded up, and there I seed one a the old men.

"Looky there, Zeb," I said. "That there's Charley Coy. He must be the one what they thought was you."

Zeb hawked and spitted on the ground.

"Ain't no way," he said. "He's too old and too damn ugly."

'Course, that's just what I thunk about that damn Gish, not the too old part but the other part, but they had mistook him for me anyhow, but I never said nothing more about it. The other old man nor the kid nor Morgan was with the live ones. We went to hunting around amongst the kilt ones over thataway, and then we seed that they was a couple shot but not quite kilt, and a couple a Potter's men was busy patching them up so they could save them to hang up by their necks. We went over to look at them, and one of them was the other old man, that Ben Wright. He looked to be hurt bad, and I figgered he wouldn't never make it to the hanging place. We went and found ole Potter and Weaver was there with him.

"Well, Kid," Potter said, "you told me you didn't want to wait for the rest of the posse. You figured out how to get your way, didn't you?"

"You might not never believe me on that," I said, "but I never started this here fight a-purpose. I told you I was worried about ole Churkee over here all by hisself, didn't I? Well, me and Zeb come over here on account a that, and I was just a-getting myself a good position up on that mountainside over yonder whenever ole Shark spotted me and tuck a shot at me. That's all. I meant to wait it out like you said."

"Okay," he said. "I'll take your word for it."

"Hey," I said, "have you saw anything a that Gish or of ole Morgan?"

Potter give a look to Weaver, and Weaver shuck his head.

"I didn't see Morgan," he said.

"And I never saw the kid," said Potter.

Damn, I wisht he hadn't a called him that.

"You reckon could they be a-hiding around here somewheres?" I asked.

"I don't see how or where," Potter said, "but I guess anything's possible."

Churkee turned and walked away without saying nothing, and I watched him where he was a-going. He walked on over to where the prisoners was standing all tied up, and he stepped right up and looked one a the bastards in the face. I follered him to see what was he up to.

"Where's Morgan?" he said.

"I don't know," the man said.

Churkee stepped in front of another one and asked the same question. He got the same kinda answer. I walked on over to his side and poked him on the shoulder. He give me a look.

"Hold on there a minute," I said. "This ain't doing no good."

I grabbed another one what Churkee hadn't spoke to yet and pulled him outa the crowd. "Come on," I said, and I drug the bastard well off from the rest, and Churkee follered me. "Cut him loose, Churkee," I said. Churkee and the owlhoot both give me funny looks, but Churkee cut the ropes. The owlhoot kindly rubbed his wrists a little bit, and I said to Churkee, "Give him your six-gun."

"What're you doing?" the man asked me.

"I'm a-fixing to give you a chance to beat the hangman," I said. "If it was me, I'd ruther go by a bullet than a rope. Give it to him, Churkee."

"Wait a minute," the man said. "I didn't ask for this."

I looked around and seed a saddled horse off to the far side a the tents.

"Looky yonder," I said, and he looked. "You know, you might could get lucky and kill me, and if you was to do that, you might could make it to that there horse before anyone gets you. Thataway, you'd really beat the hangman. It's worth a try, ain't it."

"Of course," Churkee said, "no one's ever beat the Kid before."

"You're that Kid Parmlee, ain't you?" the outlaw asked me.

"That's what they call me," I admitted.

"I don't want to fight you," he said. "Tie my hands back the way they was. Leave me be."

"Give him a gun, Churkee," I said.

Churkee drawed his six-gun and flipped it around holding it out toward the owlhoot grip first. The man backed away.

"No," he said. "I won't."

"Well, then," I said, "I'll just step me a few paces back and commence to shooting. You know, I can cut a ear a-purpose when I take it in my head to do such stunts."

"Sheriff," the man hollered. "Help."

Outa the corner a my eye, I seed ole Potter come a-walking our way.

"There's a easy way outa this for you," I said. "Just

answer us a couple a questions. Where's Morgan, and where's Gish?"

"They never came up here," he said. "Morgan told us to come up and wait for him. Him and the kid rode on back into Nugget."

Potter come up just about then in time to hear that. He grabbed that outlaw by the front a his shirt and pulled him around to look in his face.

"Morgan and Gish rode into Nugget?" he said.

"Yeah. That's right."

"What for?"

"Morgan said he didn't like being run out of a town," the man said. "He said his business wasn't done in Nugget, and then the kid said he had something to settle there too. They sent us on up here, and they was going back to Nugget."

"Tie him back up," Potter said. "We've got to get ready to ride."

Me and Churkee and Zeb didn't have nothing to get ready, but 'cept me and Zeb had to go back over to Weaver's camp to get our horses and saddles. We tuck us a couple a the outlaw horses to ride over there on, and Churkee went out and fetched his own horse, and the three of us rid into Weaver's camp. Me and Zeb saddled our own nags, and we throwed together a few supplies and headed on out. We didn't worry none about how soon Potter and them others would be headed back. We rid out on the road headed for the south route down the mountain, and we only got about halfway to the turning-down place by nightfall. We had to stop and make us a camp for the night.

Ole Zeb, he whomped us up a quick meal and some coffee, and it was all mighty good, and we set up a while a-drinking coffee after we et. Churkee, he was real quiet.

I knowed he was a-thinking about that Morgan and what the bastard had did to his daddy. I didn't want to bother him in his thinking so I just kept quiet or else I said something to Zeb whenever I felt like saying something. But it did come to me that it was getting mighty tedious a-follering them two owlhoots around the countryside. Final, we laid out our beds and tuck to them for the night.

Zeb fixed us up a breakfast in the morning and some more coffee, and we et in a kinda hurry on account a Churkee especial wanted to get on the trail. Whenever we at last come to the place where the road went on down the mountain, we met up with the rest a Potter's posse with the supply wagon a-coming along behind them. We stopped long enough to fill them in on what had done happened at Morgan's camp, and then let them get on past us, and then we headed down.

We made it on down and onto the flat road what led into Nugget going north or Fosterville going south. I thunk for just a minute about ole Chastain, and I thunk that I was sure enough lucky that I hadn't come too close to him up there right after the fight, but then I went and put him outa my mind, so I could concentrate all my thinking energies on Morgan and on Gish. 'Course it was Gish that I really wanted bad, on account a he was the one what had caused me all a my recent miseries. The two ole men was done tuck keer of. It was Churkee who wanted Morgan real bad, and me, I just wanted to see him get his man. I had somewhat against ole Morgan too, but it was on account a what he had did to my new friends at Weaver's, and on account a it looked sure as hell like he hadn't give up on that scheme, but Churkee's reason was even more personal, so I figgered it was me for Gish and Churkee for Morgan.

Night come on us again before we made it all the

way into Nugget, and so we camped again. Zeb done the cooking again, and we et. It was getting chillier in the night air, and we put our beds more closer to the fire and figgered some one of us would get up now and then to put on more sticks and keep it going all night long. We was tucking ourselfs in when old Zeb spoke up.

"Reckon what them two is doing to Nugget just now?" he said.

"Ain't no telling," I said, "what with the sheriff and most near all the able-bodied fighting men outa town."

"Whatever it is," said Churkee, "they won't be doing it for much longer."

Well, we managed to stay warm and get us a pretty good sleep, and in the morning, much of a hurry as we was in, we waited till Zeb could get us all fed again, and we washed it all down with coffee. Then we cleaned up our campsite, packed up, and headed out. We had to make ourselfs hold it down to save the horses on account a we was in such a all-fired hurry to get our ass on in there. But we went to riding along for a while at a pretty fair clip, and then we'd slow down and walk the horses a while. We done like that most a the way on in. At last we seed the place just ahead.

"We'd better ride in slow," Churkee said. "We don't want them to see us first. Not if we can help it."

'Course, me and ole Zeb, we both knowed that Churkee was right about that. He didn't really have to tell us that. We rid into town real slow like all right and looking around us in ever' and all directions for any sign a them two. I looked especial in winders and doors and in them little narrer places in betwixt buildings. I never seed no sign a them we was a-looking for. Neither did Churkee nor Zeb. It was long about mid-morning whenever we come a-riding in, and the streets was kinda busy for a small town. We rid all the way through town and turned around and come right on back into the middle a town and still never seed no sign a Morgan nor Gish. We stopped there and set still for a few seconds, I guess. I looked at ole Zeb, and then I looked over at Churkee.

"Let's ride over and try the Watering Hole," Churkee said. "That's where they were hanging out the last time they were in town."

Well, he had tuck the thoughts right outa my own head, but I never said nothing about that. I just turned ole horse around to head in that direction. Zeb and Churkee turned their horses too.

Chapter 20

We rid on around the corner and hauled up there at the hitch rail in front a the Watering Hole. We clumb down outa our saddles and hitched our horses. Then we went on in, but we done that slow and easy and looked around when we got through them batwing doors. None of us seed nothing a Morgan nor Gish. We walked on in kinda slow like and bellied on up to the bar. They wasn't too many customers in the place, I guessed on account a ole Potter's posse. They was a few men setting around one table, and down at the other end a the bar from where we was they was a couple a cowboy-looking fellers. The barkeep was a-pouring them some drinks. We waited patient till he come on down to see us.

"What'll it be, gents?" he asked us.

"Three whiskeys," ole Zeb said. He didn't wait to see what me and Churkee wanted, but he didn't get no arguments though neither. Of a sudden that there barkeep, he stopped, and he tuck a hard look at Churkee.

"Say," he said, not a-talking to Churkee even though he was a-looking at him, "is that an Injun?"

I started in to open my mouth up and say what if it is, but only Churkee beat me to the punch on it.

"No, sir," he said. "I'm a Jew. I'm a member of one of the Lost Tribes of Israel, and I'm wandering around this great looking country of yours trying to find my-self."

The barkeep wrinkled his face up, still a-staring at ole Churkee.

"You going to fetch our whiskey, mister," ole Zeb asked, "or do I got to turn Kid Parmlee here a-loose on you?"

Well, then the old boy give me a look.

"Is this Kid Parmlee?" he said.

"Whyn't you ask me?" I said. I'd had me just about enough a this guy a-looking someone in the face and talking to someone else about him at the same damn time.

"You Kid Parmlee?" he asked me then.

"That's what I go by," I said.

"You the one they say is a regular Billy the Kid?"

"That's what some says," I said, "but only I sure do wish folks'd quit saying it."

"I—I won't say it again. Three whiskeys coming right up."

Well, he poured us our drinks and left the bottle a-setting there in front of us, and it sure did look good, but I called back into my mind what had happened to me the last time, and I knowed we was a-looking for them two outlaws. I didn't know too much about ole Morgan when it come to gunfighting, but that there Gish was said to be some good. I knowed that I couldn't hardly afford to be drinking too much, so I done the way ole Churkee done. I just kindly sipped at that whiskey. Ole Zeb, he gulped his right down and poured hisself another'n.

I glanced over at Churkee and spoke to him in a low voice. "Wanta go over to the other saloon and check there?" I asked him.

"Let's ask the bartender here first," he said.

"Hey, barkeep," Zeb yelled.

The old boy come a-running.

"Yes, sir?"

"We're a-looking for a couple a fellers," I said. "One skinny little runt. 'Bout my size, I reckon. Goes by the name a Gish. His pard is called Morgan. He's a bigger man. Wears a black suit and sports a fuzzy mustache. They been in here? We got word they was headed this-away."

Well, that ole boy hesitated, and I did believe that I could see it on his face that he was a-thinking real hard what he had ought to say to me. He was a-skeered a me. That much was plain. It was clear, too, that Morgan and Gish had been there all right. Otherwise the barkeep wouldn't a had no problem just in telling me no they ain't. So I knowed they'd been there. He final answered my question.

"They was here last night," he said. "I ain't seen them today."

"Do you know was they staying in town?"

"They didn't say. Not that I heard."

"What was they doing in here last night?" I asked. "Was they a-trying to hire on hands or anything like that?"

"All I seen," he said, "they just sort of kept to themselves and had a few drinks. That's all."

I give him a nod like as if to say that's all I need from you, ole pard, and now you can run along. He got the meaning all right, and he hustled on off down to the other end a the bar. I tuck me another sip a whiskey, and it sure was tempting to me to just drink it on down and have another'n, but I never. Ole Zeb, he gulped down his second and poured a third. By the time he had finished that one, me and Churkee had sipped ours all down. I throwed some coins on the bar, and we turned and walked on out. We clumb onto our horses and headed for the other saloon, but before we come to it, we seed Potter and all a them a-heading into town. He seed us too, and he said something to that Ed feller and then left the bunch and come a-riding at us. Ole Chastain was a-riding alongside him. I seed Ed and some a the others dismount and start in to hauling them tied-up outlaws into the jailhouse.

"Still trying to jump the gun on me, are you?" Potter said as he come up close.

"We're just a-trying to find out is Morgan and Gish really here, is all," I said. "That old boy might coulda lied to us up yonder."

"Well, are they here?" he asked.

"We ain't come across no sign of it," I said.

"Your town's still in one piece," Churkee said.

"They was here last night though," Zeb said. "Barkeep over to the Watering Hole admitted as much to us. That's all he'd admit to though. Said he hadn't saw them since."

"I'll ride over there and have a talk with him myself," Potter said.

"Betcha he don't tell you no different," said Zeb.

Potter turned his horse to head for the Watering Hole, and Chastain just set still for another minute a-staring right at me. He never said nothing. Then he turned his horse to foller ole Potter. Me and Churkee and ole Zeb rid on down to the other saloon and left our horses out front. Inside, the place was about like the Watering Hole. It weren't too busy, and we didn't see no sign a Gish nor Morgan. Zeb went to the bar and ordered three whiskeys before me or Churkee could stop him. We bellied up there beside him.

Now I knowed damn well that I hadn't oughta drink no second glass a whiskey, not with trouble maybe com-

ing at me just any time, so I kinda looked over at ole
Churkee outa the corner a my eyeball, and I seed him
pick up his glass and just kindly hold it under his nose
and sniffle at it a bit. I figgered I could do the same
thing, so I picked mine up and put it under my nose. I
couldn't hardly stand it though, so I did stick the end a
my tongue down in it, but that's all I done more than
what Churkee was a-doing.

"We gonna ask this barkeep?" I said, keeping my
voice low down.

"Let's hold off," Churkee said. "I'm betting that Potter and Chastain will be here just anytime. They'll do
the asking for us this time."

Well, Churkee was right. By the time ole Zeb had
gulped down his drink and poured hisself another'n, here
they come. They looked around the room and then set
their eyeballs on us and come a-walking over. Potter
stood beside Zeb to Zeb's right, and Chastain stood to
the left a Churkee. Me, I was standing right square in
the middle.

"You surrounding us for some reason?" I asked.

"You been asking questions in here?" Potter said.

"We ain't done nothing but just order us a drink, is
all," I said. "Figgered you didn't want us asking no questions. You'd say we was trying to get the jump on you
again. So we quit. We're a-leaving it all to you."

"Why don't I believe you?" Potter said. I just give a
shrug, and then Potter, he waved a arm at the barkeep
who come a-walking down to where we was at.

"What'll you have, Sheriff?" he asked.

"Nothing, Jake," Potter said. "We have information
that Randall Morgan and Jerry Gish were in town last
night. Have you seen anything of either one of them?"

"They came in here last night," Jake said. "I think I
heard them say that the kid was riding over to Fosterville

this morning. I haven't seen him since then, so I guess he's gone."

"What about Morgan?" Potter asked.

Jake nodded toward the stairs. "Right up there," he said.

Well, me and Zeb and Churkee and Potter and Chastain all ever' one of us looked up them stairs at the same time.

"He's up there now?" Potter asked.

"Yes, sir," said Jake. "Went up just ten minutes ago with ole Katy."

"Be interesting to see how long can he keep it up," Zeb said.

"Be a good time to bust in on him and ketch him unawares," I said.

"With his pants down, so to speak?" said Churkee, and I could tell that he was a-trying to make out like he didn't have no special interest in just how this all come about, but I knowed that he was a-scheming in his own mind how he was a-going to get ole Morgan before the law done it. I just didn't want to see him get hisself in no trouble.

Potter, he looked me in the face for a long minute, and then he said, "That's not a bad idea, Kid. Jake."

Jake come back over.

"Yeah?"

"What room?"

"Three."

"Chastain," said Potter, "stay here. I'm going around back and up the stairs."

"I'll be here," Chastain said.

I give Churkee a look, but he never let nothing show. I looked back up the stairs. Potter went out the front door. He'd have to walk all around the building to get to the back stairs. I knowed that. I watched till he disappeared, and then I looked up again and damned if I didn't see that Morgan a-coming up on the landing. I nudged Churkee, and he give a glance, and he seed him too. Only thing is, Chastain did too. "He didn't last too long, did he?" Zeb said. Chastain stepped out away from the bar and squared hisself to get ready to face off with ole Morgan.

Morgan was coming on down the stairs, and Churkee was a-watching him and watching Chastain too. I could tell that he couldn't hardly stand it. Of a sudden, he stepped out fast right smack in front a Chastain, and he hollered, "Morgan." Chastain made like he was a-fixing to do something, but I stepped up behind him, whipping out my Colt, and I whopped him hard over the head with the barrel. He dropped straight down to the floor. I stepped back over to the bar.

"Keep out of this, Kid," Churkee said.

"I will," I said, "lessen he kills you."

"Who the hell are you?" said Morgan.

"You had a Cherokee business partner once," Churkee said. "Do you remember that?"

"Oh, yeah," said Morgan. "He wasn't much of a businessman as I recall."

"He did all right," Churkee said, "till his own partner robbed him blind."

"No one could prove that," said Morgan. "What's your interest anyhow?"

"That man was my father," Churkee said. "I've been looking for you for a long time now."

Of a sudden ole Morgan reached for his shooter, and Churkee come up with his own ever' bit as fast as ever I done it, and he blasted it off before Morgan's was even full pulled out. Churkee's bullet ketched ole Morgan right under the chin, and it come out the top a his head. Morgan flopped around, then pitched headfirst down the stairs. Churkee put away his gun. Chastain moaned and rolled around a little bit. Then Potter come a-running from upstairs. He stopped on the landing and looked down at ole Morgan's leftovers.

"Damn," he said.

He come a-running on down. He tuck a quick look at Morgan on the way, and he could see right off that he was a-looking at a done dead man, so he come on over to us where we was at. He looked down at Chastain who was starting to try to set up. Potter give him a hand. Chastain leaned back against the bar and rubbed his sore head.

"What happened?" Potter said.

"I don't know," said Chastain.

"Morgan come out a-shooting," Zeb said, "and I guess one a his bullets grazed poor ole Chastain. Churkee stepped out then and done for Morgan."

Potter looked at me.

"That's the way I seed it," I said.

"Jim?" said Potter.

Chastain shuck his head. "I just don't know," he said. "I don't know."

Potter looked back behind the bar at Jake, and he said, "Jake, get someone to haul that out of here."

He meant what was left a Morgan.

"Sure," said Jake.

Potter tuck a holt a Chastain by the arm and headed him toward the front door.

"Come on," he said. "Let's get the doc to take a look at your head."

The two sheriffs walked on out the front door, and a couple a ole boys commenced to dragging the body out too. Churkee picked up the drink what he hadn't even sipped outa yet, and he tossed it down all at once. I tuck up mine and done the same thing.

"You got him, Churkee," I said.

"Yeah," he said. "Now we have to get yours."

It come to me that I didn't really have no more to worry about, not too much anyhow, on account a ole Chastain already knowed that it was Gish and not me he shoulda been after in the first place. I kinda wanted to kill ole Gish, but then I guessed it wouldn't matter none too much to me if ole Jim was to get him arrested and hanged up instead. Anyhow, he was s'posed to have went on over to Fosterville, what was ole Jim's town, so I for sure didn't have to worry none about him just then.

"Churkee," I said, "let's drink to your job all did and over with."

"That's a good idea," he said.

"Well, I'll damn sure drink to it," said Zeb. "By Godfrey, I got me the best damn pardners in the whole wide world, the two fastest with six-guns that there is anywheres, and I'll drink to that two or six times."

He poured us drinks all around, and we each of us drank them down.

"Say," I said, "how about we go get us a table over there?"

They agreed, and so we done it, and just in time too, 'cause them fellers offa the posse started to coming in just then, and the place kinda filled up in just a little while. Setting at our table, we each had us another drink. Some a them fellers had done heared about ole Morgan, and they come around to slap ole Churkee on the back and brag on him. He didn't seem to keer too much for that kinda praise though, but then, he put up with it all right.

I was starting in to get just a bit woozy, but I thunk it through, and I figgered it was okay this time. I reached out for the bottle and poured me another one. Then here come ole Chastain back in again. He was by hisself. No Potter. He seed us and come on over to our table and set down.

"Howdy, Jim," I said. "Did you ever figger out what happened to you a while ago?"

"No," he said. "I didn't. I guess just what Zeb said. I don't remember it that way though. Funny thing, the doc couldn't find a scratch on me. He did find a lump on top of my head."

"A creasing bullet does funny things to a head sometimes," Zeb said. "Ain't no telling what it's going to do."

"I guess that's right," Jim said.

"You want a glass, Sheriff?" Churkee asked.

"I could use a drink," said Jim.

Churkee jumped up and went off for another glass. Zeb picked up the bottle and poured our three glasses full up again. Then here come Churkee back with a glass for ole Chastain, and Zeb poured that one full. Jim drank it down right quick, and Zeb filled him up again.

"When you headed back for Fosterville, Jim?" I said.

"First light in the morning," he said. "It's too late in the day right now, and besides, my head ought to be cleared up some by morning."

"You want to put up with some company?" I asked him.

"All three of you?" he asked.

I looked at Zeb and at Churkee, and they both give me a nod.

"That's right," I said. "The three of us."

"Sure," he said. "Why not?"

"We'll be ready to ride out at first light then," I said.

"You'll be hunting Gish, I suppose," Jim said.

"I don't need to kill him personal no more," I said.

"For a spell there I wanted to real bad, but I give it some thought since then, and I reckon it's just all the same with me now if you was to ketch the little shit head and just lock him up tighter'n a squirrel's ass there in your jailhouse and then give him a trial and all and then hang his ass up by its neck till he's dead as a rock, well, that'd be all right by me. I just want to make sure that you do for real get him. That's all. You know, he has swore to kill me, and not just that, but to mash my brains all out. He don't keer none about a-fighting fair neither. He said so. He'll shoot me in the back whenever I ain't a-looking."

"You promise?" Jim said.

"Hell, yes," I said. "I'll make you that there promise. I swear it. I ain't looking to kill no one. I never do go looking for no shootings, Jim. You know that much about me."

"In that case," he said, "I won't tell you to stay out of Fosterville."

Well, much as I was a-trying to get on with ole Jim, I just somehow couldn't help myself from being a little smart-ass at that point.

"How the hell would you keep me out a town if you was a mind to, Jim?" I said. "You can't face me down. Would you slip up on me again from behind with a damn shotgun?"

"I would if I had to," he said.

I tuck me another drink.

"Well," I said, and it weren't funny to me no more, "you won't have to do nothing like that."

"Kid," Jim said, "when Gish is taken care of, we have some business together, you and me."

I was a-hoping that he had done forgot all about that, but then, I shoulda knowed better. I tried to figger out how to answer him on that one. I knowed that what I done was plumb mean. I knowed he had a right to hate my guts and to do whatever he could do to get even with me. I didn't want to hurt ole Jim, 'special not to kill him, but at the same time, I sure couldn't just lay there or set there and let him do whatever it was he was a-fixing to do to me. I couldn't play it thataway, and I knowed I couldn't. Jim knowed it too.

I figgered it promised to be a interesting ride on back into Fosterville, what with Jim Chastain a-riding along with me and my two pards. It looked to me like as if ole Jim, he was showing us that he trusted us in spite a what I had did to him and whatever he was a-planning to do to me. He was a-showing me the best way he knowed how that he knowed for sure and real that I weren't no outlaw, and what I had to do was to show him for real that I really weren't. Whatever it was that was left betwixt me and ole Jim was just only that personal business, the sad fact that I had left him nekkid and vulnerable to the whole entire world on two separate and distinct occasions in two total different places.

Chapter 21

Well, we was all of us as good as our word. Come first light the next morning, me and ole Zeb and Churkee met up with ole Jim Chastain. We all agreed to have us a good breakfast there in town before we hit the trail, so we done that, but we didn't dawdle none over it, so it was still early enough whenever we rid on outa Gooseneck. Ole Potter, he showed up just before we left, and he thanked us all for all the help we done him and then told us all goodbye. I had me some funny kinda mixed-up feelings about this here trip too. The last time I had gone into Fosterville with having a drink with ole Jim on my mind, that was when he had come up behind me with that there shotgun. He had throwed my ass in jail, along with ole Zeb and my ole paw too, and I'd had to get myself broke out and them with me.

So I did feel some funny about riding right back in there with Sheriff Chastain hisself right alongside. 'Course he had done said that he knowed for sure that I was innocent a all a the charges a robbing the stagecoach and them banks and them killings and all. He had said that. But ever since he had come up behind me the way he had did that time, I had me this funny kinda feeling that maybe I couldn't really quite trust ole Jim. Maybe he had some kinda secret up his sleeve. Then again,

maybe I was just being kinda small-minded about it all.
I don't for sure know.

So anyhow, I had me that there nagging feeling, but
I also had me some real good kinda thoughts regarding
ole Red, and I was a-thinking that maybe this time me
and her would get to have us a good time together without me getting throwed in jail or run outa town or nothing like that to spoil things for us. I did really like that
gal, and she liked me too. I could tell. Why, hell, we
had not just only had us some fine romps together up in
her room, but she had come through for me in a pinch
more than once. I give a sideways look at ole Jim whilst
I was thinking on ole Red, and I wondered if he had any
idee who it was had slipped me my Colt whenever I was
locked up there in his jail. I sure hoped not.

I was also looking real damn forward to finding that
damn cold-blooded little shit Gish and getting rid a him
outa my young life once and for ever. I was almost telling the truth whenever I tole ole Jim that I didn't really
keer whether if I kilt him or Jim throwed his ass in jail.
Almost. Down in my most deepest heart I most wanted
to kill him my own self, but I couldn't tell that out loud.
I couldn't let it out to ole Chastain.

And then the finalist and most worrisome thought in
my head on this here trip was what was likely a-going
to happen once we had final done tuck keer a Gish,
'cause that there was just the veriest time what ole Jim
was a-waiting for in order to do his getting even on me
for them two times I had left him nekkid the way I done.
Now that was a-worrying my head somewhat, I can tell
you. I sure damn didn't want to have to shoot it out with
him, on account a I didn't want to have to kill ole Jim,
I kinda liked him, and I knowed that if it was to come
to that, that's the way it would end. He weren't no match
for me. But then, he knowed that too, so I didn't really

believe that it would come to no shoot-out. It had to be
some other something he had in his mind to do to me.

That there was the troublingest part of it all. I knowed
that he damn sure wanted to get even with me for what
I had did to him, and he weren't going to call me out
for a shooting fight, I was pretty sure a that. So just what
the hell did he have in his mind? Riding along that trail
with ole Jim and a-headed right smack into his own town
the way we was, I come to know a true fact a life. You
can face all kinds a danger up front, long as you know
what it is a-coming at you, but whenever you don't know
what's a-coming, but you do know that it's something
a-coming, but you don't know when neither, that's when
you can get really a-skeered. It's like walking into a dark
room when you're a snot-nosed kid, and you wonder is
there a bobcat or something a-hiding in there. Well, there
prob'ly ain't nothing, but only it's dark, and you sure
do wonder about it, and that skeers you. That's how ole
Jim had me a-going in my head.

Well, we rid that damn long road till long about high
noon, and then we stopped, and ole Zeb, he cooked us
up a hell of a good meal. We et it and had us some
coffee, and then we cleaned up and packed up again. We
had fed and watered our horses too, while we was there,
so we saddled them back up, clumb on their backs, and
headed on our way. And it seemed to me that the closer
we got our ass to Fosterville, the more ole Jim was a-
giving me smug like looks, like as if he knowed that his
time was a-coming. His face was kinda constant wearing
one a them sly half-smiles, you know. I sure didn't like
them looks none too much.

We made some small talk along the way, like whenever ole Zeb, he asked out loud but to no one in pertikler, "You reckon that damn kid really is there in
Fosterville?"

"Call him Gish," I said, not liking it whenever anyone called him "that kid," on account a he had been mistook for me back then, and Kid was what I was called.

"Yeah, that one," Zeb said. "That kid Gish. You reckon he really is there?"

"That's the only information we have on him," said Chastain. "Even if our information was correct, there's no guarantee that he'll still be in town by the time we get there."

"There's never no g'arantees about nothing in this here life," I said.

"Kid," said Churkee, "you're becoming quite a philosopher."

I thunk that I knew what that there word meant, so I said, "A man gets his ass shot at enough times, it does that to him. There just ain't no way around it. I sometimes wish I could cut it out though. It can get my head to almost hurting. I'd ruther just be out somewheres a-punching cows with a empty head."

"Then you'd have all the time in the world in which to philosophize," Churkee said. "If you don't want to be thinking, the worst thing you can have is time on your hands."

I reckoned he might be right about that. It was best to be busy with something. A fight or a gal or something.

"Be better to be up in the mountains a-sniffing out the mother lode," Zeb said.

"You'll die still looking for that bonanza, old man," Chastain said.

"Ha! That's what you think," Zeb said, coming up of a sudden real animated like. "I'll find it. You'll see. I can smell gold whenever I get close to it. I'll sniff it out. And when I do, I'll come back down and buy Fosterville, all of it, and I'll have you out catching stray dogs. That's what I'll do."

"And who'll be sheriff?" Jim asked him, still with that sideways grin on his damned ole face.

"That?" Zeb said. "It don't matter. Anyone. That's a job anyone can do. Hell, I might just give your badge to ole Red. That is, if she'd want it. I wouldn't want it myself. Like I said, any ole anyone can do that job. Now sniffing out gold. That's a different matter. It takes someone special to be able to do that job."

Chastain just grinned and kept on a-looking straight ahead down the road. I seed him outa the edge a my eyeballs. Well, we rid on like that till night come a-falling, and then we made us a camp, and ole Zeb, he cooked up some more eats. We set around a-jawing till kinda late, a-setting around the fire. It was almost cold that night. I wished that I had me a good drink a whiskey 'stead a just that coffee, but then if I'd a had it, I might not a been able to keep such a eagle eye on ole Chastain. Final we all hit the hay, so to speak. Next morning we was on the road again, and since we was by then on the downhill side a the trip, I fancied that I could see even more and stronger mischief in ole Jim's face. I come real nervous then.

We never stopped at noon that day on account a we was so close in to Fosterville we just kept on a-riding. The closer in we come the nervouser I got, and I wanted to try to put my mind somewheres else.

"Churkee," I said, "whenever this here business with ole Gish is over and did, what're you a-going to do then?"

"I've been giving that some thought," he said. "I've got a little cash saved up. I think I'll send it along with a letter to my parents and give them the good news that Randall Morgan has met his demise and that I'm all right. Then I think I'll take a ride down into the Cherokee Nation. I've never been there, you know. I think it's about time."

"Down in the Indian Territory?" Chastain said.

"That's what they're calling it now," Churkee agreed. "I think that just means that they're a step closer to stealing our land again."

"Just by calling it that name?" I said.

"An organized territory is the next step to statehood," he said. "That's the way it works."

Well, I sure didn't know nothing about that, but I was kinda sorry to hear that the govament was a-fixing to steal his land again. I liked ole Churkee. He was one a my pardners. Then it come to me that the whole way our country come about was by the stealing a land offa Injuns, and I sure didn't want to get started thinking along them lines, on account a I just didn't know quite where I had oughta be a-standing on such a troublesome issue as that there. I decided just then to change the subject a conversation real quick like.

"Say, Jim," I said, "how's ole Red a-doing?"

"Red never changes," he said.

"No," I said. "I reckon not."

I sure was a-getting anxious to see her and partake a her many feminine charms. I went to trying to recollect all the details a what things we had did together on the several times we had did them, and that kept my brain busy enough till we rid on into Fosterville. Then we all kinda perked up on account a we all knowed that we was a-looking for that crazy Gish what had it in his fool and deranged mind that he was a-going to kill us ever' last one. We never seed him, though, a-riding in.

Chastain went straight on to his office, and ole Zeb, he wanted to hit the saloon first thing, so me and Churkee went on along with him. Soon as we walked in the front door and them batwings still a-swinging, ole Red seed us and come a-running. She throwed her arms around my neck and like to knocked me over with the full impact of it, and she slobbered some kisses on the side a my head too. Then final she turned me a-loose and went to hugging on ole Zeb. Whenever she was done with saying howdy to us like that, she give a look at ole Churkee.

"Who's your friend?" she asked me.

"Red," I said, "this here is my new pardner, ole Churkee. Say howdy to him."

Well, she did, and it come on me of a sudden that she seemed to be a little too almighty interested. She tuck his arm and started in to walking across the room.

"Let's get us a table," she said, and she give a nod as she passed by the bar. The barkeep went after a bottle a good whiskey. He knowed us all right. Red tuck us all on over to a table kinda at the far end a the room but up close to the bar, and by the time we all got our ass set down, there was a bottle and glasses on the table there for us. I paid for it, and ole Zeb, he went to pouring the glasses full. I looked at that there glass a whiskey in front a me, and I sure did want to drink it down, but I thunk about that Gish too.

"Red," I said, "we was told that ole Gish was here in town. You know, that skinny kid outlaw what Chastain had me mistook for. Has you saw him?"

"He was here, all right," she said, "but I ain't seen nothing of him now for two days."

Well, now, part a me wanted to say goddamn it that he had got clean away from us once again, and ain't this damn chase ever going to come to no end, but another part what was more up front said good. He ain't here. I can commence into getting my ass drunk, and it's about time for it too. I picked up my whiskey glass, and I never sipped it neither. I had myself a good healthy slug. It burned my throat and my gut real good. I pulled out the makings and rolled me a cigareet and struck a match on the underneath a the tabletop. I lit my smoke and give a look over to ole Red, and she was snuggled up right against ole Churkee's side and a-looking up at him with them big blue eyes a hers. Ole Churkee was my pardner, all right, but I weren't at all sure that I tuck to this too well.

You see, I had been a-planning for all a them miles from Nugget clean down into Fosterville what me and ole Red was a-going to do together whenever I final come into town. The way she was huddled up on him, it weren't exact a easy thing for me to bring up just then. I tuck me a drag on my cigareet and blowed out the smoke, and then I tuck another pull at my whiskey. Ole Zeb, he was already pouring hisself a second one. Churkee hadn't even touched his drink, and neither had ole Red hers. I picked up my glass again, and this time I drunk it all down. I reached for the bottle and poured me another'n.

Ole Red, she was a-talking whispers into the side a Churkee's head then, and I kinda felt my face skin commence into burning. I tuck a drink. Then I seed Churkee turn his head a little so he could put a secret word or two into the side a Red's head. Of a sudden, they stood up most together.

"Excuse us," Churkee said.

Red smiled real wide and cute.

"See you," she said, and then I be diddly dog damned if she didn't take his arm and walk over to the stairs and then start right on up there to her room with ole Churkee on her arm all the way. I glugged me down another swaller a whiskey. Ole Zeb, if he ever even noticed, he never paid it no mind. After all, it was her line a work, so I reckon it shouldn't a bothered me none neither, but it sure did. I finished that second drink, and then I poured me out another'n. Just then, ole Jim come in. He made right straight for our table, and when he come to it, he set down.

"Far as I can find out," he said, "Gish disappeared a couple of days ago."

"That's what Red said," I answered him. I tuck me another drink.

"So you decided you could afford to relax a bit?" he said.

That question a his and the tone of it put a uncomfortable thought into my head, and my head was already starting in to feel a bit fuzzy.

"You planning to take advantage a my getting drunk?" I asked him.

"No, Kid," he said. "I won't do that. I want you to be sober and totally aware of what's happening."

Well, that there relaxed me again, but only I shoulda knowed that it really shoulda worried me even more, on account a just what the hell was he a-planning to do to me that he needed me to be sober and aware to get the full shock of it? I didn't think it all through just then though. I said, "Have a drink with us?" He nodded and waved for a glass, and one was brung to him.

"Where's Cherokee?" he said.

I never answered him.

"Where's Red?"

My skin on my face burned hot, and it musta showed.

"Oh," Jim said, "I see."

"Well, maybe you do and maybe you don't," I said, and I'm damned if I know what the hell I meant by them words, but they was just all that come outa me, that's all. I drained my whiskey glass and reached for the bottle, but ole Zeb grabbed on to it first by the neck, and then he poured me a glass full. I figgered that he had been a-skeered that I would maybe spill it, drunk as I was. Well, I wobbled that glass up to my lips and drunk me a slurp, and soon as I had did it, I knowed that it were a big mistake. That there swaller went straight to my head, and I felt like as if my ole head was a-going to float offa my shoulders.

My guts kinda felt loose, too, of a sudden. I sure didn't want to make myself get damn-fool sick right there in front a Chastain and Zeb and ever'one else, so I put the glass down again, and I tried to get a handle on my ass. The room a-started to lean one way and then the other, and so I just stared hard at my glass there in front a me in a feeble attempt at making the floor steady up. I was a-trying to look and act sober, but I knowed that I weren't meeting with much success.

"You mean to keep hunting Gish?" Chastain asked me.

"I'll hunt his ass clean to China if I have to," I said, and I could hear that my own words was slurred something awful. That pretty much embarrassed me. Ever'one I knowed and ever set down to have a drink with could drink way more than me without getting near so drunk as what I did on just a few glasses a whiskey.

"Reckon how Cherokee and Red are getting along?" ole Jim said, and that were a mean-spirited thing for him to say. I picked up my glass in spite a what the last slurp had did to me, and I drunk ever' last drop in it, and I slammed the glass down on the tabletop and stood up. I like to a fell over, but I managed to keep on my feet. Now I ain't never been on a big ocean-going boat, but what I imagine it would be like is like the floor a that saloon felt to me at just them moments in my life.

I turned to head for the stairs, but just then the floor tilted way far over to my left, and I staggered the four or six feet over to the bar and slammed against it. If it

hadn't a been there, I'd a fell flat for sure. I steadied my
ole ass up and made another run for the bottom step,
and I was a-moving the top a my body faster'n my legs
and like to went over on my nose, but I grabbed onto
the rail just in the nick a time and helt myself up. I
straightened up my body, but I straightened it almost too
much. I like to went over backwards, but I never.

Then I started up them steps a-taking two or three of
them at a time, 'cept only now and then I missed and
stumbled. Once I even fell down, but I ketched myself
on a step with my hands. I stood up and went at it again.
I felt a gurgling down deep, but I fit it back. I tuck two
more steps, and I spun clean around and fell back and
landing on my ass a-setting on a step and looking down
at ever'one down there in the bar. They was all a-looking
at me too. That embarrassed me so much that I knowed
I just had to get up and get on with what it was that I
was a-doing.

Only thing is, I didn't really know just what it was
that I was a-meaning to do. I was a-headed for ole Red's
room. That was all I knowed. Something in my brain
commenced to asking me just what action were I going
to take whenever I got there. Was I a-going to kick in
the door? Was I a-meaning to shoot ole Churkee? Or ole
Red? Or just what the hell did I think I was a-going to
do? Well, something come along just then and spared
me the everlasting embarrassment a having to find out
the answer to them questions.

I was most nearly to the top step whenever I just fell
over backwards, and I remember rolling over and over
and bouncing my back and my ass and my head on them
steps as I was a-making my way back down to the bottom, and then I lit all laid out on my back, and after that
I don't remember nothing more about it.

Chapter 22

I come to just a-laying on my back pretty much like the last thing I remembered on the face a this earth, and for a space there my mind was a blank. It tuck me a while to open my eyes, and whenever I did open them up, it were just a crack on account a the world out there seemed a little too bright for them. Then my mind begun to wake up just a little bit at a time, and then it come right awake, and it come to me that I didn't have no idee where I was at or what time it was nor nothing. The last thing I remembered was I was a-lying out on the hard floor a the saloon. Coming awake just then, I felt like I was laid out on something more softer than that. I felt of it with my hands, and it sure enough felt like a mattress, but only, not a real plush one like is on a good bed, but a skinnier kind a mattress. I set up fast and opened my eyes on up, and I seed that I was a-setting in a jail cell, and it were a mighty familiar-looking one at that.

I looked through them jail-cell bars, and there set ole Jim Chastain behind his big damn desk just a-looking for all the world as smug as he could manage to look. I jumped up to my two feet and run over to the bars and tuck aholt a one in each hand, and I yelled out madder'n hell, I can tell you.

"Jim Chastain," I hollered, "you sneaking, lying, damn dirty bastard you. I know you want to kill me, prob'ly by shooting me in the back, but I never thunk you'd do me this dirty. You said you wouldn't put me back in no jail, and you promised me you wouldn't be taking advantage a me in my drunkenness. You lied to me, you son of a bitch. You Ook san bastard, you. Damn it all to hell, now if I ever get me another chance I will kill you for the lying snake what you are, and I hope you wake up in hell too. Damn it. I never tuck you for no lying chicken shit."

I stopped to take me a breath and 'cause my head was a-hurting and all that yelling didn't help it none.

"You all done, Kid?" Jim said.

"I reckon I said what needed saying."

"Then come on out and have yourself a cup of coffee," he said. "The door's not locked."

"Huh?"

I stepped over and tried the door, and sure enough, it was unlocked. I swung it wide open and walked out. I went over to the stove, got myself a cup and poured me out some coffee. Then I found me a chair and set down. I tuck me a sip a that hot coffee and like to a blistered my tongue.

"How you feeling, Kid?" Jim asked me.

"I'm all right," I said, but only I was a-lying to him. I didn't want to give him the satisfaction a knowing that I was suffering so much. "I take back all them things I just now said to you," I told him. "Hell, waking up in that there jail cell throwed a skeer into me."

"That's all right, Kid," he said. "I understand. I just didn't know what else to do with you last night."

"I understand," I said.

"What were you trying to do anyhow? Did you mean to kill Cherokee or something like that?"

"Naw," I said. "Hell, no. Churkee, he's my pardner—like ole Zeb. I just wanted to find out were he having hisself a good enough time. That's all."

'Course, I was lying to ole Jim again. I kinda wished he'd ask me something where I could tell him the truth. Really, I wished that I had a easy way a getting up and getting outa there, but then I guessed that he had really did me a favor by loading me onto the cot in that there cell.

"Kid?"

I finished slurping some hot coffee.

"What?" I said.

"What are you planning to do now? Are you going to keep hunting Gish?"

"Aw, hell, Jim," I said, "I don't know. I'd surely like to have him gone and outa my life, but it begins to look as if how this damn chase could go on forever. I'm just glad that you know the truth a the matter now. Maybe I'll just let it go, you know, lessen I happen to chance on him by accident one a these days."

"It looks like that's going to have to be my stance on the matter too, Kid," he said. "I have a town to watch over here. I can't spend all my time chasing after one outlaw, especially if he rides out of my jurisdiction. Of course, his description will go out to every lawman around. He can't get away forever. Someone'll stop him somewhere."

"Some day?" I said.

"Yeah."

"Well, listen, Jim," I said a-standing up outa my chair. "I got a terrible hunger on me. I best go find myself a breakfast. Thanks for what you done for me."

"Anytime, Kid," he said, but whenever he said it, I seed that look on his face again, and I sure was glad to get my ass outa there, I can tell you. Well, I walked

around for a spell a-looking for ole Zeb or Churkee or
even Red, but I never did see none a them, and I was
so hungry and my head was still some light and a-
hurting some that I couldn't wait no longer. I went into
a eating joint and ordered myself up some food. I et real
big too. Most usual, whenever I get too drunk like that,
well, the only thing for it is to eat real big first thing the
next day. I drunk me aplenty a coffee too, and it did
help.

Then I went to the stable, and I found my horse there,
but I never found my saddlebags and my blanket roll
nor none a my stuff but just only my ole horse and
saddle. I guessed that some son of a bitch had come
along and robbed me most nearly blind, and I cussed
some, but I was glad I had my money in my jeans, so I
went back on over to the saloon what also was a hotel,
and I got me a room. I thought about having me a bath,
but I never went and ordered it up. Instead I just throwed
myself down on the bed in my room, and I went right
off to sleep again.

Whenever I come awake again, I didn't have no idea
what time a day it was, but I looked out the winder, and
the sky looked kinda dim like. I guessed that it was
getting on into the evening. I straightened myself up in
my dirty and wrinkly clothes the most best I could, and
I went on out. I was a-feeling better by then, but I was
hungry again. Downstairs I seed Churkee and ole Red,
and whenever I was just about to walk past the table
where they was a-setting, Red called out to me.

"Kid," she said, "are you all right?"

I stopped, but I really didn't want to talk none to them
two just then. I kinda looked off to the side so as not to
look at neither one of them.

"Sure," I said, "I'm just fine."

"You were pretty drunk last night," ole Churkee said.

"And you took a real fall down those stairs."

"Oh," I said. "Did I? I don't really recall that."

"Well, you did," said Red. "It looked awful."

"If you'd been sober," Churkee said, "it would probably have broken your neck."

"I'm sure glad you're all right," said Red.

"Aw," I said, "it wouldn't a bothered you none if I had a broke my neck."

Then outa the corner a my left eye I seed Churkee get a kinda look on his face like as if he'd just only then figgered something out. He looked at Red.

"Excuse me," he said. He stood up and come over to me where I was a-standing. "Where are you headed, Kid?" he asked me.

"I'm just going to find me something to eat," I said.

"Mind if I go along?"

"Naw. Come on ahead."

We walked together outa that place and back over to the same eating place where I'd et before, and we got us a table and ordered up some steak and taters. We had us each a cup a coffee and was waiting for our food.

"Kid," Churkee said, "did I do something last night to offend you?"

"What do you mean?" I said.

"Well, that girl, Red," he said. "Is she, well, is she something special to you?"

"No, hell," I said. "I don't keer nothing about her. I mean, she's all right. She's a friend a mine, I guess. Whenever ole Zeb was all beat up that time and I left outa here to get the men what done it, she looked after him for me. And then whenever ole Chastain throwed me and Zeb and Paw in jail, it were Red what sneaked me my Colt so I could get us out, but only Jim, he don't know that. And—well, she's been a good friend, is all."

It come on me of a sudden that I was a-talking too

much and too fast about ole Red to be a-talking about someone I didn't give a shit about, and it come to me at the same time, that ole Churkee likely seed that same thing and knowed I was a-lying to him.

"I didn't know that, Kid," he said. "If I had known, I wouldn't have gone with her. I'm sorry. I—"

"Aw, hell, Churkee," I said. "Don't give it no more thought. I was just drunk last night, is all. Hell, what's a pardner for, anyhow?"

"You sure of that?" he asked me.

"Damn right, pard," I said. "Hell, I wouldn't let no little thing like that come betwixt me and a pardner. After what all we done been through together?"

"I'm glad to hear it," he said. "Now what do we do about that Gish?"

"We just try to forget him, is all," I said. "I done talked that out with ole Chastain. There ain't no telling where the little shit is gone off to, and I can't spend my whole life a-chasing after him. Jim said he can't neither. A description a the little runt is being sent out to all the lawmen around, and someone's bound to ketch up with him. So lessen I run onto him by accident somewheres, I'm a-putting him outa my head."

Just then the waiter come back with our plates, and we cut out the talking and tuck to eating. Whenever we finished up, we had us a couple more cups a coffee. I pulled out the makings and offered them over to Churkee. He tuck them and rolled hisself a smoke, and then I done the same thing, and so we set there a while a-smoking our cigareets and finishing our coffee.

"I think I'll ride on out, Kid," he said, and it tuck me plumb by surprise.

"When?" I said.

"Right now."

"Well, whyn't you wait till morning?" I said.

"There's no sense in putting it off," he said. "If you were still planning to track down Gish, I'd stick with you, but that's over with. Remember what I told you about territories and statehood?"

"Yeah," I said. "I kinda do."

"Well, I'm a Cherokee, and I've got a Cherokee Nation," he said. "The only thing is, I've never been there. I've never seen it. Now they've included it in a territory, and that means the end of it is in sight. I want to see it while it's still ours. So long, Kid. It's been good—partner."

Well, let me tell you, I sure did hate to see ole Churkee go. Whenever he walked outa that eating place, I felt a real lonesome hole in my middle. I wondered would I ever again see him in my whole life, and I wondered, too, besides ole Zeb, would I ever again find me a pardner as good as what he was. It come near to making me cry, and I was real sorry that I had got so mad over ole Red the night before, but I was glad that I had lied to him about that. I hoped that he had believed my lie.

Well, I had to do something to shake off my sadness, so I got up and left that place and walked on back over to the saloon. Red was still there, and ole Zeb had came in and set down with her. I went over to join them.

"Ole Churkee just went and rid out," I said.

"Where for?" said Zeb.

"The Churkee Nation," I said. I tole them what all he had tole me about how come him to want to go there on account a he hadn't never saw it and it was a-fixing to get stoled away from the Churkees, and then we all three of us set around with long faces for a spell. Zeb, he couldn't hardly take no more a that, and he went over to the bar and come back a minute later with a bottle and some glasses. I didn't say nothing whenever he

poured me a drink, but then I just let it set there in front
a me. I weren't quite ready yet for another night like the
one I'd had the night before.

Well, I was a-setting with my back to the main part
a the room and a-facing the back door a the place, but
I wasn't worried none about no one a-coming up behind
me, on account a we'd already heard that ole Gish had
lit out somewheres, and I figgered that I'd done kilt all
the Piggses and Hookses in the whole world, and I didn't
really believe that ole Chastain would shoot me in the
back. So anyhow, I was a-setting there a-thinking about
taking me a drink a that whiskey whenever I seed Zeb
and Red both turn kinda pale and pop open their eyes
real wide, and then I heared a real familiar voice from
behind me along with the sound of a six-gun a-being
cocked for action. I friz.

"You shit stick," come the voice. "I told you I'd kill
you."

It were him, the damn kid, the other kid, Gish. Red
and Zeb pushed back their chairs and got up and spread
way out. I knowed I was dead.

"You going to let me get up and face you?" I asked
him.

"I'm fixing to shoot you in the back a the head," he
said, "and watch your brains splatter."

"Ole Jim Chastain'll get you for sure," I said. "This
here is his town."

"Not if I get him first," the kid said.

Just then the back door come open. I was a-looking
right at it, and a figger come into the doorway, and I
could see that it was a-holding a shotgun. That's all I
could see. I throwed myself facedown on the tabletop,
and then come a terrible deafening blast and a stink a
black smoke, and I could feel some a them pellets a-
scratching my back as they was a-ripping through the

air right over me. Ever'thing got real quiet. I set up and I seed that I was a-looking smack in the face a my ole paw who was a-standing there with a smoking greener in his hands. I looked back over my shoulder, and there was that damn Gish laid out on his back with his head damn near blowed clean off. It was a sure sickening sight, I can tell you. I looked back at my old man.

"Paw," I said. "You ain't in Texas."

Ole Paw, he give out with his cackling laugh.

"How could I go to Texas," he said, "whenever I knowed my own boy was up here in big trouble."

"You been dogging my trail all this time?" I asked him.

"Sure," he said. "Now let's get our ass outa here before that sheriff comes a-running."

"It's okay, Paw," I said. "He ain't after us no more. It was this here what you just kilt and two old men who done them things he thought was us. He knows it all now, and we ain't wanted no more."

"I hope you're right about that, boy," he said, "on account a he just come in the door."

I looked around and seed Chastain a-coming. He come right on back there where we was at, and he looked at Gish there on the floor with only about half a head left on him.

"What happened here?" he said.

Well, Zeb and Red come in on him and the both of them started in to telling him the story all at once, but eventual he understood it all right.

"Well, Kid," he said, "it's finally all really over for you. I'm glad."

"And you ain't a-wanting to put us back in jail?" Paw said.

"No, Mr. Parmlee," Jim said, "I'm not."

"Well, let's have us a drink on that," said Paw, and

he set right down at the table without paying no more attention to the mess he had just made. Chastain went to get some help in cleaning it up. Me and Zeb and Red set down with Paw. I tuck me that drink then. I figgered it was all right. Then I got to thinking about going upstairs with ole Red. I had done forgive her for what she done me the night before, and her charms was a-getting to me again, but only I knowed I weren't fit to get too close to no sweet thing like her. I needed me a bath.

"Paw," I said, "if I was to give you some money, do you think you could go and pick me out a new set a clothes? I got to go upstairs and get me a bath, and some-one done stoled all my stuff outa the stable. I don't wanta put these nasty things back on when I come outa the bath."

"Sure, son," he said. "I can do that."

I give him a wad a money I had in my pocket, and I asked Red could she have me a bath drawed, and she said she could, and it would be right on up there in her room. Well, that was just what I wanted to hear. I poured me another drink 'cause I knowed it would take a while to get the bath drawed. Paw headed out, and Red went and ordered up my bathwater, and then she come back to the table. I rolled me a cigareet and lit it, and I set there a-smoking and a-drinking and a-feeling better than what I had felt since that day that old Jim Chastain had come up behind me with that there shotgun.

Whenever I finished my smoke and my drink, I got up to go upstairs, and I tuck along my glass and the bottle. Ole Zeb called for another bottle for hisself, and me and Red wrapped our arms around each other and headed up for her room. Whenever we got there, the bath was a-waiting for me all right, and so I stripped my ass off nekkid and clumb in, and it sure did feel good. Red poured me another drink and handed it to me. Then she looked around the room.

"What is it, darlin'?" I asked her.

"I forgot to bring me a glass," she said. "I'll be right back."

She went out and closed the door behind her, and I just laid back in that hot sudsy water and relaxed. I tuck me a sip a whiskey, then I leaned my head back on the edge a the tub and closed my eyes. Damn, but I felt good. By and by, I heared the door come open again, and I didn't even bother to open up my eyes.

"Did you fetch you a glass?" I said.

The next thing I knowed, someone had throwed a towel over my head and was a-pulling on me. I kicked and I hollered, but I never was no good in a fistfight or a rassling match, just only with my six-gun, and so he had me dragged clean outa that tub in most no time atall. I didn't have no idee what the hell was a-going on. Some big lug had aholt a me from behind and my head all wrapped up in a towel and me nekkid and wet and kicking and a-flailing my arms all around and yelling to high heaven.

Whoever it was had me, he dragged me across the room and poked me out the winder onto the roof what was there what stuck out over the sidewalk a-facing the main street a Fosterville, and then I heared the sound a the winder a-slamming shut. I unwrapped that towel offa my head as fast as I could, and then I seed ole Chastain on the other side a the glass a-looking at me and laughing his ass off. I looked around, and I seed all kinds a folks out on the street a-looking up at me and a-pointing and a-laughing. I turned red all over me.

"Jim," I yelled. "Open the winder."

He just laughed the harder. Well, I went to grab up the towel what I had tuck offa my head so I could at least wrap it around my middle parts, you know, but I was so nervous and all that I dropped it, and it went clean offa the edge a that roof. There I was in front a the whole world, or at least in front a the whole entire population a Fosterville, high up on the roof nekkid as a slug.

"Damn it, Chastain," I hollered out. "You had your damn joke. Let me back in."

He was still a-standing there at the winder a-looking and a-laughing. And down in the street folks was roaring around and having a great time over my miserableness. They was even a-hollering into the doors a places and calling the folks inside to come out and get a look. One old lady squealed and fell over like she was dead, and some mothers was a-grabbing their little kids and a-pulling them offa the street.

Just then I heared horse hoofs a-pounding down below, and then I heared a voice yelling up at me through all a the other noise.

"Come on, Kid."

It tuck all what was in me, but I went on over close to the edge a the roof and looked down, and there was Paw a horseback and Zeb, too, and they had my ole horse saddled and waiting. I looked all around, and I knowed I had to do something. So I jumped. I sure did hurt my poor ole balls whenever I landed in that saddle. Then right there on the sidewalk was ole Red, and she was a-holding out my gun belt.

"Here, Kid," she said.

I grabbed it, and me and Zeb and Paw lit out as fast as we could make our horses go. I tell you what, I was never in my whole life as glad to get out of a town as I was to get outa Fosterville that day.